Last Year's Mistake

GINA CIOCCA

SIMON PULSE

NEW YORK LONDON TORONTO SYDNEY NEW DELHI

SIMON PULSE
An imprint of Simon & Schuster Children's Publishing Division
1230 Avenue of the Americas, New York, New York 10020
First Simon Pulse paperback edition May 2016
Text copyright © 2015 by Gina Ciocca
Cover photograph copyright © 2015 by Michael Frost (couple), Thinkstock (car), and Steve Gardner/PixelWorks Studios (ground)
Cover photo-illustration by Steve Gardner/PixelWorks Studios
Also available in a Simon Pulse hardcover edition.
All rights reserved, including the right of reproduction in whole or in part in any form.
SIMON PULSE and colophon are registered trademarks of Simon & Schuster, Inc.
For information about special discounts for bulk purchases, please contact Simon & Schuster Special Sales at 1-866-506-1949 or business@simonandschuster.com.
The Simon & Schuster Speakers Bureau can bring authors to your live event.
For more information or to book an event contact the Simon & Schuster Speakers Bureau at 1-866-248-3049 or visit our website at www.simonspeakers.com.
Cover designed by Jessica Handelman
Interior designed by Mike Rosamilia
The text of this book was set in Janson Text LT Std.
Manufactured in the United States of America
2 4 6 8 10 9 7 5 3 1
The Library of Congress has cataloged the hardcover edition as follows:
Ciocca, Gina.
Last year's mistake / by Gina Ciocca. — First Simon Pulse hardcover edition.
p. cm.
Summary: Although Kelsey has fallen in love with her best friend, David, she cuts ties with him before moving from Connecticut to Rhode Island, believing they need a fresh start, but David moves nearby at the start of senior year, threatening Kelsey's relationship with Ryan.
[1. Best friends—Fiction. 2. Friendship—Fiction. 3. Love—Fiction. 4. High schools—Fiction 5. Schools—Fiction. 6. Family life—Rhode Island—Fiction. 7. Rhode Island—Fiction.] I. Title.
PZ7.1.C56Las 2016
[Fic]—dc23
2014032573
ISBN 978-1-4814-3223-8 (hc)
ISBN 978-1-4814-3224-5 (pbk)
ISBN 978-1-4814-3225-2 (eBook)

For my family and friends,
especially Mom, Dee, Dom, and Sarah, because
you believed this would happen even when I didn't.
And for Dad, the original number thirty-three.

One

**Rhode Island
Senior Year**

The first day of senior year, he came back. I should have known it wasn't over. Nothing ever is.

I smoothed my white sundress beneath me as I took my seat beside Ryan, my boyfriend of almost a year, in his Camaro. The air was tinged with last night's September chill, a reminder that I'd soon be watching summer melt into fall for the second time as a resident of Rhode Island. Sometimes I still wondered if the whole thing was a dream.

The Camaro's engine idled loudly as I pulled down the visor to check my makeup. Satisfied that lip gloss and mascara hadn't budged on the way from the house to the car, I snapped the mirror back into place.

Then my insides went cold.

Something was clipped to the visor that I'd never seen in this car before but would have recognized anywhere.

"Where did you get that?"

"This?" Ryan unclipped the half-dollar-size medal, laughing as he held it out to me. "Keep it. You need it more than I do."

I made no effort to take it from him. "Where did you get it?"

The dimple in Ryan's left cheek disappeared as his smile faltered. "I found it. What's your deal?"

My eyes darted from him to the medallion and back again. When I still didn't touch it, he added, "Oh, come on, babe. It's a Saint Christopher medal. It's to protect you while you're driving. Or, in your case, running squirrels off the road. Lighten up."

My sister and I were bumming a ride with Ryan on the first day of school because my car was in the shop—the result of an unfortunate incident involving one too many tequila shots and a squirrel. At least, that was the story I'd told him.

I tentatively touched the medal, engraved with an image of Saint Christopher and his staff.

Ryan thought he was teasing by giving me this, laughing it up over an inside joke. But nothing about it was funny.

The car suddenly felt too warm, too small, and memories I'd locked away for more than a year poured into my head like water through a broken dam. Images of smiles and touches and kisses that weren't his.

I stared at the medal in my palm, running my thumb over the uneven surface. "I—I knew someone who had a medal like this." Not *like* it. This one was identical to the one in that long-buried past of mine. And now I held it in my hand like sunken treasure churned up from the ocean floor. I rolled the window down a little more, wondering why air couldn't seem to find its way to my lungs, and stared absently at the wicker rockers on our front porch before adding, "Someone I haven't seen in a long time."

"I miss him." Miranda sighed from the backseat. "He was the best."

I whipped around. "Be quiet. You don't know what you're talking about."

"Him?" Ryan adjusted the red Clayton High baseball cap sitting sideways over his blond curls.

Wistfulness clouded Miranda's blue eyes. "Our friend from back home in Connecticut. He's—"

"Not important." I twisted around in my seat again. "Do you want to die on your first day of freshman year?"

"Him *who*?" Ryan pressed.

I didn't look at him when I answered. "Not that kind of him. A friend. One I don't speak to anymore."

Ryan shifted in his seat. "It's not like it's the *same* medal.

Those things are mass produced. You look like you saw a ghost."

If only I'd known how prophetic those words would be.

I'd tossed the medal into my purse, and had almost forgotten about it by the time Ryan and I were kissing at my locker half an hour later.

"I swear, you two should get tracheotomies so you'll never have to come up for air." My best friend, Candy, wrinkled her nose as she slammed her locker shut.

"Jealous, Candle Wax?" Ryan retorted. I hated when he called her that. Candy's last name was Waxman, hence the rather dim-witted nickname.

"In your dreams, Smurf." Equally dim-witted: Ryan Murphy. Smurf. Ugh.

Candy fiddled with her cell phone, simultaneously running a brush through her pin-straight dark hair. "You guys wanna grab some breakfast? I've been dying for one of Ruthie's egg 'n' cheeses all summer."

"'Egg 'n' cheeses'?" I laughed. "Is that even a word?"

Candy threw her phone in her bag and tugged on my hair. "Who gives a flying fig? They're fried, greasy goodness, and that's all I care about."

Ryan snorted. "Easy, Wax. Too many of those and that bodacious booty won't fit into your rah-rah uniform."

He gave mine a squeeze and I smacked his arm. Kissing and hand-holding and other tame forms of PDA were fine, but I had no interest in being groped in front of our entire high school. Nor did I appreciate him teasing Candy about her butt. As someone who'd spent the better part of puberty hiding its traitorous effects behind shapeless T-shirts, I didn't take kindly to body comments.

Nothing fazed Candy, though. She and Ryan sparred all the time, and as usual, Candy didn't miss a beat. Not that I knew what she came back with, because I didn't hear a word of it.

I happened to glance over her shoulder at that moment, right as one of the glass double doors at the end of the hall opened. Bright sunlight shone through, and for a second I could only make out the outline of the person who stepped inside.

But it was all I needed to see.

My heart froze as I took in his broad shoulders, his dark hair sticking out in all directions. He was taller than I remembered, more built, the angles of his face sharper. Evidence of the time that had passed since I last saw him.

It can't be.

I might have said it out loud as I pulled myself from Ryan's arms, my legs turning to mush beneath me.

"Who is *that*?" Candy said, just as Ryan asked, "Are you all right?" But they sounded a million miles away.

My pulse quickened as the person at the end of the hall took a step forward, and even as the words *It can't be* repeated over and over in my head, there was no room for doubt. This morning in the car, I'd felt my past shift in its grave. Now the piece I'd wanted to bury deepest stood right there in front of me, breathing the same air.

I took a step forward, and he stopped. He'd seen me, too.

The beginning of a smile curved his lips. Lips I knew all too well. Lips I hated.

But that didn't stop me from taking another step forward. And another, until I stood right in front of him, still not convinced he wasn't some sort of hallucination. It wasn't until he reached out and slid hesitant arms around my rigid body that I knew he was real.

I had no intention of hugging him back, but my body had other ideas. The second my face pressed against his shoulder, every lie I'd told myself for the past year dissolved into the scent I'd know anywhere. I closed my eyes and wound myself around him, burying my nose in his shirt. The stiffness in his embrace melted away, and he crushed me against him.

"Hey," he whispered against my hair. "It's been a long time."

Two

Rhode Island
Summer before Freshman Year

I lifted my foot to the bumper of my parents' car and braced myself as I wrestled my suitcase out of the trunk, anxious to start my vacation. A cloudless blue sky stretched above me, and a salty breeze tempered the August heat. The perfect way to begin an end-of-summer getaway.

Every August my family made the two-and-a-half-hour drive from our home in Norwood, Connecticut, to stay with our (loaded) uncle Tommy and aunt Tess at their summerhouse. They were right at the heart of everything that the pristine, manicured beach town had to offer: the ocean; the preserved Gilded Age mansions; and Thames Street, Newport's main drag. We spent two weeks each year enjoying the fruits of my aunt and uncle's good fortune, wishing we'd come across some of our own.

That summer, I was fourteen, and my family was broke. My dad—Uncle Tommy's brother—liked to refer to himself as a "starving artist." He'd been a teacher at Norwood's local high school until a few years earlier when he'd been unable to dodge a hailstorm of layoffs.

Once he'd lost his job, he had this epiphany that he should pursue his long-forgotten dream of publishing a novel. Sure, he'd put in job applications when my mother reminded him that his unemployment check and her paralegal salary weren't enough to put two girls through college, but nothing over the past three years ever seemed to pan out. Including the novel.

So we were all ready to forget about life for a while when we pulled up to Uncle Tommy's cabin that summer. It was nothing like a cabin, of course, but that's what we'd always called it. Originally built in 1902, it had been a Victorian before various additions and build-outs turned it into the turreted, twenty-four-hundred-square-foot Thing with a Porch that currently stood on the property.

Whoever owned the house before obviously hadn't been into the whole historical preservation craze that permeated the rest of Newport. Not that I complained; everything was modern and clean, and I didn't have to share a room with Miranda. Plus, having restored mansions and the beach practically in your backyard had the crazy effect of making everything seem right with the world.

If only I could get the damn suitcase out of the car.

I wasn't sure what happened next—if the hard smack that impacted my upper arm caused me to jostle my suitcase loose, or if the case had just broken free of whatever it had been caught on and flew out of the trunk. Either way, my butt hit the ground and so did my luggage, right after it bounced off my foot.

"Ow!" I grabbed at the stinging spot below my ankle and massaged it.

"Are you okay?"

I looked up with a jolt at the sound of the unfamiliar voice. It belonged to a boy about my age. He and an older man peered over the white fence that separated Uncle Tommy's driveway from theirs. The boy's thick black hair flopped over his forehead, and both his hands stretched toward me, though I didn't know how he planned to help with a fence between us. Or while wearing a baseball glove.

"Sorry about that," he said.

"Completely my fault," the man added, waving his own gloved hand in the air. He pushed his glasses up his nose. "I missed it by a mile. Are you all right?"

Only then did I notice "it"—the worn-looking baseball nestled in the grass a few feet from where I sat.

"I'm fine," I lied, not wanting to make a big deal. I let go of my foot and stood to retrieve the ball, wishing I had more hands to rub all the places that hurt.

"Jimmy!" a voice carped through one of the open windows in the house behind the fence. "Where's my Swiss Army knife?"

The older man sighed and shook his head, his thin shoulders sagging. "In a box in the hall closet, Dad, exactly where I told you I put it," he called back.

"I can't find it. Get in here, would you?"

The man's mouth twisted as he abandoned his glove and turned toward the house, stopping to give me a look of regret. "Again, my apologies."

I waved, unsure of what else to do, before winging the ball toward the boy. A *thwack* sounded as it slammed into his glove, and his eyes went round as quarters.

"Nice arm!" He grinned, revealing a row of metal braces and drawing my attention to a small beauty mark beneath the left side of his bottom lip.

"For a girl?"

"For anyone."

I laughed and walked toward him. "I'm Kelsey."

"David."

I threw a glance at the house behind him. "Do you live there?"

"That's my grandfather's house." He grumbled when he said it and looked at the ground, like it embarrassed him.

"Really?" I pointed at the house behind me. "This is my uncle's house. We're here at the end of every August. I don't think I've seen you before."

"We usually come at the beginning of the month. My dad helps pay Grandpa's bills and stuff." Under his breath, he mumbled something that sounded like, *Makes sure he hasn't killed himself yet.* David cast a tense look over his shoulder at the house. "He's needed some, uh, extra help lately, so we've been coming more frequently. And if you've been here every summer, I should probably apologize on his behalf."

So he knew.

A nervous laugh bubbled up in my throat. "He doesn't bother anyone."

David smiled. "I see niceness runs in your family. Your uncle is the only one who never calls the police."

"My uncle's also not here most of the year."

But I'd heard stories from when he was. Jay, David's grandfather, had a bit of a drinking problem, one that had gotten worse as time passed. In earlier years his behavior had been more or less harmless; Aunt Tess told us he'd passed out with the TV blaring a couple of times, or failed to hear an alarm clock that could wake the dead—for over an hour. Most recently, though, my uncle had found him out cold on his back porch, wearing boxers and a parka. In the middle of an eighty-degree day in August.

"David! I see you've met my niece."

I turned at the sound of Uncle Tommy's voice. He stood at the door, smiling beneath his strawberry-blond beard.

David raised his gloved hand. "Hey, Mr. Crawford. I sort of knocked her over with a baseball. Sorry."

Uncle Tommy waved off the apology as he trotted toward us. "Don't worry about it. Girls always get flustered around good-looking guys like us."

I blew an indignant *pfff* through my lips and shook my head.

"Besides, David's no fool," Uncle Tommy teased as he righted my suitcase and pulled out the handle. "He probably spotted you a mile away and made a beeline." He winked before adding, "That's why you're gonna go back inside and keep your raging teenage hormones away from my beautiful niece. This young lady is spoken for."

I wanted to die on the spot. My parents must've told him about Eric, my friend who'd recently ambush-kissed me in front of the entire cafeteria. My best friend, Maddie, made the mistake of mentioning it in front of Miranda and the news had reached my mother in a nanosecond. Maybe I should've told them that I found out later he'd done it on a dare. I'd hardly call that "spoken for."

I rolled my eyes and gave David an apologetic shake of my head.

"All right, I'll catch you guys later. Let me know if you need me to work on your yard this weekend, Mr. Crawford."

"You got it, David. I know where to find you."

David gave me a hesitant wave. "Nice meeting you, Kelsey." And thanks to Uncle Tommy, I couldn't help but notice he *was* pretty cute. Minus the braces and shaggy hair, of course.

I waved back. "See you later."

Turned out later came sooner than I expected. When we returned from Thames Street that night, stuffed full of fish-and-chips and all things delicious, I spotted David's hunched form on the back porch of his grandfather's house. The voices of two shouting males rang from inside and met my ears the moment I stepped out of the car.

"Maybe I should go over and see if everything's all right," Uncle Tommy said. Before he finished his sentence, Miranda ran over to the fence, grabbed the peaks at the top, and strained on her tiptoes to see over them.

"Hey," she crowed, "there's someone sitting out there!"

"Shh! Let go before you knock it over!" I pulled her hand from the fence and held it at my side, the same way Mom used to whenever Miranda tried sneaking candy onto the conveyor at the grocery store. Seeing David had looked up, I waved at him. "Hey. Um, is everything all right?"

"Yeah." He tried to smile, but only half his mouth cooperated. His hands were jammed in his pockets, and the porch swing creaked back and forth under the weight of his slouched body. "I'm waiting for it to quiet down in there. Sorry."

Miranda hopped on the balls of her feet, trying to get a better look at him. "Come over and play video games with us! We're having a tournament! You can be on my team, because my mom stinks."

Collective laughter rang through the darkness. Leave it to my sister to make clueless cute.

"Sounds good." David stood up, leaving the wicker swing swaying behind him. "Let me, uh, leave them a note." He grimaced in the direction of the upper floor, where the shouting raged on.

"If you'd grown up and gotten your act together years ago, you and Mom never would have divorced!"

"Still high and mighty, even with the ink wet on your own divorce papers! I don't need you and your kid telling me how to run my life!"

I shuddered and gave Miranda a gentle push in the direction of Uncle Tommy's house. "Go inside and help Aunt Tess set up. I'll wait for him." Even with her bubble of obliviousness protecting her, I didn't want her hearing something she shouldn't.

David reemerged from the house a moment later, jogging up our driveway with his hands bunched into the pockets of his jeans.

"Sorry about that," he said, nodding toward the other house. "He's never been this bad before. It's . . ." He shook his head and frowned. "Out of control."

"Hey, don't apologize. He said it himself; you're not his babysitter."

"But it's getting to the point where he needs one. We're too far away to come running every time he screws up."

"Where are you from, by the way?" I started toward Uncle Tommy's back door, David walking at my side.

"Originally Portman Falls, Connecticut," he said.

"Oh, not far from us. We live in Norwood."

David stopped in his tracks. "No way. My dad and I are in the middle of moving to Norwood."

"Shut up!" I stopped too, and gaped at him.

"I swear. Your uncle helped us find the house."

"That makes sense," I said. "It is what real estate agents do. What street are you moving to?"

"Meadowbrook?" He said it like he couldn't quite remember, but I knew exactly which street he was talking about.

"That's right around the corner from us! The house next to the big empty field, right? Kind of purplish?"

David grinned. "You mean purplish, scary-ish, and dilapidated-ish? That's the one. But we're gonna fix it up—it won't be an eyesore for long."

I tilted my head and gave him a quizzical look. "You really need to stop apologizing for things that aren't your fault. Our place doesn't exactly look like the White House either. None of the houses in our neighborhood do."

It wasn't that Norwood was known for being poor on the whole. But the deeper into it you got, the more obvious it became that someone had forgotten to post a NO BOTTOM-FEEDERS ALLOWED sign. Beautiful houses on generous plots of land eventually gave way to narrowing, woodsy roads; shrinking, unkempt properties; and houses that could fit inside the master suites of the ones you'd driven past five minutes ago.

That was the part we lived in.

"Anyhow, I'm going to Norwood High," David said. "Are you? Or will you be at one of the private schools?"

"Ha! Private school." Maybe if I *really* wanted to feel like a bottom-feeder. I shook my head. "Norwood Public High is good enough for me. If you want, I'll introduce you to my friends."

A genuine grin lit his face. "Cool."

"Kelsey, hurry up!" Miranda called from inside the house.

I wrapped my fingers around the door handle, then paused. "I should warn you—I usually win."

"Then I should warn *you* that you need to kiss your winning streak good-bye, because this is the end."

"We'll see about that."

We headed into the house side by side. David was wrong, of course. It was only the beginning.

Three

"Kelsey! Kelseeeeeeeey!"

Crap.

Miranda hurried through the outdoor lunch area as fast as she could on her skinny legs. Her enormous book bag slapped against her back as she ran, and honey-colored wisps that had escaped her forever-disheveled ponytail fluttered in the breeze. Her hair was the exact color mine used to be, before I kicked it up a notch with some platinum-blond highlights. Though I had never allowed mine to look like a tornado had taken up residence on my head.

Miranda came to a halt in front of our lunch table, wide eyed and breathless. "Did you see who's here?"

Ryan tensed next to me. He hadn't exactly appreci- ated my earlier reaction to the "who" in question. Candy coughed and focused on stabbing a cherry tomato.

"I saw him," I said, taking a bite of my pretzel in an attempt at nonchalance. And failing, because I nearly choked on it. "Shouldn't you be inside with the other freshmen? The picnic tables are only for seniors."

Miranda ignored my attempt to get rid of her, plow- ing ahead with barely a pause for air. "Can you believe he's living here in Rhode Island? In his grandfather's house? Or that his grandfather died? I mean, that part I can believe because he was always drunk, but holy *crud*, Kelse, we were just talking about him in the car this morning!"

Ryan's head snapped up. "Wait. That's who you were talking about?" His leg began to bounce beneath the table, and he readjusted his cap for the umpteenth time.

Nice, Miranda. It had taken me the entire morning to lower Ryan's level of suspicion from red to orange, and she'd sent it flying off the charts again.

"Anyone wanna tell me who we're talking about?" Matt Crowley, Ryan's baseball buddy, called out from the other end of the table.

"Kelsey knows the new kid." Ryan jerked his head in my direction and then ripped a bite from his sandwich in a way that made me feel bad for it.

"Ooooh, Kelse. An old flame?" If the tone of Matt's

voice hadn't made me want to punch him, the smirk on his face would've.

"No." I crumpled my bag of pretzels. "An old *friend*. *Ex*-friend."

"I know exactly who you're talking about!" Violet Kensing squealed before I could reiterate that he was a friend I didn't speak to anymore. "He's in my homeroom! Oh my God, Kelsey, he is so hot! Can you introduce me?" She tossed her hair like she expected him to materialize at the mere mention of his existence. Candy rammed an elbow into her ribs, and Violet promptly shot back a death glare.

"How well *do* you know this kid?" Ryan asked, his eyes narrowed.

Miranda snorted. That sound, that death knell, made me turn back to her so fast, I thought my neck might snap. The panic on her face didn't stop my own from welling up inside me. She and my mother were the only ones who knew what had happened between David and me, and I'd made her promise never to tell. I'd always thought Miranda could keep her mouth shut when it counted most, and watching her stare at her feet and bite her lip, I knew she'd thought the same thing. Both of us must've had our heads lodged firmly up our rear ends when we'd come to that conclusion.

Heat prickled the back of my neck. I glared at Miranda even though she wouldn't look back at me, silently threatening her life if she dared to take the things I'd told her while drowning in uncertainty and awash in my own tears and let them slip like a greasy bowling ball. "He was a friend," I repeated through gritted teeth.

Ryan tore another bite from his sandwich and threw it down without looking at me. The whole table shook from his leg bouncing beneath it, and he mumbled *Sure*. A loaded silence settled over the group, and my friends appeared extra fascinated by their lunches.

"Bye, Kelse." Miranda turned on her heel and high-tailed it out of there. She'd sold me out, even without saying a word, and she knew it. Thanks, little sister.

"Ryan, I—" A quick glance down the length of the table reminded me that I didn't want to have this conversation there. Even with every set of eyes trained downward, I knew all their ears were primed and ready. I tugged at his shirt. "Come for a walk with me. Please?"

Ryan's jaw tensed. He balled up his sandwich wrapper and threw it into his lunch bag. But he took my hand and rose from the bench, and I knew he'd at least hear me out.

I could only imagine the conversation that exploded the moment we were gone.

I pulled him by the hand through the main doors, and then into the deserted hallway that led to the chorus room. The moment the doors closed behind us, Ryan let go of my hand, leaned against the wall, and folded his arms across his chest.

"I'm listening." He stared down the hall, refusing to meet my eyes.

"There's nothing to tell."

"I'm not an idiot, Kelse. You've been lying to me all morning, haven't you? Something happened with you and this kid."

I twisted my hands. "Nothing worth mentioning."

"I knew it!" He pulled his hat tighter to his head and paced back and forth like a caged animal. "I knew there had to be more to it. No girl reacts like that to a friend. Why didn't you tell me?"

"Ryan, I didn't even know you when—" I bit the inside of my cheeks and looked at the floor.

He stopped pacing and jammed his fists in his pockets. "When what? When you were with him?"

I stepped closer to him and put my hands on his upper arms. "Ryan."

He backed away from me and against the wall, his shoulders hunched as he frowned at the floor. "I can't believe you lied to me."

I let out a sigh of resignation. Normally I would've given him hell for throwing such a ridiculous temper tantrum, but I needed our fight to be over more than I needed to be right. The sooner I could rebury all this, the better.

Pressing myself against the length of his unyielding body, I sandwiched him between me and the wall. "Why are you being like this?" I grazed my nose against his cheek. "I was never with him—not like that. He . . . he liked me, but I freaked out when he told me. We haven't talked since."

True enough.

Ryan searched my face. "Because you didn't like him back?"

Heat crawled up my neck and spread to my cheeks. I eased back a little, praying he couldn't feel the suddenly erratic beats of my heart. "Because it never would have worked. He and I, we were good friends. And then we were nothing at all."

"Then why did you hug him like that?" Ryan's hands settled tentatively on my hips, and I knew the worst was over.

"It caught me off guard, that's all. I haven't seen him since I moved here. Knee-jerk reaction, I guess. But you saw how awkward it got after that."

Ryan smirked, undoubtedly recalling the red-faced detangling of limbs and general uneasiness as he and Candy joined our little private party. To call it "uncomfortable" would be like calling a sumo wrestler "sort of chubby."

"You really didn't know what hit you, huh?"

You mean it wasn't a frigging Mack truck?

I wrapped my arms around his neck and managed a tiny smile back. "No. Like I said, it caught me off guard. There's nothing to worry about."

Ryan's hands roamed up my back and he moved his lips closer to mine. "I didn't like seeing you in some other guy's arms," he murmured.

Our lips brushed together. "I'm in yours now."

"And you won't keep things from me anymore?"

I kissed him, knowing he'd take it as a yes. Or a no,

however you wanted to look at it. Right as the kiss became entirely inappropriate for school, the metallic sound of the double doors opening made us jump apart.

David stood in the hall, one hand curled around the shoulder strap of his bag, and the other clutching a piece of paper. And just as it had earlier that morning, my gut folded in on itself like an accordion.

"Um, sorry," David said. "I still don't know where I'm going." He held up what I assumed to be his schedule. "Think I took a wrong turn."

He made a move to retreat but stopped when I started toward him. "It's okay. We were . . . talking. Where are you headed?"

The bell signaling the end of lunch sounded. David glanced at the paper. "Chemistry? Room A one-oh-one."

"Oh. You were close. If you go back into the main hallway—"

"I'm headed that way." Ryan sidled up behind me and rested a hand on my shoulder. "I'll walk with you."

My head snapped toward him. "I—um. You will?" My palms grew sweaty at the suggestion. Two seconds ago he'd wanted to rip David's head off, and now he wanted to walk him to class?

"Yeah." Ryan draped his arm around me as he moved to stand at my side. "Like I said, I'm going that way anyway." He kept his eyes on David as he answered, and I could've sworn frost formed in the space between them.

David stared right back, his posture rigid. The corner of his mouth twitched. Whether it was the beginning of a smirk or a frown, I couldn't tell. "That'd be great," he said, a hint of sarcasm edging his words as he eyed Ryan's cap. "We can talk baseball."

If I'd looked down at that moment and seen my stomach land on the floor with a huge splat, it wouldn't have surprised me in the least. "You're joining the baseball team?" I croaked.

What a stupid question. He was obsessed with baseball, and he'd played at Norwood. Clayton would be lucky to have another pitcher as good as Ryan.

Not that Ryan would appreciate it. Oh, God.

Ryan strode toward David, almost like he'd forgotten I was there. "Sure." He looked back at me when I grabbed his wrist, trying my hardest to make him read my mind. *What the hell are you doing?*

Half of Ryan's mouth crooked up into a grin. "Don't worry." He bent and smacked a quick kiss on my lips. Under his breath he added, "I'll be nice."

The image of the two of them walking away together made my brain go haywire. I never imagined I'd see David again, period, let alone see him strolling down the halls of Clayton High, side by side with my boyfriend. It seemed inherently wrong, like the world should implode at any second from the sheer wrongness of it.

There was no implosion, though. Just the terrifying realization that my two worlds had finally collided.

Four

**Rhode Island
Summer before Freshman Year**

"It's Shake It Till You Make It tiiiiiime!" Dad bellowed as he burst into the living room.

"Yes!" Miranda pumped her fist, promptly abandoning her video game remote on the couch cushion and running over to him. "I'm getting the Chocolate Disaster!"

From the kitchen, my mother groaned. "Kevin, why do you insist on doing that challenge every year? Then I have to listen to you moan about how sick you feel for the rest of the night."

"Tradition, Amanda!" Uncle Tommy called as he galloped down the stairs. "Victory will once again be mine!"

Three summers ago, Dad had decided on a whim—

more like a mutual dare—that he and Uncle Tommy should go up against each other in the Shake It Till You Make It challenge at the Bellevue Ice Cream Shoppe. Store rules dictated that anyone who could drink three of their thick, ginormous shakes got a fourth on the house, but my father had upped the stakes by deciding the loser would get dinner and dish duty the following night. Three years out of three, Dad wound up flipping post-challenge burgers—in Aunt Tess's pink-flowered apron. That part was Uncle Tommy's stipulation.

"Come on, girls." Dad clapped his hands, my cue to turn off the TV. "Hope you're hungry."

As we headed down the driveway like a little caravan— we always walked to preempt some of the sugar—David's father emerged from the house next door, holding a big cardboard box.

"Hey, Jimmy!" Uncle Tommy called. "You guys wanna join us for some ice cream?"

"Thanks, Tom." Mr. Kerrigan hoisted the box onto the trunk of his car and fished his keys out of his pocket. "But I have to get this junk to Goodwill before my father changes his mind again. I'll bet David might like to go, though." He nodded at Miranda and me. "Why don't you girls run in and get him?"

Miranda needed no further coaxing. She took off on her bony legs, leaving me to catch up at the Kerrigans' back door. The TV was so loud that I wondered if David would even hear her musical little knocks, but a moment later he appeared. When we told him where we were going and asked him to come along, he didn't hesitate to accept.

David retreated to the living room, where his grand-father grunted in response to his statement that he was going out with the neighbors. A second later he reappeared, and I stepped aside to let him through the screen door. Before he could shut it behind him, his eyes dropped to my leg and his face filled with horror.

"Oh, shit!" He clapped his hand over his mouth and apologized for cursing, probably more for Miranda's benefit than mine, before motioning to the huge purple and blue bruise on my thigh. "Did I do that? The other day, when I hit you with—"

I shook my head and tugged my shorts lower before he could finish the thought. "No, no, that was already there. Tripped over something. I bruise easily. It looks worse than it is."

"Besides, that's not where you hit—," Miranda started, but I led her toward the steps by the crook of the arm.

"Come on, everybody's waiting."

Once we got to the ice-cream shop, Dad and Uncle Tommy's competition drew a little crowd. Probably because we weren't exactly inconspicuous, pounding our fists on the table, chanting, "Chug, chug, chug!" Among the onlookers were three girls eating cones, looking like they'd just come from the beach, bikini straps tied around their necks visible beneath tank tops and sundresses. My socks, sneakers, and T-shirt made me look like a tomboy in comparison. But after seeing David's reaction to the bruise on my thigh, I was glad I'd worn something that covered the ones on my arm and foot—the ones he *had* given me.

The girls stood behind Mom, and she wasted no time swiveling around to chat them up. The woman would talk to walls if she thought there was any chance they'd talk back. We were similar in a lot of ways, but that wasn't one of them. A fact she refused to accept. Which was why I slouched in my seat the moment I heard her say, "Oh, you're the same age as my daughter!" She turned to me with excited, expectant eyes, like she wanted me to burst off my chair and hug them for sharing my birth year. "Kelsey, this is Marisol. Her name means 'sea and sun' in Spanish. Isn't that pretty?"

I nodded and tried to form my mouth into some semblance of a smile. I hated when she did this. She was forever dragging me into conversations like a reluctant dog on a leash, lecturing me to socialize as if the fact that I preferred keeping to myself was a defect in me she was determined to fix.

"Marisol," Mom said, "do you go to school here?"

"Yep." Marisol wiped a stray drip of mint chocolate chip from her chin. "But I'm actually going to Costa Rica to study abroad next semester."

My mother's widened eyes met mine. "Isn't that *exciting*?"

"Wow, *qué bueno*," David piped up, causing the girls to twitter with laughter.

"Mm-hm. Really cool." I meant it, but I had no interest in learning this girl's life story when I'd probably never see her again and had nothing even half as noteworthy to contribute to the conversation. So I stood up and said, "Excuse me, I need to run to the ladies' room. Good luck in Costa Rica."

I didn't have to look to know my mother's mortified eyes were following me as I left the table.

By the time I came back, my father was on his feet, fists raised above his head in victory, people clapping and patting him on the back before drifting back to their own business. He'd actually won, and I didn't get to see it because I'd been hiding in the bathroom.

"Good thing I took a picture," my mother said pointedly. "You missed Daddy winning."

I mumbled something unintelligible under my breath as we filed up to the front of the store to place the rest of our orders. That was the other part of our tradition: Once the competition was over, everyone else got their ice cream and we headed over to the Cliff Walk, the walking/biking trail between the mansions and the beach.

"So why didn't you want to talk to those girls earlier?" David asked as he licked a glob of salted caramel from the softball-size mound on his cone. We had separated into groups as we walked, with Dad and Uncle Tommy at the front, Mom and Aunt Tess with Miranda between them in the middle, and David and me lagging in the back.

"Because I can't stand when my mother tries to turn me into a social experiment. She thinks my personality is faulty because she enjoys starting random conversations with strangers and I don't." I kicked a pebble out of my way. "I get all paranoid that I'll come off boring and stupid and they'll end up thinking I'm lame anyway. Is it really so wrong to not like talking to people I don't know?"

David nudged me with his elbow. "But you don't know me."

"Sure I do. You're David. You *think* you have mad video game skills, and you definitely have a terrible Spanish accent."

He threw his head back and laughed. "And you're cool with that?"

"Uh-huh." I didn't know how to explain that I didn't click with people very often, but when I did, it was instant and lasting. David was one of those people who was just easy to be around.

"Ditto. And for what it's worth, you're not lame at all." He looked thoughtful as he took another swipe at his cone. "I guess I'm the opposite. You seem really close with your family. I talk to everyone, and the only people I think suck are the ones I'm related to." A hint of bitterness hardened his voice. It disappeared when he added, "Except my dad. He's awesome."

We stopped walking, eating in silence for a few seconds as David stared through the chain-link fence separating us from the expansive lawn behind the Astors' sprawling mansion.

"Can you believe this place was built as a summer 'cottage'?" he said. "I mean, if they made something this behemoth to live in for two months a year, can you imagine what their permanent house looked like?"

I hooked my fingertips around one of the wire links and stared dreamily at the stately windows and pillared wraparound porch. For an instant I pictured myself floating down the grand staircase inside with layers of Victorian ruffles billowing around my feet. Newport always had that effect—making me wish I could go back in time and spend a day in the shoes of the filthy rich Gilded Age elite. "I think I must've lived here in a past life. Maybe that's why I love it so much."

David's eyes darkened. "Some people live here now and don't even appreciate it."

"Well," I said, hoping to lighten the mood as we started moving again, "if my present-day luck is any indication, Past Kelsey was probably a scullery maid."

That got a chuckle out of him. "You know, you're pretty funny for someone with a defective personality."

My father saved David from a retaliatory shove by yelling, "Slippery footing up ahead! Hold on to your cones!"

We'd reached the part of the Cliff Walk that lived up to its name—where the cement trail gave way to boulders and rocks without a guardrail in sight. The part that never failed to bring out my inner chickenshit.

"Um, you can go ahead if you want to," I said, pulling the hem of my shorts over the mottled splotch David had noticed earlier. "I'm going to head back. I don't think the ice cream is agreeing with my stomach."

"No, I don't want you to walk alone." The look of concern on his face made me feel awful for being such a wimp. "I'll go with you."

I tried to protest, but he called up to my parents, who, ever paranoid, told me to stay with him until they got back. Not that I minded.

We chatted the whole walk home, and I'd forgotten I was supposed to be feeling sick by the time we reached David's grandfather's house. Until we stepped into the kitchen, and the sensation that something wasn't right caused a real knot to form in my stomach.

David's father sat crouched in the door frame that separated the kitchen and dining room, a dustpan in one hand and a small broom in the other. At his feet lay a pile of broken glass.

"Dad? What happened?"

Mr. Kerrigan exhaled and scratched his head, but before he could answer, Jay appeared in the doorway from the living room. "The two of you think you're funny, hiding things on me?" he shouted, pointing his finger in David's face. "Next time I'll tear this whole house apart!"

I jumped and hid behind David without thinking, then immediately felt ridiculous. He might've been yelling like a maniac, but Jay was a slight, silver-haired old man. His eyes were bloodshot, his robe sagged on his frame, and despite being mid-outburst, he looked weary and sad. Like

32

someone who'd spent too many years fighting his demons, only to be bested by them in the end.

Over the next few minutes, as I cowered near the back door, I learned that David's father had hidden Jay's alcohol before he left for Goodwill. After he drove off, Jay had gone looking for it and, when he couldn't find it, opted to throw almost every glass in the cabinet against various kitchen surfaces instead.

"I'll finish cleaning this, Dad. You go take care of *him*," David spat.

Mr. Kerrigan reluctantly handed over the broom and dustpan, and David knelt to the floor as his father ushered his grandfather upstairs.

I fidgeted uncomfortably. "Um, can I help?"

David shook his head, his lips set so tight that I could see the outline of his braces bulging between his nose and mouth. He made two sweeps into the pan before shoving his tools aside and slumping against the door frame with a heavy sigh, letting his head fall against the wood.

"I don't get it," he said, grinding the palms of his hands against his temples. "How can someone throw his life away?" He looked at me with dark, incredulous eyes, not waiting for an answer. "How can you just not care about anything? How can someone own a great place like this and not even give a crap what happens to it?"

I walked over and settled on the floor against the opposite side of the door frame. "I'm sorry." I didn't know what else to say. After what he'd said about his family on the Cliff Walk, I got the feeling he wasn't just talking about his grandfather. "Is there . . . something else going on?"

He didn't respond right away, absently stroking the smooth curve of a broken chunk of glass on the floor instead. Then he looked at me. "You know my parents are divorced, right?"

"I heard."

"My mom was the one who wanted it, and she was such a bitch about it. Brought my dad to court over every little thing, nickel-and-dimed him for all their stuff, including our house. Then she turned around and fucking sold it. My dad never did anything to her, and she acted like she had something to prove. But you know how hard she fought for custody of me?" He picked up the piece of glass and tossed it against a cabinet. "She didn't."

My heart broke a little bit for him at that moment. I reached out and took his hand, because it felt like the right thing to do. "Her loss."

"You think so?"

"Totally."

Light came back to his eyes, and he sat up straighter as he looked from me to our loosely twined fingers. He cleared his throat but kept his hand in mine. "Do you think this can stay between us? I don't want everyone in Norwood to know how messed up my life is."

"You're no more messed up than anyone else, David."

"Still." His grin widened. "I'm trying out for the baseball team. I'll forget all about how I demolished you in the video tournament if you come to some of my games. Since no one there will know me from a hole in the dirt."

I couldn't help but smile back. "Definitely. We'll have to hang out sometime."

But we didn't hang out sometime. We hung out *all* the time.

I knew I liked David as soon as I met him, but I had no idea the boy who knocked me over with a baseball would become my go-to plus one any time I was bored or lonely. Or breathing. I didn't know he'd give the best hugs, or share my love of summer and my irrational fear of bats and my obsession with chocolate chip cookies.

I had no way of knowing he'd become my best friend in the world.

Five

Rhode Island
Senior Year

I didn't see David again for the rest of the day after Ryan walked him to class. I half wondered if Ryan had chopped him up and stashed the parts in an empty locker. But he seemed back to normal when he drove me to get my car after school.

I wished everything could go back to the way it was that easily. My family and I had been living in Rhode Island, right outside Newport, for the past year, just as I'd always dreamed of doing. That night, however, my dreams were filled with images of Norwood. More specifically, the piece of Norwood that had turned up like a metastasized tumor in the last place I expected.

Deep down, I knew I shouldn't have been so surprised. We'd met in Newport, after all, and his grandfather's house hadn't been a vacation home like Uncle Tommy's; Jay had lived there year-round. In the back of my mind, I'd always known I might see David again, especially since he and Mr. Kerrigan were Jay's only family. And I'd mostly succeeded in not thinking about it.

But every image I'd tried to suppress for the past year found a way to break through the dam that night. I saw the delicate white and purple flowers in the empty field near the house David had shared with his father. The way he'd pick them and sneak them in my hair when I wasn't looking, because he knew I was petrified that bugs would crawl out and nest in my scalp. The photo I took of him, beaming after he'd pitched a perfect game.

Then the images became more distorted and nightmarish. I looked down and saw blood everywhere. It stained my clothes, my hands, my face. I started to cry, and when David tried to comfort me, I got blood all over him, too.

Suddenly everything disappeared: David, Norwood, all of it. I stood in the hallway at Clayton, not a speck of blood in my perfectly highlighted hair, and not one red smear on my pretty white sundress. I stared at the glass doors at the end of the hall, knowing something was about to go terribly wrong. David walked in, just as he had that morning. Only this time it was the David I'd met three years ago. The one with an air of uncertainty about him and too much black hair hanging in his eyes and braces on his teeth.

His clothes were disheveled, and the closer he got to me, the easier it became to see dark splotches of blood all over him.

"David," I gasped, keenly aware that the hallway had filled with gawkers. "You're covered in blood."

"I know. It's happening to me, too."

"What's happening to you?"

David's eyes hardened, and I barely recognized the voice that spoke his next words. "Do you even care?"

That's when my eyes flew open and I struggled to sit up, fighting off the tail end of dream paralysis.

No Freud required to analyze that one.

I knew, even in my sleep, that what I'd had with David in Norwood would never translate to the life I'd lived for the past year in Rhode Island. Beautiful as he might be, he served as a reminder of my ugly past. He didn't fit in my new world, and having him here would only ruin everything. The same way he'd ruined everything once before.

According to the clock, I still had ten more minutes before my alarm went off. But the last thing I wanted was to fall back to sleep and revisit my dream. So I dragged myself into the bathroom. I cast a skittish glance in the mirror, and even though I didn't see blood pouring out of my nose or mouth, I still ran to the kitchen and downed some vitamins before jumping in the shower.

Normally a shower would have soothed me, but that morning it stimulated my pissiness, as if the receptors determining my shitty mood were activated by the hot water hitting my skin.

Who the hell does he think he is? I thought as I yanked a comb through my hair afterward. *First doing what he did before I left, and then showing up here?* I threw a towel around my hair and then let out a mini scream of frustration when it unraveled immediately. *He's crazy if he thinks I'm going to act like everything is fine. I'm not going to speak to him. I'll acknowledge him if he talks to me, but we will not be friends again. I'm not even going to look at him.*

That didn't happen.

I got to my first-period English class early, since my morning dose of Candy and Ryan hadn't done much to improve my mood. Neither had the fact that Mom and Miranda spent breakfast blathering about how excited they were to have David and his father in town, and how they wished Aunt Tess and Uncle Tommy hadn't sold the cabin, so we could all get together for old time's sake.

I had muttered that old times were old for a reason. They ignored me.

Most of the desks were still empty as I took my place in the back, reserving the seat next to me for Violet by dumping my bag on the chair. I dug out the book we'd been assigned to read and prepared to numb my mind for a few minutes.

That is, until David walked in the door and handed Mr. Ingles a transfer slip.

"Ah," Mr. Ingles said, twisting his thick mustache. "Mrs. Pruitt's class too full?"

"Yes," David replied. "They told me I should come to this room starting today."

"Well, then. Welcome aboard Mr."—he glanced at the paper—"Kerrigan. Have a seat."

No. No, no frickin' way. My palms started to sweat as I hoped David wouldn't see me. Or that he would, and he'd choose a seat as far from me as possible.

But he strode right over, plopping himself down at the desk in front of Violet's. "Hey." He smiled an effort-less smile, and something I'd noticed yesterday caught my attention again. The tiny beauty mark he'd always had beneath his lip was now accompanied by a small, angry red line, like a cut that hadn't healed properly.

I wondered how and when he'd gotten it before I slipped my bookmark between the pages of my novel and sat up. And broke my promise to ignore him by replying, "Hey."

That didn't take long.

We started talking at the same time, turned red, and stopped. "Go ahead," I said with a nervous laugh.

"I was just saying we didn't really get a chance to talk yesterday."

"I know. I'm sorry to hear about your grandfather."

"I'm not." He raked a hand through his hair and shook

his head. "That came out wrong. I just meant he's been in a bad way for a long time, and unhappy even longer. Maybe now he's at peace. Or something."

"So you're living in his house?"

He nodded. "It's ours now."

"I can't believe you're here."

It was an honest statement, but I hadn't meant for it to sound quite so blunt.

David smirked. "Neither could your sister. She made me feel like a rock star."

I wanted to ask him why he hadn't called, or sent a text, or given me some sort of warning, but I knew it was a stupid question. I wouldn't have broken radio silence after a year either. So I said, "Miranda always loved you."

Bad choice. His smile faded and he flipped his notebook cover open and closed as I tried to think of something, anything, to diffuse the mention of the *L* word.

"So, um, what else is new?"

David's eyes flitted over me. "Your hair is different."

My hands fluttered to the highlighted blond strands that suddenly felt foreign and phony, and I tried to ignore that his words sounded like an accusation. "I needed a change. Do you like it?"

He shrugged. "It's nice. But I liked it before, too."

Painful. This conversation was truly and utterly painful. *Teach us something, Mr. Ingles!* I begged silently. *So what if there are only five people in the room?*

With no relief in sight, I made a last-ditch effort. "How's your dad?"

"He's better."

"Better?"

David made a noise somewhere between a sigh and a snort.

"What?" My heart sped up as I waited for him to tell me whatever it was I didn't know but apparently should've.

His eyes narrowed, like he couldn't decide whether or not to take me seriously. "We found out he had cancer a few months after you left. They caught it pretty early and everything, but he went through some brutal treatments. I spent months learning to write computer programs because he was too sick to do his job. He was in rough shape for a while."

I laid my hand on my chest as guilt and panic coursed through me. "Oh my God. No, no one told me. Is he . . . ?" I struggled to find the right words. "Is he okay?"

"His last scan was all clear. So far so good." He gave me another dubious look. "You really didn't know?"

"I swear I didn't. Why would you think I did?"

David leaned back in his seat and fiddled with his pencil. "Because of the huge basket of stuff your parents sent."

"Wait—what? When was this?"

"Months ago. I thought you would've called."

I sank in my chair, feeling small and god-awful. The real meaning of his words came through loud and clear: *I thought you'd be there for me when I needed you.*

42

But I hadn't been.

The unmistakable bitterness in his words sat heavy in my stomach. Prickles of heat spread over my body, and for a second I thought I might really be sick. My mind refused to digest what he'd told me. Instead of thinking his father's cancer might have brought David and me back together, my own parents had thought I wouldn't care?

My hand moved toward him and my lips parted, but to say what, I didn't know.

I didn't get a chance to say anything at all, because Violet bounded into the classroom at that moment. She spotted David, froze, and threw a frantic glance from him to me and back again. I stood up and removed my bag from her chair. "David," I said. "This is Violet. Violet, David."

"Hi!" Violet thrust her hand out with an enthusiasm only the quintessential cheerleader could muster. Which she was. Take short, cute, bouncy, and blond, inject them with caffeinated lattes and dress them in a purple and yellow flowered sundress, and behold Violet Kensing. "You weren't here yesterday! Did you switch so you could be in Kelsey's class? I heard you two were friends!"

Way to up the awkward factor, Vi.

David flashed his most swoonworthy grin as he shook her hand. "Nah. My schedule was all screwed up. I spent my whole lunch in the office yesterday trying to straighten it out. They had me in Pruitt's class, but it was full. I have a feeling I'll like it better here anyway."

Violet giggled. "I think this might be my favorite class now."

Oh, for the love. That hadn't taken long at all. Girls had always thrown themselves at David. Some things never changed.

And some things did.

A bubble of something hot and sour rose up in my chest, something I either couldn't or didn't want to identify. Whatever it was, it made me want to take the hair Violet kept tossing flirtatiously over her shoulder and yank it out of her head.

My concentration drifted for the rest of class. Especially once Violet slipped me a note. It said, "I'm inviting him to my party."

I wrote back, "What party?"

"The party I decided to have five minutes ago. MUST GET HIM ALONE! P.S.: Is he a good kisser? P.P.S.: You don't mind, do you?"

A good kisser? Why would she say that?

She'd drawn a deranged-looking smiley face in the corner, and I wondered if it was to distract me from the fact that she was asking permission to treat my best friend as her shiny object du jour. *Former* best friend. Why was I gripping my pen so tightly?

I sent the note back with, "I don't know. He's all yours."

A smirk appeared on Violet's face when she read my response, and a moment later the note landed back on my desk. She'd drawn an arrow pointing to the words "I don't know" and written "LIAR!" in big block letters. Another arrow pointed to "He's all yours," which she'd boxed off so heavy-handedly that she'd almost gone through the paper. Next to it, with equal vigor, she'd spelled out "I HAVE IT IN WRITING! HE IS MINE!"

My fingers twitched as I fought the urge to write *Until you get bored with him*. Instead I forced a smile and passed the paper back to her. This was a good thing, after all. If David had his hands full with Violet, he wouldn't be thinking about me, or the things we'd said and done, or not said and done, last year. We could start all over, and for that I should have been grateful.

Violet propped her chin on one hand, pretending to be engrossed in Mr. Ingles's lecture. With the other hand, she wiggled her fingers against David's back until he turned enough to take a note from her. I watched him read it, then turn around and nod, grinning that grin I knew so well.

I definitely should have been grateful.

"Should" being the operative word.

Six

I spotted David at his locker a couple of weeks after school started and had to do a double take. I loved his recent short haircut, but I still wasn't used to it, and that morning he'd added another new thing to the mix: a navy and white Yankees jersey I'd never seen him wear before—and I'd seen him a lot. Not only did we have three classes together, but when he and his father had arrived in Norwood, my family welcomed them to the neighborhood by helping to unload the U-Haul. For their whole first week we'd taken turns grilling in our backyards until they had a chance to get their kitchen unpacked.

"Hey," I said as I came up next to him.

David looked up and promptly eyed the stack of college pamphlets I was trying to shove into the front pocket of my book bag. "Holy brochures, Kelse. Are you planning on graduating four years early?"

I answered him with my best soft-voiced imitation of Mrs. Malone, my guidance counselor. "It's never too early to think about the future." The zipper closed over the bulging compartment, and I nodded toward his jersey. "Go Yanks. Nice shirt."

David puffed his chest, pretending to model it. "Thanks. My dad gave it to me for my birthday."

"Last year?"

"Uh, no." A shy smile pulled at his lips. "Today."

My books almost slipped out of my hands. "David! Today is your birthday? Why didn't you tell me?"

"Eh, it's just another day. Nothing to make a big deal over."

"Of course it is! Everyone should feel special on their birthday! I would've brought balloons and decorated your locker if I'd known."

"No offense," he laughed. "But in that case, I'm kind of glad I didn't tell you."

I gaped at him. New kid or not, someone as nice as David didn't deserve to have his birthday pass with no fanfare at all.

I found Eric at his locker after lunch. He and I had known each other forever. But ever since Amy Heffernan had dared him to kiss me and he'd done it, the awkward factor kept ratcheting up between us. He'd apologized, and even asked me out a few times, which I suspected was more about the desire to save face than actual interest in me. But then he'd tried to kiss me for real, and the way he used his tongue like an overexcited puppy made me pull back and wipe my mouth with the back of my hand. I also may or may not have said "yuck" out loud. . . . And even though I'm sure his assessment of the kiss was similar, he was highly insulted.

So the fact that I still felt more comfortable talking to him than to Maddie lately was saying a lot.

"Hey," I said as he dropped books onto a mass of compacted papers and gym clothes. "Can we do something tonight for David's birthday?"

"Sure." He slammed the metal door and hoisted his backpack onto his shoulder. "Maddie's brother already bought a bunch of beer for her party this weekend. I'll bet we could get some people to go down to the lake and celebrate."

He emphasized the word "celebrate" with a giant grin that showcased his unusually square teeth—and also told me he was way more excited for an excuse to drink beer than to actually acknowledge David's birthday.

When had my friends become so enthralled with the challenge of smuggling booze into their bloodstream? It was like puberty had triggered some need to experiment, and I was clearly missing the hormone.

"Oh. That wasn't really what I had in mind."

"Then why not just invite him to the party? Do we have to do something today?"

I didn't get a chance to tell him that, technically, Maddie hadn't even invited me to her party, because she came around the corner at that moment with Amy Heffernan. The carefully curled ends of Maddie's chestnut hair tumbled over her shoulders, and her pink-glossed lips pursed conspiratorially as she and Amy exchanged the gossip du jour. They sported matching charm bracelets around the arms holding their designer bags in place, like they were modeling them. Must've been nice to have gainfully employed parents.

I remembered the days when Maddie couldn't even wear earrings because her ears would get infected, or drink milk because it made her sick. Now she had three piercings in each ear, plus a tiny diamond stud in her nose, and her stomach had no problem at all with frequent vodka ingestion.

"Hey," Eric said before I could open my mouth. "Do you mind if we invite the new kid to the party this weekend?"

An awkward laugh that Maddie tried to pass off as happy surprise skittered from her throat and she wound her finger into the green and white fabric of her dress. "Oh! You're coming, Kelse? That's great."

I bit back my response of *Am I invited?* to spare myself her inevitable and insincere *Of course!* Instead I twirled the frayed hem of my jean shorts and asked, "Will Sloppy Ho be there?"

Maddie's lips thinned. "Kelsey, you really need to stop calling her that. Everyone is over it."

During the summer Maddie had started dating Jared Rose, younger brother of Norwood's sophomore queen bee, Isabel. That was the start of Maddie's metamorphosis. Her hair, her makeup, her party girl reputation—none of that resembled the Maddie Clairmont I'd been friends with since first grade. The one who, like me, didn't make a full-time job of impressing people. Lately it was like she'd tried on some sort of Isabel Halloween costume and forgotten to take it off.

Anyhow, on the first day of school, I'd stood behind Isabel in the lunch line and Maddie stood behind me. My blood had come to a slow boil as I pushed my tray toward the register, listening to Isabel and the girl in front of her ruthlessly pick on the freshman exchange student.

"She has a mustache," Isabel's friend said with a shudder. "There're, like, things you can do for that. Fucking do it already."

"And she's a moron." Isabel stopped texting long enough to wave her hand in disgust. "I've heard the place you're conceived affects the person you become. Her parents must've done it on a toilet bowl, because she's dumb as shit."

They burst into laughter, and that was it. Before I could stop myself, I rammed my tray into Isabel's as hard as I could. It bumped against her mammoth purse, which slid off her shoulder and hit the edge of her tray, catapulting the contents of a sloppy joe sandwich all over the bag, which probably cost more than a year's worth of lunches.

She'd given me a lifetime supply of evil eyes since then, claiming I'd done it on purpose. Which, of course, I had. She and her friends practically hissed at me every time we passed in the halls. In return, I called her Sloppy Ho behind her back.

But the worst part? The way Maddie had rushed to Isabel's defense and not mine. The way she was doing right now.

"And of course she's invited," Maddie continued. "You can bring David if you want to, but don't start any trouble."

My mouth dropped. We might not have been on a level playing field anymore statuswise, but I didn't deserve to be lectured like some punk from the wrong side of the tracks. "Why don't you get your head out of your ass, Maddie? Or maybe I should say out of Isabel's a—"

"Hey!" Eric laughed as he pulled my arm. "No catfights in the hall. Here, kiss and make up." He propelled me toward Maddie, and I took two stumbling steps in her direction before snapping out of his grip.

"On second thought," I said, looking right into Maddie's eyes, "I think I'll skip the party."

I turned around and shoved past Eric, knowing I was headed in the wrong direction but not willing to sacrifice my dramatic exit or my pride.

"What about David's birthday?" he called after me.

I didn't turn around. "I'll figure it out myself."

* * *

The moment I stepped off the school bus that afternoon, I hurried into the kitchen, tossing my book bag along the way. I needed something I could whip up in a hurry for David. I reached into a cabinet and grabbed a cookie sheet, deciding baked goods was the way to go.

"Kelsey?" Mom called as the metal clanged its way onto the counter. "What are you doing?"

"I need to use the oven. Today is David's birthday and I didn't have a gift. I want to make chocolate chip cookies."

"I have balloons left over from Daddy's birthday. Do you want me to blow some up for you?"

"Sure. And maybe I can make him an IOU for a gift or something."

A little while later, with cookies, balloons, and IOU in tow, I headed through our backyard to the woods. David lived around the corner, and with all the times we'd been to each other's houses, it hadn't taken long to figure out that walking or riding our bikes through the streets was actually the long way. If I cut across my backyard and kept going, I'd end up in his yard, and vice versa.

A few minutes later I emerged in the clearing and tip-toed around to the front, fumbling to ring the doorbell with my armload of goodies. Mr. Kerrigan answered the door.

"Kelsey!" he said. "What's all this?"

He held the door for me and I stepped inside the house. With the exception of the décor, our homes were identical:

small, boxy split-levels. Except the Kerrigans' layout was the reverse of ours, and it always made me feel like I'd stepped into a bizarro alternate universe where everything was the opposite of what it should be.

"Your son failed to mention he had a birthday coming," I said.

"Ah, he never lets me make a fuss over him either. Too old for that now, I suppose."

"Who's old?" David poked his head down from the stairwell. A look of surprise rippled over his face when he saw me. "Kelse? I thought you were going out with Eric this afternoon."

David had asked if I wanted to do math homework together after school, and I'd fibbed about having plans. But after what had happened in the hall earlier, I didn't care to make plans with Eric or anyone else. Except David.

I held up the dish of cookies and flushed, suddenly feeling embarrassed. "I lied. Happy birthday."

The smile on David's face, the way he looked completely mortified and thoroughly flattered all at once, made it entirely worth it. We stood there grinning like idiots at each other until David finally said, "Come on up. Now that you're here I can help you with those math problems."

Mr. Kerrigan snatched a cookie from a spot where the hastily applied plastic wrap had come loose, winking at me as he took a bite. He sent me off with a pat on my back, and

I followed David upstairs. As I set the plate down, I noticed a silver medal sitting inside an open box on his desk. It was a religious medal, the kind my aunt Tess kept in the glove box of her car. It was supposed to be like a guardian angel watching over you on the road.

"Is that for when you start driving?" I asked.

"Yep, another gift from my dad. I'll need all the help I can get with the hunk of junk I'll be cruising in."

"You're getting a car? Nice!"

"Not for a while, and 'scrap metal' might be a better term, but yup. 'They see me rollin'. They hatin'.'"

"Oh my God." I laughed. "Quoting bad rap lyrics? I think you need a cookie."

As I started to unwrap the dish, I saw three birthday cards standing up on his desk. One from his mother, one from his father, and one that looked handmade. Let me rephrase that: and one that had clearly been handmade by a girl.

I tilted my head to see the signature, then wrinkled my nose in confusion. It was signed, "xoxo, Amy."

"Amy Heffernan made you a birthday card?" I picked it up to look more closely. "How did she even know?"

"Because it was a Spanish assignment. We had to pick names and find out when that person's birthday is. Then we have to make them a *feliz cumpleaños* card when it comes."

"'Xoxo,' huh? That's some advanced *español*."

"It doesn't mean anything."

"Hugs and kisses don't mean anything in Spanish? I think

Miss Amy is trying to say a little more than *feliz cumpleaños*."

David cocked his head. "Do you sign your cards to Eric with *x*'s and *o*'s?"

I was fairly certain that if I'd ever given Eric a card, I definitely hadn't signed it with *x*'s and *o*'s, and never would. Especially since our "relationship" had fizzled like a defective firecracker before it even started.

"No," I said. "And I didn't sign my IOU with *x*'s and *o*'s either, but I think you'll get the point." I grabbed the piece of paper off the cookie dish and handed it to him.

"Kelse! All this is enough." He motioned toward the cookies and balloons. "You don't have to make a big deal."

"But it's your birthday! Presents are, like, a rule."

"I don't need anything."

He could be so exasperating. "Okay, but do you *want* anything?"

David's lips twisted in thought as he ran his fingers over the edge of the IOU. "You have English class with Amy, don't you?"

"Second period, every day."

"Maybe you could ask her what she thinks of me?"

Ick. He was actually interested in her? "We're talking about birthday gifts, David, not pimp services."

"But you said you wanted to give me a gift!" His eyes widened with disbelief. "Favors count."

"Ew, you're serious, aren't you? You could do so much better than Amy Heffernan. She's gross."

"Geez, Kelse. No one can accuse you of not telling it like it is."

"It's a talent."

David threw his hands up with a laugh. "Fine. Maybe she'll be at Maddie's party this weekend. If I have enough to drink, I can ask her myself."

I froze. "You're going to Maddie's party?"

"She invited me this afternoon. Why, you're not?"

I stared at the medal, tracing the etching on the face with my finger. "Maddie and I . . . aren't as close as we used to be."

David didn't push when I sat quietly for a few seconds, absently dropping the medal into its box and fishing it back out again.

"Then I won't go either," David said.

I looked up at him. "No, you should go if you want to. They like you better than me, anyway."

A slow smile stretched across his face. "Well, I like you better. So I'm not going."

His grin must've been contagious, because I felt it reflected on my own face. "Don't think this means I'll talk to Amy for you."

"Forget I said anything about Amy. I take it back. But"—he looked down and picked at something on his comforter—"it's not like you're interested, right?"

"David!"

He looked at me long enough to make me a little nervous.

Then his lips quirked up again. "Kidding, Kelse. Kidding."

"Good. So how about a new hat to go with your Yankees jersey?"

His face turned serious. "No gifts, Kelse. Promise me."

I let out a long, exaggerated sigh. "Fine. But only if you promise you won't get me anything for my birthday either."

"Deal. I'll give you the gift of my friendship," he teased.

That was good enough for me. Because even though there's no way to say it without sounding horrifically cheesy, having him in my life was gift enough.

Seven

**Rhode Island
Senior Year**

"Seriously, how have you never mentioned this guy before?"

It was the first Friday night of the school year, and Candy sat perched on the edge of my bed, holding my post-perfect-game photo of David, which I'd dug out of my closet after my freaky dream the other night.

"There wasn't much to say." More like no easy way to say it. "But I must've mentioned him once or twice."

Hadn't I?

She tapped the picture against the palm of her hand and pursed her lips. "I definitely know nothing of Hot David from Connecticut. So what aren't you telling me, and why does Smurfy all but piss himself every time this kid comes around?"

The sound of a car pulling into my driveway distracted Candy, and she scurried across my bed on her knees to peer out the window. "Speak of shit heads and they appear," she said. "Come on. Let's go before they try to come inside and I have to watch Ryan molest you." She stretched across the bed and set the photo down on my dresser. Then she pointed at me. "And don't think this conversation is over."

I popped a mint in my mouth as we walked out to the car to meet Matt and Ryan. I still didn't know how Violet managed to put a party together on less than a week's notice, but her party was exactly where we were headed. She'd been touting it as a "last pool party of the summer," and used words like "epic" and "fab" every time she talked about it. She'd also been all up in David's business every time I'd seen her since Mr. Ingles's class—like, walking so close you would've thought they'd been surgically fused together.

I did not want to go to this party.

My interactions with David had been limited to polite hellos and what's ups since then, despite the fact that Violet had invited him to sit at our lunch table. Stressing me out even more was the fact that our parents were on a full-fledged mission to get together one weekend. Luckily, my dad's weekend trips to promote the book he finally got published made it impossible. For the moment.

Candy bounced down the steps of the front porch as I locked up the house, and Matt stepped out of the car and catcalled loudly. "Lookin' good there, Candle. When am I finally gonna get a piece of that?"

She stopped in front of him and adjusted her black tube top over her ample chest. "Eat your heart out, Crowley. I'm saving myself."

"For who?"

"For someone who's not you."

Matt grabbed her and pulled her into a bear hug, purposely mussing her hair as she squealed and tried to squirm away. "You're full of shit. You know I haunt your dreams, Waxman. Now say it!"

Normally I would have found their antics hilarious, but tonight nothing seemed amusing. "Knock it off, you two," I said as I approached the car. "Let's get this over with."

Matt and Candy climbed into the backseat of Ryan's Camaro, and I could almost feel the look they exchanged at my comment. Or, rather, Matt's look of *What's up her ass?* and Candy's responding shrug.

I smacked a kiss on Ryan's lips as the car door slammed behind me.

"Hey. What's that all about? You don't want to go?"

"Not in a party mood, I guess."

"Is it because that kid's gonna be there? Has he been bothering you?" It was about the hundredth time that week Ryan had asked if David had been bothering me. Like he was dying for me to say yes, and to finally have a real reason to kick his ass.

"No, Ry. He didn't bother me today, or the day before, or the day before that. Like I keep telling you."

"Just making sure." He squeezed my knee and put the car in reverse, then hit the brake when he looked up at my darkened house. "Wait. It's Friday night. Where is everybody?"

"My dad's doing signings and stuff in New York this weekend, so Mom went with him. Miranda's sleeping at a friend's house."

His hand crept over to my thigh and he gave me a sly grin. "Then maybe we should have our own party here."

Exactly why I hadn't told him. Wasn't in the mood for that kind of party either.

A cacophony of gagging sounds rose from the backseat, followed by Candy saying, "Sorry, Romeo, I'm staying with her tonight."

I smiled over my shoulder at her, grateful to have her as my friend. Then Ryan slipped his hand beneath mine and lifted it to his lips, kissing it with a sweetness that made me melt, and I sighed. It felt so good to be reminded of the things and the people I was lucky enough to have in my life. Especially when everything else had started to feel like I'd been flipped to an alternate universe.

For all her talk of epicness, Violet's party wasn't much different from any other Clayton High party. She'd covered all the bases: tiki torches lining the wrought-iron fence around the inground pool, music turned up too loud, an illicit supply of beer and alcohol probably procured with a fake ID, and the obligatory beer pong table, topped with red plastic cups, set out on the manicured lawn.

"Hey, guys!" Violet chirped as we walked into the kitchen. "People will be here any minute! This is going to be great!" David stood next to her, muscles straining beneath the sleeves of his T-shirt from the bags of ice he held in his arms. Like she'd already put him to work.

I was so surprised to see him that I blurted, "Your car wasn't outside." I knew immediately it was the wrong thing to say, because Ryan would take it to mean I'd been looking for it. I hadn't *consciously* looked for it, but David's beat-up Chevy Cavalier was kind of hard to miss, especially around the expensive cars my friends drove.

"I'm driving my grandfather's car now," David said. "I got rid of that other one."

Something inside me twinged. Did he get rid of it because of what happened the last time we were together?

"Boys," Violet interrupted, addressing Matt and Ryan. I could have hugged her. "I need your muscles. Can you go down to the basement and bring some more drinks outside to the deck? David was just about to put ice in the coolers."

"Better do that before my arms go numb," David said, moving toward the door that led from the kitchen to the deck. His eyes darted to Ryan as he stepped past us, and I knew Ryan must have been sizing him up, which he seemed to do constantly. It was getting old.

The tension I may or may not have imagined cleared once the boys left the room, and Violet grabbed Candy and me by the arm. "Come on, girls. I'm making daiquiris in the blender, except the blender kind of scares me so I need one of you to hit the button."

Candy shook her head. "Step aside, Vi. I got this."

Violet beamed and turned to me. "What are you drinking tonight, Kelsey?"

"Soda. I just got my car back from the squirrel incident."

"You're no fun!" Violet pouted. "Didn't Ryan drive?"

"Yes, but if I know Ryan, I'll be driving home."

Truth be told, it felt good to have an excuse not to drink. Cocktails with a thousand parts alcohol and two parts strawberry-flavored ice only served one purpose. I already felt like so many things were slipping out of my control. I didn't need my presence of mind to be one of them.

Candy glanced over her shoulder as she poured way too much rum into the blender. "I think Sober Sally should be made to schlep ice with your boy toy, Vi."

As if on cue, the door opened and David stuck his head inside. "Hey, Violet? Want to hand me another couple of bags?"

"I'll get it, Vi," I said. I felt like I needed to ask David something. I wasn't sure what. But I knew I didn't want an audience.

David took the ice from me when I got to the door, but I followed him outside anyway. As he set the bags on top of the ones he'd brought before, I found myself blurting another question at him. "So why did you get rid of your car?"

He didn't look at me as he broke one of the bags open, but he made that sound again, the half sigh, half snort, that he'd made when I'd asked about his father. "Things change," he said.

"What's that supposed to mean?"

"I mean, look at you, Kelse." He straightened and stared at me in disbelief, scratching his head. "Take a look at yourself if you want to know what I mean. You never used to wear dresses, or all that shit on your face. You hated parties and girls who walked around with fancy designer purses. And didn't you tell me once that Tiffany jewelry was an experiment to see how many morons would overpay for a bracelet? 'Cause if I'm not mistaken . . ." He reached out and held up my wrist, his cold hand sending a jolt through me.

I yanked my arm back and wrapped my other hand around the silver toggle bracelet. "Ryan gave it to me," I said defensively.

"I'm sure he did." He ripped open a bag of ice almost violently and sent it clattering into the cooler. "I mean, I'd ask if you want to go throw some balls around, but I wouldn't want you to break a nail or anything."

My fingers tightened until I felt the links of my bracelet imprinting on my skin. "What. Is. Your. Problem." My voice came out in a low growl, but it didn't seem to faze David at all. He closed the lid to the cooler and sat on it, arms taut at his sides. His eyes were challenging, but something else flickered behind those long lashes, something that scared me even more. Like he'd looked inside me, and hated what he saw.

"Heard you got drunk and wrecked your car. Very responsible of you, Kelse."

Heat flashed through my skin and I swallowed hard. "That's not what happened!" I said before I could stop myself.

His expression didn't change. "Then what did?"

I looked away, twisting furiously at my bracelet. He'd heard the lie I'd sold my friends. And worse, he believed it.

"What does any of this have to do with what I asked *you*?"

David's eyes roved over me. Assessing. Judging. Then he held up his hands. "A year's gone by. A lot of things are different. That's all I was trying to say."

I stepped toward him, my jaw clenched and my hand still clutching my wrist. I was sure I'd breathe fire if I picked up enough momentum. "What the hell are you even doing here?"

To my surprise, the condescension on his face disappeared. His eyes darkened and his lips turned down until he looked heartbreakingly sad.

"I don't know."

A noise from the ground below made my head snap to the left. Ryan and Matt had emerged from the sliding glass doors that led from the basement into the backyard, lugging cases of beer and another cooler with them, and effectively ending my and David's conversation.

The way his eyes moved over me as I went back inside—filled with questions and judgment—told me it wasn't over for good.

From there, I can't say the fun factor picked up. Maybe it was because of the pains I took to avoid being within twenty feet of David for the rest of the night. Or maybe it was because I was the only one not drunk, or even the slightest bit tipsy.

I wanted to gouge my own eyes out by the time Ryan and Matt were playing their umpteenth round of beer-buzzed video game race car driving in the basement. Nearly everyone had left, Violet had disappeared, and Candy was curled up in an armchair snoring softly.

"Grab a controller, babe," Ryan said. "I want to race against you."

"Not tonight." I stood up and stretched. "I'm going to find Violet and say good-bye. Finish up your game, okay? I want to go home when I get back."

"Kiss me first." Ryan gave me a bleary-eyed smile and puckered his lips. When I leaned in, he grabbed me around the waist and tried to pull me on top of him. "Candle Wax is sleeping," he slurred, his booze breath hitting me full in the face. "How 'bout she stays here with Vi and I come home with *you*?"

I kissed his cheek before freeing myself from his grip and smoothing my dress. "Not tonight, Ry. I'll drive you home, and Matt can bring you to get your car from my house tomorrow."

"Totally," Matt agreed, his eyes never leaving the TV screen.

Ryan scowled, and I felt his eyes following me as I headed toward the stairs that led up to the main level. The moment the quiet darkness of the stairwell surrounded me, I felt relieved. I could not wait for this night to be over.

I made my way through the kitchen and opened the screen door to the deck. The sound of David's voice and Violet's giggle made me stop in my tracks. I got the distinct feeling I'd be intruding on something if I made my presence known. Goose bumps stood up on my arms in spite of the warm night air as I maneuvered behind a tall potted plant and looked down at the pool.

"Come on," Violet said conspiratorially, leading David by the hand to the steps that descended into the water. He still had his T-shirt on, but he'd traded his jeans for swim trunks. "Everyone's gone. Let's go for a swim." She released his hand and glided into the water.

He hesitated at the second step, protesting that the water was cold, even though Violet seemed fine at waist-deep. She stuck her lower lip out and tugged at his hand. "Just for a little bit? I won't make you miss curfew. Promise."

"All right. But I can't stay much longer."

Violet bounced and clapped as David threw off his T-shirt, hurried into the water, and submerged himself. The ripping-it-off-like-a-Band-Aid approach, as he'd always called it. The one he always tried to get me to use on our summer vacations, when he'd be up to his chest in ocean water and I'd still be at the shore tiptoeing my way in.

David ran his hands over his face and hair as he came up for air. "Your turn," he said.

"No way!" Violet tittered furiously and made a half-assed attempt to get away from him, but he grabbed her around the waist and pretended to overpower her as she laughed like a yelping Chihuahua. No wonder girls like Amy Heffernan and Isabel Rose turned into doe-eyed tramps around him. The boy knew his way around the flirting game. It was a side of him I didn't care to see.

And yet, I couldn't. Stop. Looking.

"I'm just kidding." David released her and put his hands on the outer edge of the pool, leaning up against it. If it was a tactic to put distance between them, which I doubted, Violet didn't take it that way. She draped her arms around his waist and propped her chin against his chest.

"See? This isn't so bad, is it?" she said.

"Nope. It isn't."

One of her hands moved up toward his face, and she traced the scar beneath his lip with her finger. "How'd you get that?"

Even with only a slice of his profile visible from where I

stood, I knew David was embarrassed by the way he turned his head and rubbed at his chin, as if he were trying to scrub away the mark. I leaned closer, curious to know the answer.

"Ran into a door," David mumbled.

Violet seemed oblivious to his discomfort and touched his face again. "Scars are sexy."

"Right. I knew that. I did it on purpose."

More giggles. Then she leaned up on her toes and wrapped her arms around his neck, and my stomach started to cave in on itself.

Stop looking. Walk away. Escape, now!

Violet put her lips against the scar and kissed it. "There," she said. "All better now." And just as I managed to convince myself that maybe that was the worst of it, her mouth moved to his, and she kissed him for real.

It was like driving by an accident. Even when he put his hands on her waist and tilted his head in response, I couldn't peel my eyes from the scene.

It occurred to me then that even though we'd both dated other people, I'd never actually seen David kiss another girl. I'd never given any thought to how it would make me feel.

It felt like my vital organs had simultaneously imploded.

I felt hurt, too, though I had no right to. Violet had asked if I'd be okay with it, and I'd said yes. So why did I want nothing more than to hurl something heavy and blunt directly at her head and tell her to keep her whore slut hands off him?

Something rough and sharp dug into my finger, and I realized I'd gripped the edge of the deck hard enough to turn my knuckles white. That unsanded knothole brought me back to reality. I took a step away, irritated at the effort it took to get myself under control. But before I could turn around and walk into the house, something in the bay window across the way caught my attention.

Candy stood in the Kensings' kitchen, her hand pressed against the glass. My eyes met hers, and I knew she'd seen exactly what I'd seen. The look on her face, though, told me she'd seen something else, something far worse.

She'd seen the look on *my* face when it happened.

Eight

Connecticut
Winter, Freshman Year

David and I weren't the only ones to become fast friends after he and his father moved into our neighborhood. My parents loved his dad, and whenever David stayed for dinner, my mother always invited Mr. Kerrigan, too. They fit into our lives like they'd been there all along. So naturally they were both invited the night my mother cooked up a storm for my fifteenth birthday.

I looked around the table, feeling happy and glowy at having all my favorite people gathered in my honor: my parents, David and his dad, Aunt Tess and Uncle Tommy. And Miranda, of course.

My mother had asked me a hundred times if I'd wanted

a party, but I hadn't. I knew my parents were still struggling financially, and the last thing I wanted was to put
another burden on them. I also didn't want to admit that
most of my girlfriends had followed in Maddie's footsteps
and boarded the Sloppy Ho train, deciding school was
little more than their personal runway. Or maybe they'd
always been like that and I hadn't noticed. Either way,
we'd drifted, and it didn't make sense for me to sponsor
the next occasion where they'd break their backs trying to
outdress and outmakeup each other.

Nope. I just wanted the people who cared about me the
most, and whom I cared about the most, sitting at one table.
And that's exactly what I got.

Halfway through dinner my dad stood up and cleared
his throat. "Amanda and I have an announcement we'd like
to share with all of you." He put his arm around my mother,
who'd stood up too.

Miranda's fork clattered to her plate. "Oh my God, are
you having a baby?"

"No!" my mother cried.

The whole table laughed and Dad shook his head. "No,
no babies, sweetie. But it's something almost as exciting."
He stopped to kiss Mom's temple. "After a very long, very
trying couple of years, this morning I signed a contract for
my very first book deal."

An explosion of screams and cheers immediately filled
the dining room. My mother teared up on cue. Within sec-

onds we were all out of our seats, piling hugs and handshakes and back slaps on my father, and the intensity of my happiness could have burned a hole through the floor.

"Daddy, how did this happen?" I asked when we'd all taken our seats again. "You never even told us someone was interested!"

"I didn't want to get anyone's hopes up. We've been down that road before, and this time I wanted to know it was real." His grin widened and he winked at me. "Happy birthday, Kelsey."

He looked at me with a mixture of such pride, such love, that I almost wanted to cry. I couldn't have asked for a better birthday present.

As if he'd read my mind, David leaned over and whispered, "My gift seems pretty lame right about now."

My head whipped toward him. "What? You weren't supposed to get me *anything*!"

David shrugged and motioned to his father. "It's from both of us." He smiled, clearly proud that he'd found a loophole. "Come upstairs. I put it in your room."

We excused ourselves from the table, and I followed him up the short flight of stairs. The upper level of our house had three bedrooms and one bathroom clustered off a tiny hallway at the top. Once we'd reached the landing, he pulled me in front of him and covered my eyes with his hand.

"For real?" I said.

"Yes, for real." I heard the light switch flip up and shuffled into the room, afraid I'd trip over my own feet even with David guiding me.

"Okay, look."

I blinked as his hand lifted from my eyes and my bed came into focus. Then I gasped. And then I burst into laughter. On top of my quilt sat a beige-colored stuffed cat wearing a red and blue cheerleading uniform. The red bow perched atop her right ear matched the outline of the white letter *A* printed on her shirt. A card with my name scrawled in David's handwriting stood propped up against it.

"Oh my God!" I threw myself on the bed and hugged the cat to my chest. "Did you get this because—"

"You hung a picture of the Grand Canyon by your bed right after I saw you take two hundred flyers from the guidance office about the University of Arizona?" He laughed. "Yeah."

I eyed the postcard I'd taped up next to my headboard, a gorgeous photo of a sunset casting rainbow-colored shadows over the cavernous walls of the canyon. Uncle Tommy had sent it from one of his many vacations. He'd written:

It's a beautiful world, beautiful girl. Can't wait for you to get out and see it.

I'd promptly grabbed some tape and hung it up. My fascination had been growing since.

"They weren't *all* for the University of Arizona."

74

"A lot of them were. And the ones that weren't were all schools on the other side of the country." He grabbed a pillow from my bed and propped it between his head and the leg of my dresser, sprawling out on the floor. "What's up with that?"

I picked at the bow in the cat's hair—Wilma the Wildcat, the mascot for the University of Arizona. I knew I had plenty of time before I needed to seriously consider college, but I'd been thinking about it a lot over the past few months. Obsessively. "I've never left the East Coast. Do you know how small Connecticut is in relation to the rest of the United States? Like a crumb of apple compared to an entire pie."

"Apples don't make crumbs."

I faked like I was going to throw the cat at him and smiled when his arm shot out with baseball-player instinct. "You know what I mean. I figure if I'm ever going to get out of here, college is my chance. Arizona has a great journalism program, it's close to California—which I've always wanted to see. I think I'd really like it there."

"You say that now, but Arizona is *far*. Don't you think you'll be homesick?"

I shrugged. "I wouldn't miss this place. I'd miss my family." A flash of blond hair and blue polka dots in the corner of my eye betrayed Miranda lurking outside my door. "Except my nosy sister."

"Hey!" came the indignant cry from the hallway.

"Go back downstairs!"

So what did she do? Came in the room, sat next to me, and stuck her hand out, of course. "I helped get her in here; you can at least let me hold her." I handed over the cat and she stroked its head.

"So, Miranda," David said. "What do you think of your dad's news?"

"I think it rocks. I hope everyone on the planet buys Daddy's book and he gets famous and we become rich, rich, rich!"

I rolled my eyes. "Don't get your hopes up. Daddy's told us a hundred times that getting published doesn't mean getting rich."

David bobbed his head from side to side, his face contemplative. "You never know. It could happen. Especially if it's a bestseller and they decide to make a movie out of it."

"Could I be in it?" Miranda squealed.

"Don't give her any ideas," I warned.

But David didn't have it in him to frost her cookies. "If it were my movie, I'd let you be in it, Miranda." That was all it took to set my sister beaming. I swear if she worshipped him any harder, she would've broken something.

I shot David an admonishing look. "There's not going to be a movie. Although I wouldn't complain if the book were a *little* successful. Like, successful enough to buy a house near Uncle Tommy's cabin."

David pretended to be aghast. "What happened to waiting for college? You'd leave me high and dry like that? Just take off with Wilma and ditch me for Newport?"

"You? No. Norwood? In a heartbeat."

"What? But Norwood has so much to offer! There's restaurants and stuff to do on every corner. Oh, wait—no, there's not. But wait, we're right on the water. Oops, that's Newport too. I know—no one has a Weed-'n'-Feed supply store on every other street like we do. Try to find that in Newport."

"See," I said through snickers, "you've only been here six months and you already have a firm grasp on the lameness."

He shrugged. "Portman Falls wasn't much better."

"Miranda!" my mother called from the bottom of the stairs. "Leave your sister alone. Come help me with the cake."

Miranda scowled, but dropped Wilma in my lap and stalked off to help my mother. Only then did I notice something peeking out from beneath Wilma's skirt, and I peered closer at her stubby thigh.

"Um, why is there a Band-Aid on her leg?"

David didn't bother keeping a straight face. "She had a bruise the size of Texas."

Laughter bounced off my bedroom walls as I hurled the cat at his face. "Ass!"

He threw her back, and I sank into my pillow, stroking the soft fur, allowing myself a momentary lapse into fantasies of my father's roaring success.

"You're thinking about it, aren't you?" David said. "About your dad's book."

I flushed guiltily. "It *would* be nice."

"Would you really leave?"

"If my parents went, I wouldn't have a choice. But it's not going to happen."

"It could happen."

"It won't. Besides, it's more fun when you're there with me. You'd have to come too."

David smiled. "That's definitely not happening."

I smiled back. "Anything is possible."

Nine

Rhode Island
Senior Year

Candy's shoulders rose and fell rhythmically as I tucked my comforter around her and Wilma, whom she'd fallen asleep clutching the night before. She'd come home with me after Violet's party, where I'd left Crowley to babysit Ryan.

Lucky for Matt, Ryan wasn't a puker when he drank. But Candy? Yeah. I wound up holding her hair somewhere around two in the morning.

Before I could tiptoe away from the bed, one of her eyes cracked open. "I've made fun of this cat eleventy billion times and you never told me she was the product of some torrid love affair you had before I knew you."

Crap. After she'd caught me spying on Violet and David,

I'd spent a good part of the night dodging questions about him. Considering what she'd seen, I'd been hoping she'd wake up this morning with a serious case of alcohol amnesia. My wish had obviously not been granted.

"It wasn't a torrid love affair." I sighed.

She sat up, dragging Wilma by the arm. Her hair looked like brown cobwebs, and remnants of midnight-kohl mascara rimmed her eyes. "You hid his picture in your goddamn closet. Which means it was torrid. So spill it, sister, because I saw everything last night and I want the real story."

I plunked down next to her. "We were friends, Can. I know no one believes it thanks to my stupid sister, but we were." I reached for the photo on my dresser, still sitting where Candy had left it the night before. "Besides, I didn't want that from him."

"*Why?*" Candy blurted, attempting to get her fingers through her tangled mane. "Did he smell bad? You know I love you, Kelse, but short of some serious noxious fumes, I can't imagine why anyone would not want 'that'"—she snatched the picture from my hands and thrust it in my face—"from *that*."

I plucked the photo from her fingers and placed it face-down on the bed. "Believe me, plenty of girls wanted it. I guarantee he didn't spend this past year crying into his pillow over me."

Candy raised an eyebrow. "Do you wish he had?"

"No."

My stomach turned a little as I remembered my and David's conversation in English class earlier that week, but I pushed the memory away. I wasn't a mind reader, and if he'd wanted me to know about his father, he could have called, or even e-mailed. At least that's what I kept telling myself.

"Oh, come on. It's always nice to know someone misses you."

I turned the picture over and looked at it again. "I have Ryan, remember?"

"Then why are you eye-banging that picture?"

"I'm not!" I nearly bent the picture in half in my rush to flip it back over and push it away from me.

"You so are!" Candy's eyes widened. "Shut. Up. You've seen him naked, haven't you?"

"No! Oh my God, nothing ever—"

"Spill it!" Wilma's soft, furry body collided with the side of my head. "Spill it, before I beat it out of you with your four-legged love child!"

I shrieked and nearly caught a mouthful of Wilma's skirt with the next blow. "All right!" I scurried away from her on my hands and knees. "It was one kiss! One, and that's all!"

Candy sat back and gaped at me. "I take it Smurf man doesn't know about this?"

"No. And I know I should probably tell him, but it seriously happened once, and you saw how paranoid he got on the first day of school."

Candy rolled her eyes and pretended to gag. "He's

been extra attentive since a certain someone came to town, hasn't he? Your morning make-out sessions have been more barfworthy than usual." She propped Wilma haphazardly against my pillow and pointed a finger in her face. "I don't care who you are, you will never rock a cheerleading uniform like I do." Then she turned to me. "Do you still want to go to Arizona? You never said anything about putting it on the 'to-tour' list, and as your future roommate, I think this is something I should know."

I shook my head, reaching out to smooth a dog-eared corner of the picture. "It was a phase." I'd realized a while ago that my fixation on going away to college had less to do with the schools and more to do with the actual going away.

And I'd already done that.

I waited until Candy went home before I called Ryan. "Babe," he said when he picked up the phone.

"Hey. How're you feeling today?"

"I'm fine. Listen, is your sister sleeping at home tonight? Because I know she doesn't like to be home alone, but I really want to see you. I miss you."

We'd seen each other every day that week, but somehow I missed him too. All the, ahem, *intrusions* in my life lately had made me feel like I'd spent the past week in a drunken stupor, watching my life instead of living it.

"Oh. So you mean it's been a while since you got laid?" I teased. To my surprise, Ryan sounded annoyed.

"No—I—geez, Kelse, I'm trying to tell you I want to spend time with you. Do you have to be such a pain in the ass?"

"I'm sorry, I'm sorry. I miss you too, Ry. I talked to Miranda this morning and you're in luck. She wants to stay at Carrie's again. What did you have in mind?"

I swear I heard the dimple in his cheek reappear as he answered, "I'll pick you up at quarter to seven."

And did he ever. With *flowers*.

When I first started at Clayton, he'd told me he liked me by way of flowers. Orange and black carnations to be exact, sold by the cheerleading squad as a Halloween fundraiser. He and I were in the same math class, and we'd chatted every now and then, but I figured he flirted with all the girls. Candy kept telling me he thought I was hot, but I found it hard to believe. I might've looked different, I might've acted more confident, and hell, I might've even felt more confident. But I was still afraid I wore it like a super-obvious disguise, one that people would see right through if they looked hard enough.

Which probably explained why I didn't hesitate to accept the double shot of vodka Ryan offered me the first time I went to a party with Candy, even though I'd never attempted to chug anything larger than a dose of liquid Tylenol. He'd been so cute about it—eyeing the fitted Yankees tee that, until that night, had sat in a drawer with the tags on because I hated the way it clung like a second skin. "You know," he said, holding out the glass, "I'm a Boston fan, and I'm still gonna share this, if you want it. That's kind of a big deal."

He flashed a dimpled smile and I ignored my stampeding heart, reminding myself, as I accepted the shot, that my new life meant giving myself permission to do stupid things.

"Duly noted." I closed my eyes, raised the glass to my lips, and opened my throat.

And immediately went into a coughing fit that resembled a seizure.

I felt so ridiculous that I avoided Ryan the rest of the night, certain I'd obliterated any interest he might've had in me—until the day he walked into class with two flowers, set them down in front of me, and watched my face turn every conceivable shade of red as the class hooted and hollered all around us.

Tonight he'd upgraded the carnations to a drop-dead gorgeous bouquet of red roses.

"Ryan!" I gasped as I opened the door. "What's all this for?"

He bent to kiss me. "Because I love you."

For a second I panicked. I wondered if he'd somehow seen me spying on David and Violet and decided damage control was in order, but then dismissed that idea as ridiculous. If he'd seen my reaction, he'd be birthing a giant green cow, not buying me flowers. I threw my arms around him, holding the flowers out so I wouldn't crush them, and nipped at his neck.

"I love them."

"You look beautiful tonight."

I stepped back and smoothed the strapless purple sundress I wore. I'd had serious doubts about my outfit and my makeup after the comments David made at Violet's party, but seeing the way Ryan looked at me gave my self-confidence a much-needed boost.

Screw David. He was nothing but a jealous ass wipe.

After I put the flowers in water, Ryan and I headed out to his car. I felt more like myself with every passing second. He refused to tell me where we were going, so we spent most of the car ride laughing at recaps of the stupid, drunken things our friends had done at Violet's the night before.

I didn't tell him what I'd seen in the pool. Any minute now I'd be able to think about it without tasting bile, anyway.

By the time we parked the car on Thames Street, the sea air had already started to work its magic and I felt myself relax. The temperature was much cooler than the previous night, and I pulled my sweater tighter as Ryan hugged me to his side and the familiar ocean breeze teased us with the scents of garlic roasting and fish frying and hamburgers grilling. The last of the summer tourists milled through the streets, getting their final fills of the sights and sounds that were home to me now.

I squealed with delight when Ryan pulled me toward the Mooring. "I know it's your favorite," he said with a smile. "I made a reservation."

And he'd even asked for a table near the fireplace, the best spot.

"Ryan, we still have almost two months until our anniversary. What's this all about?" I asked again.

He reached across the table for my hand. "I feel like you've been kinda distracted lately. I wanted to take your mind off things, spend some time alone."

I looked down at my lap. "I guess I have been a little distracted. And it's not just because . . ." I trailed off, afraid David's name might invoke the black cloud that seemed to hover between Ryan and me whenever he came up. "It's other things too. My dad's book has been getting so much attention, and he's never home anymore because he's either working or at signings and promos. When he does come home, he's holed up in his office. Mom gets mopey when he's gone too long, so she keeps busy by hounding me about college applications, and Miranda's just in my face all the time, period."

Ryan looked down at our hands as his thumb brushed over my knuckles, his brow furrowed. It was the same pensive look that came over him any time the subject of college came up.

"Have you thought any more about where you want to go?" I asked gently.

Ryan sighed and sat back in his chair. "You know I need to go wherever my scholarship money stretches the furthest. My grades aren't good enough to get in on academics, and my parents can go on a cruise every other month, but they won't pay for the schools I want without at least a partial ride." He leaned forward again and stabbed his straw through the lemon in his soda. "Your friend could really screw this up for me."

"Who? David?"

"He's good, Kelse. Really good. And on top of it, Coach and his dad are, like, college buddies or something. There's no way he's not making the team, and he'll definitely be starting. Which means everyone will be watching him when they should be watching me. Which means he'll be eligible for all the scholarships I would've had in the bag if he'd stayed the fuck away from here." He ran his hand through his hair and grumbled, "Sorry for the f-bomb."

Oh, wow.

No wonder he'd been so on edge around David. Not only did he see my past with him as a threat to our relationship, he saw David's presence as a threat to his whole future.

This could get ugly.

"Ry, David's a good ballplayer, but so are you. And you're a senior. . . . Haven't those decisions been made already?"

Ryan's lips twisted. "Clayton doesn't announce their scholarships until the postseason banquet. And I wasn't interested in any of the universities that offered early signing. I'm sort of holding out to see what else happens."

"Maybe David's already picked his school and you're freaking out for nothing. Besides, you've played at Clayton for three years, and if anyone deserves one of the school's scholarships, it's you. They're not going to screw you over if they know what's right."

Ryan frowned. "It's not what you know. It's who you know."

I leaned across the table and took his hand again. "I don't want to talk about this particular 'who' anymore, okay? No more distractions tonight, for either of us. I want to enjoy the amazing night my boyfriend planned for me. All right?"

Ryan squeezed my hand and smiled, his beyond-adorable dimple coming out to play. My heart expanded about three sizes, and I pushed thoughts of David to the back of my mind.

"All right, babe. I love you."

"I love you, too. And I'm sorry I've been such a mope lately. I'm over it, I promise."

I meant it. Or I wanted to. As Ryan and I walked hand in hand toward the marina after dinner, the sound of live music floating through the salty air, I'd almost forgotten why I'd been such a drudge all week. I might have succeeded in forgetting completely if I hadn't spotted a pretty blond girl walking with her tall, dark-haired boyfriend. They were laughing and talking and one of her hands curled around the crook of his arm. In the other a bag from the taffy store swung in rhythm with her steps.

I swallowed down the sourness that rose in my throat as Ryan pulled aside into a little patch of concrete that jutted out between two restaurants, where we could lean against the fence and look out at the silhouettes of the docked boats. He put his arm around me and I settled against his shoulder.

He leaned in and kissed me, the soft warmth of his lips sending a thrill through me from head to toe. It was like having some of the poison from my toxic week drained out of my body.

I wrapped my arms around him and kissed him with everything I had, determined to force the rest of the demons out. By the time we pulled apart, both ready to escape to my mercifully empty house, I decided I'd never let David, or anyone else, get under my skin again.

Ryan deserved so much better than that, and I was going to give it to him.

Ten

I'll never forget the first time things got weird between David and me. It was only for a minute, but it definitely happened.

It was our second summer together in Newport. We'd bought some taffy on Thames Street and taken it to the Cliff Walk. The sky was the perfect shade of summer blue, and the sun sparkled off the ocean as we walked, biting our candy and stretching it as far and thin as we possibly could before it broke.

"That was definitely a record!" David laughed, slurping a long, sagging ribbon into his mouth. "That had to be, like, twelve inches!"

I nearly spit my own glob of strawberry taffy on the ground, or I would've if it hadn't been stuck to my teeth.

"Leave it to you to make it sound dirty! Do you boys always exaggerate when it comes to size?"

David leaned against the railing, pulling another wrapped piece of candy from the pocket of his shorts. He placed one of the twisted ends between his teeth and pulled the other, exposing the soft purple cylinder as he leaned in close to my face and wagged his eyebrows. "I have no reason to exaggerate, Miss Kelsey."

I stepped closer to him, a smirk stretching across my lips as I flicked his taffy to the ground with my thumb and middle finger. "You're gross."

"Aw, Kelse! That was a good piece!"

I rolled my eyes and dug around in my bag, producing a piece the same color. "Here, take it. Besides," I said as David plucked up my offering, "if I really wanted to know, I could ask Amy Heffernan."

While Eric and I barely spoke anymore, Amy and David had hooked up on and off for most of freshman year. Her name came out much harsher than I'd meant it to, like a bad piano note.

A huge grin spread across David's face, and he let out a hearty laugh. "Whoa! Am I sensing a little *jealousy* here?"

"Like hell!" I meant it, though for some reason the sun felt especially hot on my cheeks at that moment.

David leaned back against the railing, still grinning, cocky and braces-free. Without them, he had a killer smile. As he twisted his palms over the railing, I couldn't help but notice all that baseball training had been kind to him too. His shoulders were broader, his arm muscles more defined. No wonder girls like Amy had sat up and taken notice.

"Let's just walk," I said, hoping to drop the subject.

"What even makes you think anything happened between me and Amy?"

I rolled my eyes so hard, my whole head rolled with them. "Oh, I'm sure you've been the *perfect* gentleman."

I tried to give him a playful shove, but he looped his arm around my neck and crushed me against his side. "You're doubting my intentions?" he said with mock indignation. "I'm not feeling the love here, Kelse."

His grip tightened, and I shrieked as my nose squashed against his shoulder, suffocating me with the scent of cologne and deodorant and taffy. Under different circumstances, I might have liked that combination. Or I might have liked it right then and there. But I didn't have time to think about it, because David's lips were suddenly right against my ear, his voice low as he said, "Know what sucks?"

The tingle that rippled down my body took me completely by surprise. We'd hugged plenty of times before. So what the hell, exactly, was that about?

I pushed him away, my hands flying up to fix the Miranda-like mess he'd probably made of my hair.

"What sucks?"

David paused dramatically. "That a gentleman never tells."

My hands froze midsmooth and my eyes opened wide.

"A gentleman? Where?" I looked frantically in every direction, and while David's laughter told me I got the last word, I wasn't happy. On the one hand, I didn't want to know what happened when a good-looking guy and a girl nicknamed Hoover were left alone for indefinite periods of time. On the other, I didn't want David feeling like there were things he couldn't tell me. I'd always scoffed at the idea that guys and girls couldn't have uncomplicated friendships. But that was before outside relationships had created any lines in the sand between David and me.

We'd reached the rocky part of the Cliff Walk when David rubbed his nose and squinted up the sky. "My nose is frying," he said. "I can feel it."

"Come on." I nodded in the direction of an out-of-the-way boulder and started toward it. "I have sunblock you can put on. It's too frickin' hot for rock climbing anyway."

David snorted. "You always find an excuse to turn around here."

I ignored him, even though he was right. Every time I even thought about going farther than where we were now, my blood pulsed in my ears and my head felt swimmy. Hopping boulders just didn't seem like a wise choice for someone who bruised as easily as I did, unless I wanted to look like a topographic map by the time the trail picked up again.

I sat on the sun-warmed rock, and David settled next to me, resting his arms on his bent knees. I had my trusty mini bottle of sunblock in my bag, and I put a piece of taffy between my teeth, letting it dangle like a coach's whistle as I fumbled through the contents of my purse.

That's when I felt hands slide around either side of my face. Then a split second of soft, delicious heat against my mouth. I gasped. I didn't even realize the candy had been pulled from between my teeth until I blinked my eyes into focus and saw David, laughing victoriously as he rolled *my* candy around in *his* mouth.

I sat frozen, mouth gaping. My heart threatened to beat right out of my chest. I pictured it bouncing down the rocky incline until it landed with a splash in the ocean below.

Calm down!

But I couldn't. Hadn't he—didn't that count as . . . ?

"Payback," he garbled.

And his dumb ass sat there, chomping on taffy like he'd merely stolen a piece of candy and not put his nasty mouth that wasn't even close to nasty all over mine.

Which meant I was the only one freaking out.

David laughed harder. "I really got you, didn't I? How many times in your life have you been speechless?"

"Did you *kiss* me?"

"That wasn't a kiss. If I kissed you, you'd know it."

So I *was* the only one freaking out. I swallowed hard and shook myself, looking at the bottle of sunblock that had mysteriously appeared in my hand. Sunblock. Right.

"Very funny," I said, popping the lid. "Hilarious. Here, put this—"

But David had already turned toward me and closed his eyes.

My jaw dropped again. "You want me to do it *for* you? Do I look like your mommy?"

"Nah." He didn't open his eyes, but the smile still played on his lips. I gave up, making an exasperated sound as I squirted the white lotion onto my fingertips. Then he added, "You're prettier."

I froze again. My heart flip-flopped as my hand hovered near his face. What the *ef* was up with him today? What the ef was up with *me*?

Refusing to be the only one rattled, I brought my fingers down on his nose, maybe a little harder than necessary.

"Ouch! Again, Kelse, not feeling the love today."

"Sorry," I mumbled.

"Was that for the taffy?" His eyes opened, alive with amusement as they gazed into mine. "Or for Amy?"

"You can do whatever you want with Amy." I concentrated on the beauty mark beneath his lip, knowing he'd see my discomfort if I made eye contact. My new focal point wasn't much help in the comfort department though, either. We were way too close to each other.

"I won't see her if you don't like her. Say the word and she's out."

"You would do that for me?"

"Of course. You're my best friend. Ergo an excellent judge of character."

I smiled and shook my head, touched that he'd place such importance on my opinion. Maybe there weren't as many lines between us as I'd thought.

I hadn't noticed that my hand had wandered as we talked. I'd started to work some of the excess sunblock around beneath his lips, letting my fingers graze his jawbone. The harshness I'd started with had been replaced by gentle, exploring strokes. My fingertips lingered over his skin, and I didn't know why.

"I'd never tell you to stop seeing Amy if she's who you want to see," I said softly. "It's not like you can control who you like."

Our eyes met as I said it, and something in his seemed to darken. My thumb brushed the underside of his bottom lip, and I felt it in every cell of my body.

"I can't, can I?" His voice was low, and his eyes searched mine. For a split second something electric passed between us—something I'd never felt before, never thought I'd want to feel. If I kept looking at him, I knew he'd kiss me. Except this time he'd mean to do it.

And I wasn't even close to ready for that.

I sucked in a breath and looked away, snapping the cap of the sunblock in place. "No. No, I guess you can't. But, um, thanks. For saying you'd put me first. It means a lot."

I arranged my face into what I hoped looked like a composed smile, though the pace of my heart was more conducive to vomiting. David flashed one back. "Anytime. I meant it."

With that, like a cloud that had passed over the sun, the weirdness was gone.

Eleven

Rhode Island
Senior Year

Over the next few weeks David and I became masters at paying minimal attention to each other, even in close range, like in English class or at our lunch table.

It was easier with Violet around, because we could talk to her without really talking to each other. And because the David-induced stars in her eyes seemed to keep her from noticing the tension between him and me.

Even so, I'd been having daily anxiety attacks over whether or not I should do something for his birthday when it came around. Sophomore year, I'd made good on my promise and decorated his locker and made sure everyone knew what day it was.

Junior year, I hadn't even called.

But having him there with me, I felt like ignoring it was too deliberate. I walked down the hall toward where David stood at his locker, with a small box of taffy clutched in my hands. With every step, I practiced the first half of my ingenious speech in my head: *Happy birthday. This is for you.* It beat the hell out of the second half, which even in my own head, sounded like, *Blah blah blah, lame lame lame.*

Before I could get close enough, Violet came bounding out of nowhere with a white-frosted cupcake in hand. "Happy birthday!" she squealed, throwing her free arm around his neck and smacking a kiss on his cheek.

Every time she hung on him that way, my mind went right back to the two of them in the pool; her fingers pressing into the back of his neck, his hands touching the skin left exposed by her beige bikini. It made me throw up a little in my mouth.

When David's face lit up like a Christmas tree, I turned and hurried back to my locker. They hadn't seen me, but I felt overwhelming embarrassment, like I'd fallen flat on my face in front of the entire school. I shoved the taffy to the back of my locker and slammed the door, wanting to breathe a sigh of relief but nearly jumping out of my skin instead when Candy suddenly stood at my side.

"Is that for David?" she asked. "It's his birthday today, right?"

"Um, I brought him something, you know, in case. But Violet's got it under control, so, no big deal."

And then came the part I hated. Any time I witnessed David's and Violet's hands grazing, or caught them sharing a laugh, Candy would give me these awful, pitying looks, like she thought I must be dying inside. The same look she gave me then.

"I'm not jealous," I told her for the hundredth time.

I wasn't jealous.

Maybe "possessive" was a better word.

As much as I wanted nothing to do with David, I couldn't ignore the fact that for a long time I'd been the most important girl in his life, and I'd liked it. I loved knowing he'd drop anything, or anyone, if I needed him. My ego inflated each time he greeted me with his biggest smile. In a way—a very comfortable, uncomplicated way—he'd always been mine. Until Isabel. But that's a whole different story.

Now we barely looked at each other, and his biggest smiles were reserved for someone else.

I knew the avoidance dance couldn't last forever, though. And sure enough, I came home after school one Friday to find my father and mother sitting at the kitchen table. Under normal circumstances, there wouldn't have been anything unusual about it, but my father was supposed to be on tour for another two weekends.

"Daddy!" I cried, flinging my arms around his neck. "What are you doing home?"

"Hey, baby girl." He squeezed me extra tight, the way he did whether it had been five days or five minutes since we'd last seen each other. "There was a fire at the store where I should have been signing this weekend, and next weekend's canceled. Looks like I'll be kicking around here for the next couple of weeks."

"So guess what we're all doing next weekend, since Daddy will be here," my mother piped up. A sly grin twitched across her face, and she tried to hide it by taking a sip of her coffee. That right there made me nervous.

"Depending on what you're about to say, I think I might have plans."

My mother made a don't-even-try-it face at me. "I already looked at your calendar, and I know you're touring URI with Candy Saturday afternoon. Which is why our plans with the Kerrigans are for next Saturday *evening*."

"Ohhh, *Mom*!" I fought the urge to stomp around the kitchen like a two-year-old who'd had her favorite toy taken away. "Why can't you and Dad go? You know I haven't talked to David in forever. It'll be so awkward!"

My mother looked genuinely surprised. "Kelsey, you see David at school every day. You said he's in one of your classes! The two of you still aren't speaking?"

"We speak. But we aren't friends."

She tut-tutted. "Such a shame. You two were attached at the hip before we moved here." I winced, expecting her to launch into a pontification about how he and I should patch things up, but she went for a different guilt trip: "What about David's father? He always loved you, honey, and he's so excited to see you girls. He'll be so disappointed if I tell him you're not going."

I stood up straighter. "Speaking of Mr. Kerrigan— I heard he had cancer. And you two knew about it. Why didn't you tell me, Mom?"

My mother swallowed and set down her mug. "We didn't find out until he was well into his treatment. Daddy and I kept trying to get him to come out to Rhode Island for a visit, and he kept making excuses. He didn't say a word to Daddy or me about being sick until we offered to come back and visit him instead. I guess they really tried to keep it quiet, which is one reason we didn't tell you."

She eyed my father, his cue to be the bad cop.

"Plus," he said, "you snapped at us every time we suggested making amends with David. We thought you'd accuse us of 'guilt-tripping' you."

So there it was. Even my own parents hadn't trusted me to do the right thing. I stared at the wood-grain patterns in the table. Had I really changed that much in one year?

"So?" my mother prompted. "You're not going to let David's father down after what he went through, are you?"

The cancer card. Nicely played, Mother.

"Why should I go when I didn't even deserve to know?" I mumbled.

My father stood up and kissed my cheek. "Six thirty,

next Saturday," he said. "Did you ever think you'd set foot in that house again?"

Nope. I certainly didn't.

I went, though. And if I'd known what was going to happen, the past week of weirdness between David and me would have seemed like a picnic on the beach.

We pulled up to the familiar house next door to Uncle Tommy's ex-cabin right on time. My unease was palpable. The torturous déjà vu of seeing David every day had been bad enough, but now we were about to sit around the dinner table with our families and break bread like nothing had happened.

Of course, for everyone else, nothing had.

I was grateful for the big, awkward salad bowl clutched against my chest as I filed in the door behind my family. It spared me the moment of uncertainty when everyone else walked in and gave David a hug or, in my father's case, a handshake, and I had an excuse not to follow suit. He took the bowl from me with a polite thank-you, and we were on our merry way.

Or we should have been, if I hadn't chosen the next moment to fall apart.

David's father stood in the kitchen, greeting the members of my family with big hugs and an even bigger smile. The difference in his appearance caught me completely off guard.

Jimmy Kerrigan had always had a sort of crazy-professor look about him: thinning, disheveled hair; bright blue eyes;

and clothes that never seemed to hang right on his bony frame. I used to slip him cookies from the batches I'd bake for David, and tease him that he needed to put some meat on his bones. He in turn would hide candy in the compartments of our book bags and leave it there for us to discover.

At that moment I wanted nothing more than to feed him some cookies, or candy, or any kind of calories at all. He must have had three shirts on, but with the layers of material having nothing to cling to except one another, they hung like potato sacks. He couldn't have weighed more than 120 pounds. David might have told me about his father's cancer, but he never prepared me for the sight of the emaciated man wearing Jimmy Kerrigan's smile.

I stood rooted to the spot as the sea of bodies parted, and Mr. Kerrigan held his arms open, smiling warmer than the sun. His hair had started to grow in, and the graying tufts glinted in the overhead lights of the kitchen. "Kelsey," he said. "How I've missed your beautiful face!"

So, speaking of my face? That would be the exact moment it crumpled. My whole body felt hot and wobbly, and a choked sob tore through my chest before I knew what was happening.

The kitchen went deathly silent. Or maybe it just felt that way from the ringing in my ears. Mr. Kerrigan's arms wrapped around me, nothing but skin and bone, and he rubbed my back as he tried to soothe me. "Shh, it's okay. I'm all right. I promise you, I'm fine."

"I'm—s-sorry," I hiccupped against his shoulder, my face burning with embarrassment and soaked with tears. "David t-told me, b-but—"

Mr. Kerrigan held my shoulders and winked at me. "You think this is bad? You should see the other guy."

I managed a weak smile at his joke, and I became vaguely aware of my parents' hands patting me as Mr. Kerrigan pulled me into another hug. I looked up long enough to see David leaning against the door frame of the kitchen, his jaw muscles tense as he stared off into the hallway. He rubbed my sister's shoulder absently, because she'd started to cry too.

That's how it worked with us Crawford women. One of us cried, and that was the end of it. I didn't have to look at my mother to know she was dabbing her eyes too.

Mr. Kerrigan took my face in his hands and spoke quietly. "Would you like to run into the bathroom and take a minute?"

I nodded, and he smiled. I wished he'd let me go right then and there, but he said, "We missed you, Kelsey."

My face contorted all over again and fresh tears spilled over my cheeks. He hadn't said *he'd* missed me. He'd said *we*.

"Take your time," he said as he guided me toward the bathroom that doubled as a laundry room. Miranda and David stepped aside, and I avoided looking at either of them. "We'll start all over when you come back. You remember where it is, don't you?"

I nodded and slunk off, my heart beating madly. The moment I shut the door behind me, I slid down to the dark green tile and sobbed into my knees until I thought I might be sick.

I'd failed David, failed his father. I'd left them both without a single glance back, and I hated myself for it.

A knock on the door made me jump, and I scrambled to my feet, nearly tripping over nearby paint cans. It was the first time I noticed the old wallpaper had been stripped away and blue painting tape lined the seam where the wall met the ceiling. David and his father must've been trying to spruce up the house, but the only thing I could focus on was the sound of David's voice outside the room.

"Kelse? You okay?"

I hurriedly wiped my face and nose with a tissue before cracking the door open. I meant to say yes, to say or do something other than stare mournfully. The look in David's eyes mirrored mine. As if by mutual agreement, I opened the door wider as he stepped inside, shutting it behind him with one arm and pulling me into a crushing hug with the other.

Neither of us said a word for the longest time. I held him as tightly as I could while I buried my face in his shirt, and he held me just as tight with his cheek against my hair. All the defenses I'd put up puddled at my feet.

"David," I finally blubbered. "I'm sorry. For ruining dinner. I'm sorry for everything."

"Hey, it's okay." He smoothed my hair away from my face. "I'm sorry too. For upsetting you at Vi's party."

I shook my head, accepting and dismissing his apology, wanting to forget everything about that night.

David took my hand and led me past the washer and dryer to the sink, where he grabbed a tissue and held it out to me. He studied my Tiffany bracelet as I wiped my face, his fingers drumming against the laminate countertop, and I had a feeling he was still thinking about the words we'd exchanged on Violet's deck.

"So what did you mean when you said you didn't smash up your car?"

Yep.

I balled the Kleenex into my palm and squeezed it. "I did crash my car. Just not the way everyone thinks." I hurled the snot rag into the trash, blowing out an exasperated breath. "Look, I know you think I'm some big sellout, and yes, I'm different, but you were the one who told me I should try new things, remember? And after what happened . . . I agreed. So I did." He folded his arms across his chest and I did the same. "Some of them I liked. Some I didn't."

"What does that mean?"

"I wasn't drunk that night. I drank, but not nearly as much as everyone thought."

David eyed me, his expression hardening just enough to tell me he still didn't like my answer. "You weren't drunk, but you wanted people to think you were?"

"More like they already thought it, so I let them."

"Because they're really your friends if you have to fake it."

"Like it did me so much good when I *wouldn't* fake it?" I snapped back.

"At least you had a mind of your own. What happened to the Kelsey who didn't care what anyone thought?"

"Whatever, David. It was a lot easier than trying to explain the real reason I almost blacked out behind the wheel."

He stood up straight, towering over me. "That's still happening? I thought—"

I held up a hand. "It's not. I mean, I don't know. I'm kind of a stickler about staying on top of it now. But I got really dizzy all of a sudden, and I swerved. It could've been the booze, because God knows I'm a lightweight. But Candy and I had just spent a week vacationing with her family, and the bag with my pills got lost, so I can't be sure."

David studied me. "Is that why you reacted to my dad that way? Are you—have you been—okay?"

"I think it was just a freak thing. Honestly, I'm better now than I've been in a long time." I gave him a pointed look, in case he missed the threat edging my next statement. "Which is why I don't bring it up anymore."

He nodded slowly and sat back against the counter. "So where did the squirrel come in?"

"I added that for my parents' benefit."

David shook his head, grabbing another tissue with one hand and pulling me toward him with the other. As he started to wipe mascara streaks from my face, an odd smirk pulled at his lips.

"Why are you smiling like that?"

"C'mon, Kelse. A squirrel? In the middle of the night? Are you sure you weren't drunk when you came up with that one?"

"I claimed to be sober, not quick under pressure."

He threw the tissue in the trash and held my face in his hands, the same way his father had done moments ago. The only thing different was the pulses of warmth that rocketed through me as his palms touched my cheeks.

Not good.

"What?" I said as his smirk stretched into a full-on grin. "What is it?"

He touched his forehead to mine. "I knew you were in there somewhere."

I threw my arms around him again, the weight of the marred night and our strained friendship bearing down on me all over. "I'm sorry," I repeated.

We held each other, the silence stretching until I became aware of the clock ticking on the wall. When David spoke, his voice seemed eerily soft in comparison. "Kelse?"

"Mmm?" I mumbled against his shoulder.

He drew a breath, then gently pushed me away from him, holding my arms at my sides. His eyes were dark as they searched mine.

"Why did you run away from me that night?"

I looked at the floor, then back at him. Then back at the floor. My voice came out sounding as inadequate as my answer. "I don't know." I wanted to tell him the rest, to finally get it off my shoulders. But the words solidified in my throat, and I knew I'd never get them out without an accompaniment of fresh tears.

You ran away from me, too.

David let out a breath and his eyes dropped somewhere near my shoulder. "Did you even miss me?"

"All the time."

The answer came out before I'd even processed it, before I had time to think about whether or not it was true. After all, if I'd missed him so much, how had we come to this?

But looking at him, having him right here in front of me and seeing the familiarity of everything about him, the sadness in his eyes, I knew I meant what I'd said.

A piece of me had been missing without him. I'd just been ignoring it.

My hand floated up to his face, almost like it wasn't attached to my body. I definitely hadn't planned to trace the scar beneath his mouth, but somehow I found myself doing exactly that.

I avoided his eyes even as I felt his boring into me. Even as I felt his fingers creep around my waist. And even as I took an involuntary step closer to him.

"I missed you," he murmured.

Finally, our eyes met. Something electric crackled inside me and seemed to fill the space between us.

This was the one thing I should not miss about him. Could not miss about him.

A knock on the door made us both jump.

Whatever spell I'd been under shattered at the sound.

"David?" Mr. Kerrigan's voice reached us as we fidgeted and fumbled a respectable amount of space between us. "Kelsey? Is everything all right?"

David pushed himself away from the sink and went to the door, opening it wide. "She's fine, Dad. She, um, she— it's my fault. I didn't tell her. She was surprised, that's all."

"Of course she was. You have to give someone warning when they're about to encounter a walking skeleton, son. Especially after what she went through."

I shuddered as David's lips pressed together in a frown. Both of them knew my reaction tonight had a lot to do with releasing a year's worth of pent-up emotion, and with memories crashing down on me like a waterfall.

One of those memories still crept into my nightmares every so often.

And maybe they knew that, too, because they also knew why it had been so hard for me to see what Mr. Kerrigan's illness had done to him.

Because it had almost been me.

Twelve

I called it the perfect storm.

Literally. Since everything started around the time of our first big snowstorm of the season.

I sent David a text message one Friday morning, telling him I wouldn't be in school and to please get my homework. I'd been feeling lousy for two weeks, first with a sinus infection, and then with the antibiotic to treat it bothering my stomach. For the past couple of days, though, it was all I could do to lift my head from the pillow. I didn't feel sick anymore; I just felt *tired*. So I stayed home, and waited for the snow to start.

As much as I loved the summer, nothing thrilled me

like the first sighting of tiny white flakes. I'd sit at my window and crane my neck upward to watch them swirl from the sky, as if I were in the middle of my own personal snow globe.

The storm didn't disappoint. By Sunday morning when it finally came to a stop, we had eight inches of blinding fluff on the ground.

David called to see if Miranda and I wanted to go sledding at the golf course, and I said yes in the hopes of finally shaking my funk. Even after spending a chunk of my weekend in bed, my head still felt foggy and I hoped the cold, crisp air would clear it once and for all.

It didn't quite work that way.

My clunky boots felt particularly heavy as I lifted them in and out of the snow coating the hilly golf course. Had it always been this steep?

I looked up to see David and Miranda waiting for me a few feet ahead, Miranda with her hands on her hips and a scowl on her face, and David wearing a playful smile and holding the sled upright in the snow.

"Hey," he said. "Did you forget to eat your Wheaties this morning? You're dragging ass today."

"Tired," I mumbled.

David put his arm around me as I caught up to him. "Come on. You'll feel better after the first run." He jiggled the sled. "This thing's gonna fly."

"If we ever get there," Miranda grumbled.

"What's up your butt today?" I shot back. "You're one to talk. You usually fall at least three times before we get to the top."

As if on cue, one of the monstrous-looking boots covering half her chicken legs got lodged in the snow and she pitched forward with a shriek.

David and I burst into laughter as we each took one of her arms and set her back on her feet. I did feel a little better after that, and better still as we piled into the sled, laughing hysterically as all three of us attempted to sit in it at once. It didn't even bother me when I spotted Maddie on the other side of the hill with Jared and Isabel Rose, Amy Heffernan, and a few other people. At least, it didn't bother me as much as it should have. By the time we reached the bottom of the hill, the rush of chilled air still stinging my cheeks, I felt almost normal again.

Before we could make a second run down, Isabel walked toward us—or, more specifically, toward David. She looked like a stereotypical ski bunny, all toothy smile and athletic build, complete with a thick white headband holding back her dark, glossy hair, and puffy white mittens over her undoubtedly manicured hands.

Seriously, mittens? Call me crazy, but I preferred not to have my hands melded into a unifinger if I could help it.

I looked past her and sent a feeble wave in Maddie's direction. She responded with a limp flop of her hand that looked more like an attempt to flick snow off her glove than a greeting to someone she'd known forever. Maybe it made sense. She knew me, but I didn't know her at all anymore.

"Hey, David," Isabel said with an unmistakably flirtatious lilt. I pretended to brush off the sled as I rolled my eyes. Ever since things with David and Amy had cooled, Isabel had been eyeing him the way a hungry vulture eyes fresh roadkill. Apparently she'd chosen her moment to swoop in for dinner.

"Thanks again for helping me with my math homework on Friday," she cooed.

Exactly what had I missed when I'd been out on Friday?

"No problem. Let me know if you're still having trouble, and we can go over it again," David replied.

Oh, of course. David and I had the same free period, and we always went to the cafeteria to do homework. Normally we were in one corner while David helped me with *my* math homework. He was in all honors classes for math, and it was disgusting how he could make perfect sense of the problems with almost no instruction. Isabel's group sat in another corner—painting their nails, flipping their hair, reapplying their makeup. Definitely *not* doing homework. More than once I swore I caught Isabel giving me dirty looks, but I always thought they were residuals from the sloppy joe incident. Now I realized she'd been waiting for me to get the hell out of her way.

I stifled a laugh as I pictured a vulture screeching toward spilled innards on the pavement.

Isabel's grin stretched wider, revealing even more of her white teeth. "I might take you up on that. In the meantime, we noticed, um, your sled is kind of puny—" She peeked around him at our sled, studiously ignoring Miranda and me as if the Walmart-issue "puny" thing were standing up in the snow of its own accord. "And I thought I'd ask if you want to ride with me this time. We brought a toboggan. It's huge."

David glanced over her shoulder to Maddie and Jared and company. Their faces lit up and arms stretched into the air in greeting. Okay, so Maddie did remember how to execute a proper wave. Good to know.

"Come on over!" she called. "You're missing out!" She patted the toboggan the way a cowboy would pat the rear end of his trusty steed.

"Oooh, a *toboggan*," I said under my breath before I could stop myself.

Isabel's head snapped toward me, and she finally looked at me. "Is there a problem, Kelsey?"

She knew my name? Isabel was a junior, and I always assumed she knew me as Maddie's Friend or the Sloppy Joe Girl.

"Nope, no problem. Isabel."

Using her name didn't rattle her at all. She gave me a bored look before breaking out another smile for David. "So come on. If you want, we can race your friends." The word "friends" came out flat and was accompanied by another cursory glance in my direction. Like it physically hurt her eyes to look away from him.

David turned to me, an almost guilty look on his face. "Would you guys mi—"

"Nope," I interrupted. "Go ahead. We'll catch up with you later."

He shook his head. "Nah, I should stay—"

"David." I said it a little more sharply than necessary, then purposely softened my tone. "It's fine. We'll be here when you get back."

His face broke into a grin. "I know. I'm your ride." With that, he turned to Isabel, and I swore her lip curled in smug triumph. As they started off together, I heard him say, "So are you pretty comfortable with linear equations now? They're not so bad, right?"

Oh, David, David. Did he honestly believe she'd needed help with her math homework? For someone so smart, he could be pretty dense at times. Unless, of course, he was playing along. Flirting back. The thought made me frown.

"You're the one who said it was okay, dummy. Don't pout now." Miranda's arms were folded across her chest, as if the look on my face had personally offended her. Sometimes that child needed a major attitude adjustment.

"I'm not pouting! I just—don't like her that much."

"Do you even know her?"

"I know enough."

Miranda smiled. "Don't worry. I don't like her either."

And other times she was the coolest person I knew.

We piled onto the sled and pushed off, the cold air blasting our eyes and making them tear even as we giggled our way down the bright white hill. We were both squealing as the sled finally lost momentum and came to a stop, and I forgot that I'd been frowning a second ago.

Until, through the corner of my eye, I saw Isabel's fancy toboggan coasting down the hill. David sat at the forefront with Isabel pressed up against his back, clutching him around his middle. They both had huge smiles on their faces, and I watched as their toboggan cruised right past the point where our sled had conked out, coming to a graceful stop some twenty feet farther away.

"Kelsey!" Miranda said sharply.

I jumped. "I'm not pouting!"

Miranda looked at me with wide eyes. "No, your nose—it's bleeding!"

I ripped off one of my gloves and swiped at the spot above my lip. My fingers came away smeared with red.

"Shit!" I fumbled through the pocket of my coat for the travel package of Kleenex my mother had stashed there, grateful that she always thought of those things. I felt wet warmth run over my lip and started to panic as I realized it was getting worse.

Finally, my shaking fingers freed one of the folded squares, and I jammed it against my nostrils. I turned toward the street, hoping I could dab at my nose a few times and move on without anyone noticing.

My nose, however, had other plans. In less than a minute, my tissue had gone from white to completely red. Miranda kept grabbing more from the package and handing them to me as I knelt over the snow, afraid I'd get blood on my clothes.

"Kelse, are you okay?" Miranda handed me another tissue, terror plainly visible in her petite features.

I nodded, but it was like the motion made things worse. My nose started to gush. It bled so profusely that it splashed down the back of my throat and I gagged, spitting red all over the snow like some kind of horror movie. Then I started to cry.

Miranda must have thought I vomited blood, because she started to scream. And cry. "Help! Help! Someone help my sister! Something is wrong with my sister, someone help!"

Boots crunched in the snow as people descended on us. A middle-aged man with a little boy reached us first.

"Did you fall? Do you think it's broken?" he asked. He moved my hand to replace my falling-apart tissue with a handkerchief. I wondered if it was used before I realized I was bleeding too much to care.

"She didn't fall," Miranda whimpered. "Her nose started bleeding, and then she started throwing up blood. I don't know what happened."

"Kelse!" The sound of David's winded, worried voice made me flush. He must have run over at top speed. I could only imagine what I looked like, but even if it wasn't as bad as I thought, it still wasn't anything I wanted him—or Isabel—to see. I stared down at the Rorschach-like patterns my blood had made on the snow, wishing the ground would open up and swallow me.

David knelt beside me. "What happened?"

The bleeding finally abated enough for me to talk without gagging. "Nosebleed," I panted. "Not vomiting. It went down my throat. I've never had one this bad before. I scared her." Quite frankly, I had scared the shit out of me, too.

"Does she need an ambulance?" the man with the handkerchief asked.

I gave a weak shake of my head, afraid a more vehement protest would set the bleeding off again.

"No, no ambulance," David said. "She'll be okay. Thank you, everyone. She's fine."

I brushed my temple against his shoulder and sighed, so grateful when footsteps started to retreat. He must have known I wanted to die on the spot.

David scooped up a pile of unbloodied snow between his gloved hands and packed it together in one of his palms. Then he yanked the back of my coat down and pressed the freezing cold snowball against the nape of my neck.

"David!"

"Sorry," he said, his smile evident in his voice. "It's

supposed to restrict bloodflow to the head, or something." He leaned down until his face appeared in my peripheral vision. "Look at you. Your mom's gonna think I came at you with a machete."

"Is it that bad?"

"Um . . ."

"You're a crappy liar, David. Don't even try."

"You look like someone tried to murder you!" Miranda sobbed. The dramatics of it were too much. David and I tried our hardest not to laugh at her as we exchanged a look.

"Um, David?" Both of us looked up at the sound of Isabel's voice. She stood a good six feet away, like she was afraid she'd get blood on her expensive North Face attire if she came one step closer. "Is there anything I can do?"

She sounded semi-sincere, though I got the feeling she'd faint or throw up if either of us said yes.

"No, we're good," David said. "I'm going to get her home now. Thanks, Isabel."

Dismissed. My insides may or may not have done a little jig.

Isabel nodded, not bothering to hide her disappointment before she turned and walked away. *Good-bye to you, too*, I thought to myself. I was about to say it—okay, grumble it under my breath—when she turned around and, with all the decorum of person forced to speak in tongues by a demon inhabiting her body, said, "Feel better, Kelsey."

She turned away again before I could utter an equally

forced thank-you. When I started to laugh, David narrowed his eyes. "What?"

"*What?* Seriously?" He really was dense when it came to girls. I folded the handkerchief to a clean spot and wiped my face. "Did you hear what she said?"

"Yeah. She was being nice."

"Uh-huh. Nicest thing anyone's ever said to me."

David shrugged as he helped me to my feet, replacing his hand on the back of my snow-covered neck with mine. He held an arm out to Miranda. "You okay, kid?" Miranda buried her face in his jacket and nodded. "Good. Come on. Let's go."

I didn't know what made me look back as David ushered us to the parking lot, but I wished I hadn't. My eyes zeroed in on Isabel's group in the distance. One of the guys, a tall, beefy football player, was flailing and spasming all over the place as his friends doubled over with laughter. One of the girls made exaggerated wiping motions at his face with her scarf, dancing in fake-panicked circles around him. Not just any girl.

Maddie.

They were making fun of me. *She* was making fun of me. The same girl who'd told off Cameron Myers in second grade for teasing me when I threw up on the playground was laughing at my expense. My heart sank like I'd watched something die. And maybe I had.

I'd never stopped to think that Maddie and I wouldn't

find our way back to being friends again. We'd disagreed on things before, and had always gotten over it. But the girl prancing around at the top of the hill obviously didn't consider me her friend. Somewhere along the line, the gap between us had grown impassable, and there was no turning back.

Before I could look away, I caught sight of Isabel standing at the edge of the little reenactment. She wasn't participating, but it didn't matter. Not with the way her arms were folded across her chest, and the way she stared right at me.

No, not stared. Glared.

I turned away. She might have been able to convince David of her concern, but I left the golf course certain of two things. One, I'd never forget the hurt and embarrassment I'd felt that day. And two, I'd cinched my status as Isabel's enemy without even trying.

Thirteen

Rhode Island
Senior Year

Violet came into English class looking the way she once had when she left Starbucks with someone's decaf tea instead of her latte—pissed off.

Her gold ballet flats swept over the tile floor with short, quick steps. Her eyebrows were furrowed, and the force with which her butt hit the seat and her bag hit the floor told me she definitely wasn't happy.

"What's up with you?" I said.

She looked at me and huffed an agitated breath. "Nothing."

"Could have fooled me."

Violet shot a glare in my direction, and the look on

her face told me she was contemplating whether she wanted to say more. Finally, she leaned toward me, one arm draped across her desk. "I think David is gay."

I nearly spit out the sip of bottled water I'd just taken.

"What? What the hell are you talking about?" I wiped my mouth, not bothering to hide my laughter. I would have if I'd known Violet's face would turn purple.

"*Something* is up with him," she said defensively. Her eyes darted around the mostly empty classroom, and she scooted closer to me and lowered her voice. "So last Saturday? I invited him over to my house to watch a movie. You know, in the basement?"

A cringe started deep in my stomach and worked its way out. "Watching a movie in the basement" was Violet-speak for "hard-core make-out session." Or whatever else she did down there. That couch converted into a bed, and probably had better stories than some hotel comforters.

It was more than I cared to think about.

I must've managed to control my face, because she kept talking. "So we're kissing and everything, and things are getting, you know, pretty hot, and all of a sudden he just— *stops*. Like, hands me my shirt and says he should go."

"Oh." The fact that her shirt had been off was way more than I needed to know. "So, um, what happened?"

"I don't know! I asked if he was feeling okay, and he said he thought we should wait. No one *waits* anymore, Kelsey. I mean, what the hell? When he said he liked you before, was it legit, or was he totally trying to cover being gay?"

Laughter spewed out before I could control it. "Violet! He and I never—"

She waved her hand dismissively. "Whatev. But seriously? He has to be, right?"

I struggled to contain my chuckles. "I doubt it, Vi. Maybe he'd talked to his mom beforehand? That always puts him in a bad mood."

Violet's expression soured. "I don't know, he never talks about her. I was starting to wonder if she died or something."

"She's not dead!" I stopped and shrank in my chair when I realized the look in her eyes was pure evil. It was obvious she didn't care to know about David's mother—she cared that I knew more than she did.

I chewed at the mouth of my water bottle, trying to pretend I didn't feel flattered—and the tiniest bit smug—to know that there were still some things David didn't feel comfortable sharing with just anyone.

Violet folded her arms, continuing down the warpath. "Well, he's either gay"—her eyes raked over me in an unmistakably accusing way—"or he's hung up on someone."

"What is *that* supposed to mean?"

"Nothing." She pretended to examine her nails. "Just that you two have been all buddy-buddy lately, and it magically coincides with me getting the shaft. Care to explain?"

I had to admit, Violet was more observant than I gave

her credit for. A lot of the tension between David and me had dissipated since I'd more or less broken down in his arms. We were still nowhere near the way we used to be, but we'd been talking a lot more. Laughing a lot more too.

"Listen, Vi. David and I were only friends. That's as far as it will ever go, and we're not even there yet. So if you really think he's hung up on someone, it isn't me."

Violet frowned. "Great. Then I guess my boyfriend is gay."

The fact that David walked in before I could defend him made it even harder to bury my laugh in my bottle of water.

"Hey," he said, nodding in my direction as he sat down. He turned to face Violet. "You didn't wait for me today."

She pressed her pen against her lip and gave him a pointed look. "I hate waiting."

Oh, God. Poor David. He'd landed himself in the doghouse for being a gentleman, and he didn't have a clue. And although I'd never admit it, I was dying to know the real reason he'd put the brakes on.

"You hate waiting?" David looked baffled. "You wait at my locker every morning. What are you talking about?"

Violet rolled her eyes. "I don't always feel like waiting. Waiting bites the big one, okay?" Under her breath she added, "Don't get excited because I said biting big ones."

David's bewildered look went from Violet to me and back again before Mr. Ingles called the class to attention.

David turned to face the front of the room, but his forehead remained creased with confusion. Through the corner of his eye, he glanced at me as if to say, *What the hell is going on?*

There was no way to clue him in that wouldn't be completely awkward. Sex was the one subject he and I had always skirted around, probably because it was something we'd never done together, and never would. We'd kept it out of each other's faces. Or he'd kept it out of mine, since I'd been a virgin until Ryan.

As Mr. Ingles took attendance, I decided I could at least tell David that Violet was upset, though that much was pretty obvious. Passing a note would have been too noticeable, so my eyes wandered to my cell phone in my bag, an actual smartphone from the twenty-first century that my parents had upgraded me to when we moved. I could text him, but what if his number had changed? A twinge of shame went through me as I remembered all the times last summer when I'd seen *Missed Call: David Cell* on my screen, and *New Message: David Cell*.

I'd ignored them until they stopped coming altogether. I definitely owed him an explanation for way more than just Violet's behavior.

Pretending to dig through my bag on the floor, I scrolled through my contacts and prayed (a) David's number hadn't changed and, (b) he had his phone on him.

I typed in, *Run for the hills*, and hit send.

A second later, as Mr. Ingles wrote out questions on

the board, David took his cell phone from the pocket of his hoodie and looked at it. Then he glanced at me and mouthed, *What did I do?*

I bit the insides of my cheeks to keep from laughing as I typed back, *It's what you didn't do.*

"Okay, ladies and gentleman, I'd like to begin our discussion on *Twelfth Night* by William Shakespeare," Mr. Ingles said in his booming voice.

My bag vibrated with David's reply. *I'll bite. What didn't I do?*

Violet's hand shot into the air. "Mr. Ingles? Wasn't Shakespeare *gay?*"

In the same moment she asked the question, my response reached David: *Her.*

Horror washed over his face as he connected my answer with her question. Spots of color appeared at the tips of his ears, and I had to cover my mouth with my hand to keep from dissolving into a fit of giggles as he whipped around in his seat to look at her, then spun forward again, wide eyed and fidgeting.

Mr. Ingles grabbed the back of his chair and leaned on it. "It's a highly debated topic, Ms. Kensing. Shakespeare was, of course, married to a woman, and he fathered several children."

"But that doesn't mean anything, right? He could have been trying to hide it."

David sank in his seat and rubbed his temple. He

looked so uncomfortable that I wondered if I should have just kept my mouth shut. But then he cast a sidelong glance in my direction, and the corner of his mouth pulled up into a smile.

"There's undoubtedly evidence of homosexual themes in Shakespeare's work," Mr. Ingles continued. Or tried to, before Violet cut him off again.

"Right. So why write about homosexual themes if you're not homosexual? I mean, he was definitely bi-curious, right?"

A rumble of laughter rippled through the classroom, and Violet looked like she wanted to murder someone.

Mr. Ingles held up his hands. "While this is a very interesting topic of discussion, I'm afraid it has nothing to do with our lesson today. But, Ms. Kensing, I'll be happy to pick it up later this week. Now then, everyone . . ." He turned to the board, and Violet folded her arms across her chest, scowling.

David and I spent the rest of the class sneaking furtive glances at each other, trying our hardest not to laugh. It had been a long time since we'd shared an inside joke, and I couldn't help but enjoy it. I prayed Violet was too distracted to notice, or I'd have to get in line behind him to grovel for her forgiveness.

She bolted from her seat the moment the bell rang, throwing a hurried, "Later, Kelse," over her shoulder.

At least I was in the clear.

David stood up and ran his hand through his hair, finally letting the grin he'd been stifling break free. "So that's what's bothering her? Geez. Guess chivalry really is dead."

"Was there a reason?" Ugh. That sounded a lot less nosy in my head. I concentrated on putting my books in my bag so I wouldn't have to look at him. "I mean, is everything all right with you two?"

He shrugged. "They're fine. Besides, that was almost a week ago. Why's she getting all bent out of shape now?"

"Maybe she's been stewing all this time."

I didn't mention Violet's other accusation, about him being hung up on someone.

David grinned again. "Look's like the stew's up." He glanced toward the door. "Guess I should go take care of this. See you at lunch?"

I nodded and slung my bag over my shoulder before heading over to Mr. Ingles's desk. The question I needed to ask him and the answer he gave me couldn't have taken more than two minutes. Which made what happened next that much more unbelievable.

I shouldered my way into the hall, slipping into between-class traffic. As I turned the corner, I stopped short when the blue bulk of someone's book bag nearly collided with my face.

The boy turned around and gave me a once-over, then stepped closer to the wall without apologizing for his loitering nearly making me face-plant into his bag. Annoyed,

I shoved past him and a few more stationary bodies. That's when I saw what the holdup was.

Ryan and David stood barely a foot apart. Both of them had clenched jaws. A vein in Ryan's temple throbbed, his face was bright red, and his back was pressed up against the lockers.

I took one look at David and instantly all those feelings I'd started to reacquaint myself with—the camaraderie, the fondness—all melted away. The laughter and lightheartedness I'd witnessed moments ago were gone. I didn't even recognize the person in front of me.

He shook with rage. His eyes were filled with hatred so intense I never would have thought him capable of feeling it.

And his fingers were wrapped around Ryan's throat.

Fourteen

Connecticut
Winter, Sophomore Year

My mother freaked out, as predicted, when I came home from sledding looking like I'd gone ten rounds with a slasher movie villain. A phone call to the doctor resulted in the very plausible explanation that it had probably been a combination of lingering sinus issues and dryness caused by the extreme cold, along with the assurance that they could cauterize my nose if it happened again.

We were both satisfied with that, especially since it hadn't been my first nosebleed ever, just the most intense.

Not so satisfying? The balled-up snot rags that had mysteriously started littering the floor near my locker the Monday after the incident. The first time it happened, I'd wrinkled my nose and kicked them away, remarking to David that people who didn't have basic knowledge of how to use a trash can shouldn't be allowed to graduate. But when it happened for the next two consecutive days, the feeling I'd had when Maddie and Isabel's friends mocked me at the golf course—the one of having swallowed a bowling ball—returned with a vengeance.

"David," I murmured as I frowned at three white wads. When I leaned closer, I saw that some of them had been colored with red marker. "They're doing this on purpose."

"Who is?"

"Isabel and her friends. Maybe Maddie, too. I saw them making fun of me when we were leaving the golf course."

David frowned. "You did? Why didn't you tell me?"

"Because it's embarrassing." My shoulders sagged as I kicked the tissues away.

"I'm getting to the bottom of this right now," David said.

My head snapped up in time to see him striding down the hall toward Isabel, his back straight and tense.

"David, don't—" But it was too late. I wished I could crawl inside my locker and hide as he caught up to her. Isabel's eyes grew round and incredulous as David looked down at her like he'd caught her stealing. That part I might've liked.

My mortification turned to confusion, though, when David's features relaxed after a few seconds and his scowl morphed into a smile. Then the two of them headed toward me, together. I tried to appear busy with my books as they closed the distance, the whole time wondering why Isabel looked like she was about to hug me. And hoping like hell she wouldn't.

"Kelsey!" Her voice dripped with remorse. She motioned toward the scattered tissues. "I am *so sorry* about this. I had no idea what was going on. Sometimes my friends think they're funny when they're not. It's *so* immature."

I glanced at David. He raised his eyebrows and nodded ever so slightly toward Isabel, like a parent prompting a kid to remember her manners. Which meant he was buying this crap.

"Yeah," I agreed. "It's pretty immature."

She pressed her manicured fingertips against her collarbone. "That's why I wouldn't have any part of it."

No, she'd just tried to decapitate me with her laser eyes.

Isabel's red-glossed lips pursed earnestly. "You saw that, right? It wasn't me making fun of you."

I had to give her credit. Declaring her innocence in front of David was one smooth move. Especially since I couldn't deny it.

"I saw, Isabel. I saw the whole thing."

"I'm *so sorry*, Kelsey," she repeated. "This will never happen again. And I'll make sure that they apologize to you."

I held up my hand. "I don't need an apology, really. As long as I don't get any more 'presents,' it's fine."

"You won't." She flashed a brief grin at me, then turned

a full-on beam at David, like she'd completed the performance of her life and expected him to applaud or something. "Walk us to class, David?"

"This is where Kelse and I part ways," he said. "But I'll walk
with you." He looked at me. "See you after second period?"

"See you then." I was too tired and too weirded out to
pull off a fake smile. David might've bought her apology
hook, line, and sinker, but I would've eaten my textbooks
before I'd believe one word had been sincere.

I hated fake people.

But even more, as I watched them walk away together
and leave me with crumpled tissues at my feet, I hated that
I felt so alone.

"You look tired, Kelsey," Mom said, studying the purple-
tinged bags beneath my eyes over her coffee mug. "And
pale. Are you sure you're feeling all right?"

I dragged a piece of pancake through the syrup on my
plate, finding no desire to put it in my mouth. "I got my
period last night. It's really heavy."

"Ah." Mom nodded knowingly. Once a month my
body decided it hated me, a trait I had picked up from my
mother's end of the gene pool. And it seemed to be hating
especially hard this month, though certain other stressors
probably weren't helping the fact that my energy level was
zero lately. But I didn't want to get into that with my mom.
I wouldn't put it past her to ambush me into a meeting with

Maddie and Isabel to "talk things out." She watched me play with my food for a few more seconds before asking, "Do you want to stay home from school?"

I shook my head. I hated being absent to be sick. Playing hooky was one thing, but staying home alone to feel lethargic and useless was its own brand of suck. One person, however, definitely wouldn't complain about it—Isabel.

I'd felt her eyes drilling holes of hatred into the back of my head during study hall ever since the sledding incident, despite her apology and the cease-fire on tissue-bombing my locker. I still couldn't figure out why my bleeding had offended her so thoroughly. I just knew that she saw the time David and I spent together as a roadblock in her never-ending quest to hit on him, even though His Denseness shrugged off my suspicions.

I caught up to him at his locker before first bell. "Hey," I said. "You never responded to my text about the history project last night."

"Um, last night?" He avoided my eyes as he transferred books to his bag. "I kind of went over to Isabel's to help her with her homework."

My fingers tightened around the strap of my own backpack. "Went over . . . to her *house*? For real?"

He mumbled something I couldn't hear over the sound of lockers slamming and feet shuffling and jaws dropping. My jaw, anyway.

I waited for him to apologize for not texting back, or to at least make an excuse and then spill the details I was dying for. Like what Isabel's house looked like on the inside and whether or not he'd seen the four Porsches her parents were rumored to own. And whether or not Maddie had been there, sucking face with Jared and acting like David was her new best friend.

He said nothing.

"So," I hedged. "How was your study date?"

The red tinge that lit his ears told me they hadn't done much studying at all. "It was fine. She's um—she's nice."

Oh, Christ.

"I'll bet she is." I'd meant to sound teasing, but it came out sour.

David threw his bag over his shoulder. "You're not mad, are you?"

"I'm too tired to be mad." Which was true.

A look of concern clouded his face. "You have to snap out of this soon, you know."

"Why is that?"

He looked past me and bobbed his head to indicate something behind me. "For that. It's this weekend."

I turned around to see what he meant. A poster hung on the side of the lockers, featuring glittering black and white snowflakes whirling around the shadowed figures of a dancing girl and boy. WINTER SWIRL TICKETS NOW ON SALE.

I shrugged as I faced him again. "Eh. Isabel will be happier if I don't go. Then she'll have you all to herself."

"Wha— Isabel? What does she have to do with it?"

"You're taking her, aren't you? Because that idiotic look on your face a minute ago told me you probably should. You must've at least copped a feel."

"Kelse, me and Isabel . . . I don't think . . ." He trailed off, rubbing the back of his neck.

"You don't think what? Whatever you did counts? Oh, David. You got a piece. Just say it."

David didn't laugh at my ribbing. He seemed genuinely flustered, and even a little frustrated. "But she's—I—Isabel's a junior. She's not gonna want to go to the dance with a sophomore."

Before I could answer, a manicured hand appeared on his shoulder. "I wouldn't be so sure of that," Isabel said. She beamed up at him.

And ignored me.

"Oh, hey," David said, his ears turning beet red. "We were just talking about you."

She pressed her chin against his shoulder. "I know. And I'd love to."

David shot a half-nervous, half-apologetic look at me. "Uh, that's—"

I spun on my heel. "I'll catch you later." Between my nosebleed and my period, I didn't have enough blood in my digestive tract to keep my stomach from rejecting my breakfast if I stuck around much longer.

I'd only made it ten steps when I felt a hand on my arm. David pulled up in front of me, blocking my path. "Kelse, wait a second. I'm sorry about that. That's not how it was supposed to happen."

Now I was the one confused. "What were you planning to do? Get her roses or something?"

"I wasn't planning—" He shook his head. "Never mind. You're still gonna go, right?"

"I doubt it."

David's face fell. "Why not?"

I looked down. I didn't want to say something as self-pitying as *No one else cares if I go*, even though it was obviously true after what had happened at the golf course. I wrapped my arms around myself, feeling everything I'd felt that day, right down to the cold.

"I don't know. I haven't really thought about it."

"Well, think about it, okay? I really want you to be there."

"Oh-kay?"

He smiled, my bewildered answer apparently satisfactory.

As he walked away, a pinprick of realization started somewhere in my head, turning my whole body hot with embarrassment as it spread. Blood loss and all, any moron should have been able to see what had just happened, and why David had been acting so weird.

Maybe I'd misinterpreted his half-finished sentences. When he said he hadn't planned for it to happen that way, he hadn't meant the *way* he asked Isabel to the dance. He meant he hadn't planned to take her at all.

He'd planned to go with me.

Fifteen

Rhode Island
Senior Year

No one would tell me what started the fight in the hallway. Or rather, Ryan and David wouldn't tell me. No one else seemed to have a clue.

It ended when I ran up and smashed my palms into David's ribs as hard as I could, attempting to break whatever psychotic spell he'd been under. I demanded to know what he was doing, but it was like he didn't see or hear me. He pointed at Ryan and, through clenched teeth, told him to watch it. Then he walked away like nothing had happened.

I tried confronting both of them, but neither one would talk. The more I questioned Ryan, the more agitated he got, so I dropped it. For the moment.

As for David and me, things went right back to the way they'd been before our semi-reconciliation. Worse, actually. We'd at least been polite before our tentative mending of fences, but watching him try to choke the life out of my boyfriend had sent hypothetical fence posts flying all over the place, damaged beyond repair.

We hadn't spoken since.

Which made the fact that my parents had invited him and his father for Thanksgiving even more unbearable.

I was at least happy to see Mr. Kerrigan looking somewhat healthier since our last get-together, and made sure to give him a big hug when he walked into the kitchen. This time without blubbering all over him.

"I'm a little less scary now, eh?" he said cheerfully.

I squeezed his shoulder. "You're adorable no matter what, but I'm still gonna bake some cookies to fatten you up."

I turned and looked David up and down, hoping my face conveyed my thoughts loud and clear: *As long as he doesn't share them with you.*

We gathered around the table, and the feeling of being flipped to some backward bizarro world was stronger than ever. Normally Aunt Tess and Uncle Tommy celebrated Thanksgiving with us. This year they were on a Mediterranean cruise, and their seats were filled by the last two bodies on Earth I would have ever imagined.

"So, David," my father said as he pulled out his chair. "I hear you made the baseball team. Congratulations."

David nodded and his father slapped a hand on his shoulder. "Ed came to watch David play over the summer." By "Ed," Mr. Kerrigan meant Ed Benson, the baseball coach. "He told him he didn't even need to try out, but David didn't want any special treatment." He ruffled his son's hair, and I could almost hear him thinking, *Such a good boy.*

Yeah. The picture of moral frigging fiber. Especially when he's strangling people.

"Ed even said he'd get some scouts out this season to watch David play," Mr. Kerrigan continued. "Though I'm sure his grades are good enough to help us with college." He beamed at David.

Anyone else bragging that way would have made me point my finger at the back of my throat and gag. But Jimmy Kerrigan was so genuinely proud of his son that it didn't come across as bragging. His pride in David radiated like sunbeams and warmed my heart. Despite my wishing it didn't.

Especially since he'd basically confirmed exactly what Ryan had been afraid of.

"Clayton has a really good team. Kelsey's boyfriend is on it," my father said. He nodded toward me and my eyes dropped to the table. "You must know Ryan, right, David? Quite an arm on that kid."

Way to serve up a big plate of awkward along with the turkey, Daddy.

David swirled a baby carrot around his plate with his fork. "Yeah. He's . . . something." He didn't look at my father when he said it.

Mr. Kerrigan turned to my father. "You know, Kevin, since Kelsey is determined to plump me up"—he winked at me, and I didn't know if he'd changed the subject intentionally, but I wanted to hug him for it—"and since Tommy's not here to do it, maybe we could all head over to Bellevue for shakes this weekend." He squeezed David's shoulder. "I can't even attempt the challenge, but I'll bet David could give you a run for your money."

"We should!" Miranda sat forward in her chair, nodding enthusiastically. "We haven't done that in so long!"

I knew by the way the corners of Dad's mouth turned down that he was going to say no, and he didn't disappoint.

"Sorry, guys. I have papers to grade and a deadline coming up, and I'm so behind. I should be eating dinner in my office right now."

Miranda scowled and sat back.

"Sounds like a plan," I muttered under my breath. My own bitterness surprised me. I suddenly felt very resentful that my father spent so little time with us anymore, only to make things uncomfortable on one of the rare occasions he did, and then blow us off again right after.

Dad obviously didn't hear my grumbling, because he leaned back in his chair, put his arms behind his head, and steered the conversation right back to where it had been.

"Anyway, Ryan's good to Kelsey, and that's all that matters. She was so miserable before we moved here, poor girl. He spoils her rotten." He stopped talking long enough to look in my direction. "Show David the bracelet he got you for Valentine's Day." Looking back at David, he added, "I thought my wife was going to faint when she saw it."

I shot my mother a look, hoping she saw the SOS in my eyes as I hid my hand beneath the table.

"He's seen it," I said. *And he hates it.*

My mother stood up, taking the napkin from her lap and putting it on the table. "Kelsey, why don't you help me bring out the salad and some salad bowls?"

I was on my feet before she even finished her sentence, but still too late to avoid hearing David mutter, "Glad you're not *miserable* anymore."

As much as I wanted to hate him for the comment, I felt a sting of guilt. Of course he'd taken my father's statement about my pre–Rhode Island unhappiness personally—before we moved to Rhode Island, I'd spent most of my time with *him*.

All at once I wanted to squeeze his shoulder to let him know my former state hadn't been his fault, and spit in his food to let him know how miserable he was making me now.

I pretended not to hear him, annoyed that I couldn't muster the level of indignation his comment warranted, and followed my mother into the kitchen.

"Mom." I sighed. "You need to get Daddy a muzzle. Or

at least pinch him under the table when he's making me wish I could crawl into my own shoes and hide."

My mother eyed me warily. "I thought things were better with you and David. Are you upset because he's dating your friend?"

"No! That has nothing to do with it." I hadn't told her about the fight in the hall, and unless word somehow reached Miranda and her megamouth, I intended to keep it that way. "Things are still . . . weird."

"Kelsey." I knew by the way she said it, the way she looked at me, and the way she pursed her lips that I wasn't going to like whatever followed. "That's because you still feel guilty about hurting him."

"I don't," I said too quickly, trying and failing to keep the wobble out of my voice. "I apologized for that. We talked about it. Sort of."

Besides, he hurt me too.

I restacked the salad bowls on the table to avoid meeting her eyes.

She grabbed the salad and started toward the dining room, but stopped when we were shoulder to shoulder and leaned in. "Maybe you need to do better than 'sort of,'" she said quietly. Then she walked out of the room.

Sixteen

Connecticut
Winter, Sophomore Year

I didn't go to the Winter Swirl.

I never stood a chance. Not that I was even sure why I wanted to, when my former best friend had turned on me and my current best friend was taking a girl who'd gladly string me up in a tree by my toenails.

I was being a good daughter that afternoon, helping my mother chop vegetables for dinner when disaster struck.

Miranda came into the room and peered over my shoulder. "Let me do some!" she whined.

"No way. Last time you mangled the zucchini beyond recognition." Hand-eye coordination and my sister were not the best of friends.

But she had already gone to the butcher block and grabbed herself a knife, and was now trying to elbow her way next to me at the cutting board. Slamming mine down, I reached for her wrist to take the knife out of her hand, but she pulled away. The blade sliced into my palm and wrist, sending such sharp, hot pain through me that I barely noticed the similar sensation on my leg before the knife clattered to floor.

"Kelse!" Miranda gasped. "I'm sorry!"

I cried out as the wound opened up and dark red blood spilled out. My mother appeared out of nowhere and ran over, grabbing a dishcloth on the way, and pressed it against my hand.

"Kelsey, you need to be careful!"

"It wasn't my fault," I whimpered as Miranda stood watching with horrified eyes. Why it was my mother's first instinct to reprimand me for an accident, I'd never understand. But that was Mom.

We both looked down to where the bloody knife lay, looking like it needed to be bagged and tagged by a forensics crew.

"How is there so much blood on the floor?" my mother murmured. She took a step away from me, still holding the towel against my hand. I looked down in time to hear her say, "Oh my God, your leg!"

The knife had grazed my calf on the way down, ripping right through the leg of my yoga pants. The pants, my shoe, and the floor were covered in blood.

"Hold this!" my mother demanded, indicating the dish towel on my hand. She scrambled to the drawer for another one and pressed it against my leg. I held my hand over the sink and attempted to adjust the already-drenched cloth so I could put more pressure on the cut. But as my shaking hands fumbled with the towel, I saw how quickly the blood poured out and I started to feel light-headed.

My limbs felt as limp as noodles, and I started to see black dots dancing in front of my eyes. I leaned against the counter. "Mom." My jaw felt like deadweight as I tried to say more. "I don't feel good."

Then I collapsed.

The next time I opened my eyes, my eyelids felt like iron curtains. I was lying in a hospital bed hooked up to an IV. The bright lights blurred my vision as I turned my head in the direction of my mother's hushed voice. She stood a few feet away, talking with a man I assumed to be a doctor. She ran her fingertips over her bottom lip as he responded, which meant she was worried. Which automatically made me worry.

"Mom?" I tried to sit up, swallowing over my parched throat. "What happened?" Even as the question left my lips, it all came back to me. I groaned.

"Stay still, sweetie," my mother said as she rushed over to my side. "They're prepping you for a blood transfusion."

"What?" I immediately felt like crying. "Blood transfusion" sounded so serious, so foreboding. So not what I wanted to be doing on the night of the Winter Swirl. "What's wrong with me?"

Mom took my hand and squeezed it, which only succeeded in making me more nervous. "We're not sure. You lost a lot of blood today, and they need to figure out why."

The man, who introduced himself as Dr. Delano, cleared his throat and walked to my mother's side. "Kelsey," he said, adjusting his thick black glasses, "I was just telling your mother that I believe you may have a blood disorder. We'll need to run some tests, of course, but it could be something as simple as a severe vitamin deficiency."

"Simple" and "severe" didn't seem to belong in the same sentence. As I recounted my symptoms in my head—everything from the bloodshed event nosebleed to the times my skin had bruised like overripe fruit, even if I couldn't remember hurting myself—fear turned what was left of my blood into ice. "Or it could be something serious, like cancer, right?"

I'd seen one of those awful Lifetime movies about a girl with leukemia, and they'd given her the blood disorder line at first too. My mind reeled. I wanted answers, and I wanted them now.

Dr. Delano looked rattled, like he hadn't expected me to have half a brain and put him on the spot. "We'll have to rule it out," he said cautiously. "But understand that serious blood disorders don't have to be cancer. Either way, we'll get to the bottom of it." He gave a curt nod and left the room.

"Mom, he said 'serious.'" My voice cracked and my lip trembled. "What's wrong with me?"

"Honey, don't listen to a word he says," my mother said through gritted teeth. "He knows nothing, do you understand me? When the tests come back, we'll figure out how to make you better. Until then, the transfusion will help." She looked behind her, at the door where Dr. Delano had exited, and spat the word "douche bag" under her breath.

In spite of myself, laughter bubbled up in my throat. "Mom, did you just say 'douche bag'?"

Her lips floated into a tired smile, and I huddled closer to her.

"Do I have to stay here tonight?"

My mother sighed. "You probably won't have to, but they did say they might keep you for observation. If I can help it, you're sleeping in your own bed." She smoothed my hair away from my face. "And if you can't, I'll stay right here with you."

I nodded, swallowing the lump that formed in my throat as I thought of everyone else getting their hair done, their nails painted, their makeup applied. Even though I'd told David I wasn't going to the dance, I wanted to. I'd actually been fantasizing about shedding my usual jeans and ponytail to try out a different look, to wear a dress that made me feel pretty.

A hospital gown wasn't quite the gown I'd had in mind.

My disappointment must have been obvious, because my mother left and returned a little while later with Miranda in tow—and a bottle of red nail polish from the hospital gift shop.

My mom painted my nails and Miranda curled up next to me and brushed my hair, while I tried not to think about the plastic bags suspended from a metal pole next to my bed, feeding disgusting things into my body for reasons I didn't understand.

I'd sent David a text message to let him know where I was and why I wouldn't be at the dance, but then had to shut my cell phone off following a look of death from one of the nurses. I knew he'd be worried, but I also knew he had Isabel to think of. So when a soft knock sounded at the door to my room, the last person I expected to see was David— standing there in a tuxedo, holding a plastic corsage box.

My mouth dropped open, and not only because I was shocked to see him.

He looked amazing.

His hair was freshly cut, and for once the short black spikes were more carefree than unruly. The cut of the tux showed off his broad shoulders and slim waist, and the color complemented his dark eyes. The more tentative steps he took toward the bed, the more I realized he smelled as good as he looked. Nothing that gorgeous belonged amidst the fluorescent lights and dull tile floors of the hospital room.

I burst into tears on the spot.

"David!" I cried as he closed the distance between us and folded me into a hug. "You look so handsome!"

He pressed his nose against my neck as I wept into the shoulder of his tuxedo jacket. Low enough so only I could hear, he asked, "Are you okay?"

I nodded and started to wipe my eyes but froze when I saw he hadn't come alone. Standing in the door frame, fidgeting with the wrist strap of a corsage identical to the one David had carried in—and looking beyond beautiful—was Isabel Rose.

Her sapphire-blue halter dress hugged her curves, and her hair cascaded down her back in flowing dark curls.

The dress I'd wanted to wear was so similar. I'd eyed it on the rack in the department store but left it there when I saw the price tag—and when I pictured Isabel and Maddie dousing me with a bucket of red paint, *Carrie*-style, and making me the laughingstock of the dance. I was glad now that I hadn't bought it. I couldn't imagine ever looking that flawless in it. In fact, even with my painted nails and my brushed hair, at that moment I could not have felt more hideous or inadequate.

Isabel picked at the lacy band of the corsage around her wrist and twisted it around her finger as she shot me a tight smile. I scooted back on the bed, putting some space between David and me.

"How did you know where to find me?" I asked.

"Your dad was getting coffee in the lobby." David turned to look at my father, who handed a steaming cup to my mother and a Snapple to Miranda. "We followed him up. By the way, everyone, this is Isabel."

Isabel looked mortified at the mention of her name, as if saying it out loud had stripped her of an invisibility cloak. The tight smile stretched even tighter, and this time an equally tight wave accompanied it. My parents must have sensed the discomfort in the room, because they promptly ushered Miranda out and made an excuse about needing to stretch their legs.

"This is for you," David said with a grin as he held out the corsage box he'd placed on the bed.

I fought back the lump in my throat. "David. That is so sweet of you."

He shrugged and his expression turned sheepish. "I was gonna get you one anyway." Behind him, Isabel's lips pressed into a line. "Seriously though, are you okay? Do they know what's going on yet?"

I shook my head and dropped my voice to a whisper. "It could be a few different things. They're really making me nervous."

David's brow puckered and he squeezed my hand. "Don't be nervous. You'll be fine, I know it." The corners of his mouth turned up again and mischief lit his eyes. "You just did this so I wouldn't embarrass you on the dance floor tonight."

I had to smile. "If you dance as badly as you spell, then maybe I should be glad I'm not going."

He squeezed my hand again and leaned a little closer. "I really wanted you to go," he said quietly. "I would've come alone, but by the time you texted me, I was already on my way to her house." I knew he didn't want Isabel to hear, and if she felt like a third wheel, I didn't care. I hoped she did, actually.

David spoke in his regular voice as he told me to call him if I heard anything, and to let him know when I went home. But then as he stood, he leaned in again so only I could hear him. "Save me a dance for another time, okay?"

I nodded, feeling sad and alone the moment his weight lifted from the mattress.

"Feel better, Kelsey," Isabel said as David walked toward her. Her relief couldn't have been more obvious. From the way she'd been eyeing the room and shifting on her silver-heeled feet, you would have thought a fleet of cockroaches were closing in and David had rescued her in the nick of time.

They left the room and I sank into my pillow, ready to give in to my overwhelming urge to cry. I turned on my side, the IV needle pinching me in protest. That was all it took to push me over the edge, and I buried my sobs in the stiff linen.

As I repositioned my hand, trying to avoid the niggling stabs, the bloodstained gauze around my wrist caught my attention. Red seeping through white, the same as it had been in the snow. Seeing it made the image of Maddie mimicking me and Isabel glaring at me after the sledding incident loop through my mind. Embarrassment flooded over me just as powerfully as it had that day.

I'd always sort of blended into the woodwork at Norwood High—not exceedingly popular, but not invisible, either. Lately, though, the only person who looked at me like I was worth anything was David.

I buried my hand beneath the blanket as I thought about how illness was the last thing I wanted to put me in the spotlight. It already devastated me to know that I was the brunt of jokes. That people were laughing at me. I didn't want to be the subject of more whispered conversations, or worse, the recipient of anyone's pity. Suddenly what I did want—more than anything—was to be out at my high school dance like a normal, healthy sixteen-year-old, instead of stuck in a hospital bed with someone else's blood dripping into my body.

Please, I thought. *Don't let this be my future.*

Seventeen

Rhode Island
Senior Year

Things were all sunshine and kittens between Violet and David again, so I could only imagine he'd given her what she wanted.

The thought made my stomach turn. Not only did I not need the mental image, but it gave me the distinct sensation of bugs crawling all over my skin every time I looked at David.

So when Mr. Ingles announced in English class that he'd be pairing us off for an assignment in which we'd have to write a short biographical essay on our partner, my body tensed. The possibilities were endless for disastrous pairings.

But I would have taken anyone over David.

"Now," Mr. Ingles said as he scrawled example questions across the board, "I don't want your interviews to be boring, but I don't want anyone to be uncomfortable, either. Feel out your partner, and decide how personal you're willing to get."

Snickers erupted at the phrase "feel out your partner," and I rolled my eyes. I wanted to ask why we couldn't just write our own autobiographies, especially when I saw how very bland his sample questions actually were:

"Where did you grow up? How does it compare to the setting of your favorite novel?"

"What has been your greatest accomplishment to date?"

"Where do you hope to be five years from now?"

There were at least three more, but I stopped reading and made a *Kill me* face at Violet, who responded with a slicing gesture across her throat.

Mr. Ingles made a big show of picking up his grade book and announcing that he'd given careful consideration to our pairings, and that there would be no switching unless we had an ironclad reason.

And the very first pair of names he called?

Of course.

"Ms. Crawford and Mr. Kerrigan."

Violet's hand shot into the air.

"No, Ms. Kensing, you may not switch," Mr. Ingles said with barely a glance in her direction. "Being all atwitter for someone is not an ironclad reason to be his assignment partner."

The class snickered again, and I might have felt bad for Violet as she sat there pouting if I wasn't trying to ignore the twenty-degree increase in my body temperature. Oh, that universe had quite a sense of humor. I racked my brain trying to think of an ironclad reason David and I couldn't work together, but I had the feeling personal drama didn't qualify.

The more I thought about it, the more I realized it might not be so bad. After all, I had plenty of questions for David that weren't related to our assignment, and now I had an excuse to ask them. And considering we hadn't spoken since the hallway incident, an excuse was definitely in order.

At the tail end of class, we were allowed to meet with our partners and get started on the interviews. David turned his desk toward mine and moved it closer without even looking at me.

"So," I said. "You and Violet are . . . better?"

Of all the questions I'd planned to fire at him, I hadn't meant to let that one slip first. Or at all, even.

"Fine." He rotated the cap of his pen around the barrel. "Although she keeps asking about my mother. Any idea why that would be?"

His tone made me squirm in my seat. "How *are* things with you and your mother?"

He shrugged. "We tolerate each other. Talk every now and then. Nothing worth telling the whole world about."

"Uh, your girlfriend is hardly 'the whole world.'" When seconds ticked by without a response, I added, "Maybe Violet's hinting that she'd like to meet her."

"My mother moved to Puerto Rico with her boyfriend."

"Puerto Rico? When?"

"Right after my grandfather died." He snorted. "Probably when she realized she had no way to stake a claim on his house." Sitting up straighter, he finally looked at me. "It's all good, though. I'm used to people walking out of my life."

I gripped the edge of the desk and my teeth ground together. "You can work with someone else if you can think of a good enough reason," I offered coolly. "So if you want to fake an anaphylactic reaction to my perfume or something . . ."

David leaned back in his chair and folded his arms, arrogance oozing from every pore. "Now, why would I want to do that when I can think of one or two questions I'd like you to answer?"

I dropped my pen onto my notebook and sat up straighter. Two could play this game. "Know what? Me too. Starting with this one." I leaned forward and lowered my voice. "Why would you try to hurt Ryan?"

David snorted. "Ask him."

"Don't you think I have? I can understand why *you'd* clam up—you attacked him. But why won't he talk to me?"

"Maybe he has something to hide." The flippant shrug that accompanied the comment made me want to jab him in the eye with my pen.

"Or maybe you do." I leaned back in my chair, mimicking his overconfidence. "The David I knew never would have done something like that without a reason. But you said it yourself. Things change."

That seemed to get him appropriately riled. His eyebrows pulled together and his jaw muscle twitched. "You do know me, Kelse. Probably better than anyone. Did you ever stop to think it's *him* you don't know so well?"

"What's that supposed to mean?"

"That he's not the great guy you think he is."

My fingers curled around my pen and squeezed. I wanted to snap it in half. And pretend it was David's neck.

"If you're going to make a statement like that, I suggest you back it up."

We glared at each other for a pointed second before David gave me an equally pointed answer. "Next question."

"You're kidding, right? I'm giving you the chance to clear your name, and you're going to blow it?"

The corners of his lips turned down. "Like you've never blown your chance at anything?"

I'd walked right into that. I shook my head and stared at my notebook, trying to find something to analyze on the blank page so I wouldn't have to look at him. "I don't think this is the time or place for that."

"Why not?" The exaggerated nonchalance returned. "Question number seven." He jerked his head in the direction of the board, where I scanned for question number seven.

Apparently, Mr. Ingles and the universe shared the same sense of humor.

"Describe your ideal romantic relationship. Tragedy? Comedy? Fantasy? Explain."

So much for not getting too personal.

I knew my mother had been right when she said I owed David more than a *sort of* explanation for the way our relationship had ended. And despite his holier-than-thou attitude—no, because of it—I knew he wanted me to do better than *sort of* as well. But I'd been right about something too. English class wasn't the time or place.

"David, listen. You have Violet now, and I have Ryan. We're both happy. That's all that matters, right?"

"You really don't miss Norwood at all, do you?"

"Where did that come from?" I sputtered.

David shrugged. "Just answer it."

"I miss certain things about it."

"Like what?"

I looked at my desk, knowing I couldn't say the first things that came to my mind: *Cutting through the woods to your house. Dinner with you and your dad. Blasting music in your clunky old car and singing at the top of our lungs.* So I said, "I miss riding my bike around my old neighborhood. I miss my dad being around on the weekends instead of going off to promote his book. And I miss going down to Pennyfield Beach, and parking a mile away and walking past all those old, beautiful houses just so I wouldn't have to pay to get in."

I smiled to myself. I *did* miss those things.

"Do you still talk to *anyone* from home?" he asked.

"Do *you*?" I folded my arms, well aware of how defensive this topic made me.

"Of course. It hasn't been that long since I left. Why wouldn't I?" His eyes leveled with mine, and the unspoken portion of his question hung in the air between us: *Just because you didn't?*

The silent accusation made me feel the way I did when I didn't drink enough water with my vitamins—like I had a rock sitting in my throat.

"Easy for you to say. Everyone *loved* you."

He looked me right in the eye. "Not everyone."

My pen grew slippery with sweat and I knew I must've been glowing crimson, but I refused to back down. "Have you seen anyone from there lately?"

Tell me you don't still see her. Of all people, please tell me you're not still hanging out with that bitch.

"Yep." He ripped a square of paper out of his notebook and started to shred it, purposely staring at the strips of paper and not at me. A definite sign of guilt, in my opinion.

"Anyone I know?"

"No one you would have cared to see." He stopped midshred. "Oh, wait. That's everyone."

Before I could do anything more than gape, or even fully register how deeply his comment had hurt me, the bell rang. David stood up and shoved his notebook into his bag.

He looked at me long enough to say, "We can do this by e-mail. It's probably easier."

With that, he walked away, leaving me dumbfounded, and pained.

I forced myself to shake it off as I stood to gather my books. I told myself it didn't matter what David did, or with whom. There were reasons we weren't friends anymore, and I'd been perfectly happy before he got here. I could be perfectly happy again if I stayed away from him.

If only it were actually that easy.

Eighteen

Connecticut
Winter, Sophomore Year

I stayed completely silent on the way home from the hospital that night.

My mother glanced at me in the rearview mirror, her face pinched with concern. "Kelsey? Are you all right? You're so quiet back there."

"Fine, Mom." I wondered if she heard the utter lack of conviction in my voice. "Tired. I want to go to bed."

"I'm sure you'll feel much better tomorrow." Her words were too cheerful, and I knew she sensed my complete and total despair. "David can come over for dinner, and tell us all about the dance. That was so nice of him to come by, wasn't it?"

"Mm-hm." Sure. It was great of him to come by and flaunt his girlfriend in front of my face. The thought of glamorous, gorgeous Isabel with her fabulous figure and flowing hair squeezed my chest like a vise. She and David were probably having a grand old time on the dance floor right now, pathetic girls in hospital beds the furthest thing from their minds as they laughed and took pictures with people I used to call my friends. Holding back my tears took phenomenal effort.

I left my bloodstained shoes in the garage when we got home. I hadn't wanted to put my torn-up, bloodied pants back on, so I'd been given a pair of scrubs to wear home. I threw them in the garbage when I changed into my pajamas, not wanting any reminder of that hospital or this night.

My mother tucked me in like I was five years old again. I was exhausted and I knew she was too, but I needed her to be more exhausted than me. There was so much I had to find out, and I didn't want anyone hovering.

Once she turned out my light and closed the door, I grabbed my cell phone, a dinosaur talk-and-text-only model that was all my parents could spring for on their limited income. I knew David was still at the dance, but I also knew he wanted me to check in with him. Besides, texting would keep me awake until I could go downstairs to use the computer.

I typed in, *I'm home. Got a fill-up on blood (so gross). How's the dance?* Then I waited for his response.

And waited.

And waited some more. Oh, and then waited even more than that.

I hit the button on my phone in frustration, wondering if he'd written back and the chime had failed to sound. Nope. Not a single new message.

Guess he wasn't that worried about me after all.

I didn't know why, but I felt like I needed to hear from David before I did what I'd been dreading and faced a search engine. Obviously, it wasn't going to happen that way.

I tiptoed down to the study and closed the door. When the site loaded, I typed in the words that had been burning a hole in my brain all night. I'd hoped to come down there and find reasons why something scary like leukemia couldn't possibly be my diagnosis, but the more I clicked, the more it felt like pure dread flowed through my veins instead of donor blood.

The symptoms fit. The bloody nose, the effortless bruising, the excessive blood loss during my period. The fatigue.

Fantastic.

I checked my phone again. Still nothing.

Now I had to confirm the thing that scared me the most: the treatment.

I searched desperately for the site that would tell me a blood transfusion meant the end of my worries, that I'd been cured tonight without even knowing it. But the goddamn Internet refused to humor me. The sites all seemed to agree that while transfusions could treat the symptoms, the best way to completely eliminate the disease was through chemotherapy and radiation.

I checked my phone again. *God, David, where the hell are you?*

Sitting in that chair with my infuriatingly silent cell phone, and with the computer screen and all its horrors as the only source of light, I'd never felt so scared or alone in all my life. I rested my head on my knees and tried to control the tremors racking my frame, but nothing helped. My brain seemed to take its cue from my body, flashing dozens of erratic images behind my eyes.

I saw myself cheering David on at his baseball games, and the way he'd sneak me a sly wink before he wound up for a fastball. I thought about the sunlight catching Miranda's hair as she ran through the field near David's house, picking dandelions. Miranda, being poked and prodded as a potential match for bone marrow donation. I remembered the way she'd brushed my hair tonight, and suddenly I imagined it transforming into dry, strawlike strands before detaching from my scalp in clumps. I wondered what Isabel and her friends would do to me then.

Then, for the first time since that afternoon on the Cliff Walk, I thought about kissing David. I'd pulled back because I hadn't been ready to wander into messier territory. The last time I'd let a friend kiss me, our relationship had unraveled right after. Whether it was a direct result of the kiss or not didn't matter. It happened, and I didn't want to risk leaving the safe, comfortable place David and I were in.

Did I want that now? Did it even matter, if David had already moved on?

I tried to imagine that day on the boulders with a different ending—one where I didn't pull away. It shocked me to realize I could. And that my whole body came alive when I did, only to go numb as I remembered the way David had lowered his voice in front of Isabel at the hospital. I thought he'd done it to keep our conversation private. But what if he'd only been trying to make it look like he didn't care in front of her? And worse, what if he didn't? Maybe he'd only gone to the hospital out of some sense of obligation. Maybe he'd started to see me as a joke, just like everyone else.

I didn't know what I would do if it were true. I couldn't face this without him.

I looked at my phone again. Not a single message.

I walked into our lower-level bathroom on wobbling legs. If I hadn't been shaken to the core already, my reflection in the vanity mirror would have frightened me. Pale skin, bruiselike circles beneath my eyes, matted hair. I gathered the brittle strands in my hands, wishing it hadn't taken the thought of losing them to make me want to pay more attention. Suddenly I wanted nothing more than to let my hair down more often, to wear it like a crown jewel the way Isabel did. I promised myself that if I got through this, I'd do exactly that.

That's when the worst thought of all hit me. What if I went through treatment and it didn't work? What if I was going to die?

A choked sob escaped my throat, and I clamped my hand over my mouth. In the mirror, the hospital bracelet still circling my wrist taunted me. I'd never felt so disgusted by anything in my life.

I yanked the medicine cabinet open and located the scissors my dad used to trim his beard. Then I sliced the godforsaken piece of plastic off with a vengeance. A little too much vengeance, because the sharp tip of the scissors pierced the skin beneath my palm. My heart leaped into my throat as a drop of blood swelled at the site.

Shit, not again!

I grabbed the hand towel off its holder and held it as hard as I could against the cut. At the same time, I sank to the bathroom floor and sobbed my fear and frustration into the other side of the towel.

I cried until I was too exhausted to move. Upstairs, my family slept, quietly unaware. And somewhere out there, wherever he was, my best friend was too busy to care.

Nineteen

Rhode Island
Senior Year

I spotted Ryan hovering at my locker as the bathroom door closed behind me. A smile spread across my face, and I reached back to slow the door so he wouldn't hear it shut. His brow scrunched in concentration as he spun the combination lock with one hand. His other hand clutched a red rose.

Grinning from ear to ear and tiptoeing as lightly as I could, I scurried over to him and grabbed him around the waist.

"Whoa!" he said, practically jumping into the locker. His startled expression melted into a grin when he saw me.

I wrapped my arms around his neck. "Guess I know who my secret Valentine's Day admirer is."

"Yeah, yeah, you caught me," he fake-groused, kissing my nose.

"You don't have to do this. The cookies were enough."

"I'd buy out their whole supply of roses if you wanted them."

Valentine's Day was pretty much legendary at Clayton. It was sort of sad, because it was also a blatant popularity contest. The cheerleaders always sold roses and made cookie-grams, heart-shaped sugar cookies that could be sent to the person of your choice with a message of love, or secret admirer-ship, or insert sentiment here.

Two cookies had been delivered to me before lunch, courtesy of Ryan. One with the message I LOVE YOU and the other with HAPPY VALENTINE'S DAY. Simple and sweet. Just like the single red roses he'd left in my locker before each period.

I kissed him, drawing it out with a long smacking sound. "You don't have to buy me any more. I'm letting you off the hook."

He shrugged. "What if I want to? Think of it as supporting Candle Wax and her rah-rahs. You're always telling me to be nicer to her."

I kissed his cheek and shook my head as if to say, *What am I going to do with you?* "Speaking of Candy, I have to get back to the cafeteria. I'm helping her man the rose table until the end of lunch."

"All right. But remember, you never saw me here." He kissed me again and started down the hall, watching me over his shoulder. We smiled at each other until I rounded the corner to the cafeteria entrance.

I wasn't a cheerleader, but Candy and Violet were, and I was with them so often that I'd sort of become an honorary member of the squad. It was only natural that I spent my lunch helping Candy sell flowers.

"How many roses did Chester the Molester give you this year?" Candy asked with a devilish gleam in her eye as the lunch crowd finally started to clear. "What was it last year? Thirty? Forty?"

"No." I waved off her exaggeration. "Seven. He left one in my locker before each period. Same thing this year, so far."

"How romantic." She batted her lashes, pretending to swoon before pointing her finger at the back of her throat.

"Kiss my ass! I saw you with a bunch before. Don't act like you don't love it when Crowley falls at your feet!"

"Hmm. I do love it, don't I?" We both snickered until something caught Candy's eye.

"Uh-oh," she said with a smirk. "Here comes your lover boy."

I followed her stare toward the cafeteria doors, expecting to see Ryan. Instead, my smile faded as David hesitantly approached the table. He had on red and white, not only the theme colors for the day but also the school colors. It was strange to see him in the same red Clayton High Baseball cap that Ryan wore so often. He had it flipped backward on his head, and his raglan shirt had red sleeves and a white trunk.

I had to admit, the way he filled it out was rather impressive.

Candy stood up with a flourish. "I think I need to hit the ladies' room," she announced.

I grabbed her arm. "I think your bladder can wait a minute. You have a customer coming."

"Now he's my customer? You've been handling sales all period; I think you can manage this one too."

It was too late to protest, seeing as David had come within earshot. I let go of Candy's sleeve with a small whimper of defeat, and she took off.

"Hey," David said, pulling his wallet from his back pocket. "I guess I'll take a couple of those."

I had to smile. "This is Violet we're talking about here. You're going to need more than a couple."

David laughed. "Good call." He surveyed the two plastic buckets in front of me, one filled with white roses and one with a dwindling supply of red. "What's the matter, no one likes the white ones?"

I ran my fingers over the silky tops of the white roses. "Well, *I* like the white. I always have. I still have the—" I cut off, not wanting to finish what I'd started but realizing it was too late. "The, um, corsage you gave me. The white rose." I glanced up at him. "Do you remember? The night of the Winter Swirl?"

"Of course I remember. I'm surprised you kept it, though. There's sort of some bad memories associated with it."

173

I stared at the roses, watching my red-and-white-painted nails graze over the petals. "No sense in taking it out on the corsage." An awkward silence followed. "So," I said a little too brightly, "you'll take pity on a few of these white ones?"

"Sure. Give me three of each."

As I gathered the flowers, I felt him staring at me. When I looked up and caught him, his eyes dropped to the floor.

"Why were you looking at me like that?"

"It— Nothing. You just never talk about the past. It's like you try to act like it didn't happen."

"Some of it," I conceded.

I grabbed a pair of scissors and snipped the ends of the roses, trying to ignore the way he continued to stare.

"What?" I finally said.

"Your hair like that. It's cute."

My hand flew to my hair, which I'd put up in a high ponytail and wrapped with curly red and white ribbons. I almost never wore my hair up anymore.

"I thought you didn't like my new hair," I said, only half teasing.

"I never said that. I always liked your hair." He handed me his money in exchange for the roses, concentrating a little harder than necessary on putting his change in his wallet. "So, um, speaking of the Swirl. Are you sure you're okay?"

I managed a small nod and a forced laugh. "Taking my vitamins religiously. Healthy as a horse."

Ugh. Did I really say that?

David nodded, and mercifully did not call me out for avoiding his real question, the one that had nothing to do with my physical health. "Good. See you later, Kelse."

"David?" He stopped and turned back toward me. "I know I said this already, but no one here knows about that night. No one knows about any of it. I'd really like to keep it that way."

He nodded again, and when our eyes met, I knew from the honesty and warmth in his that I could trust him. The same way I used to, before the literal and figurative distance between us.

David's fingers drummed against the stems of the flowers. "You know, the night before you left." He paused. "I didn't do it to upset you. The point wasn't to hurt you."

But you did. More than you know.

David's gaze held steady. "You believe me, right?"

Maybe I did, maybe I didn't, but I nodded anyway. My throat felt thick and tight and I had a sudden urge to throw my arms around his neck and bury my face in his shirt.

Almost as if he'd read my mind, he took a step closer to the table. Instead of hugging me, though, he pulled his wallet out again. "On second thought, I'll take one more white one. I can't let them sit there all pathetic like that."

I handed him another white flower. Our fingertips brushed when he took it from me, and for a second neither of us let go.

"Here," I said, needing an excuse to take my hand away.

On impulse, I grabbed a red one, too. "Violet will appreciate symmetry. The red's on me."

We smiled at each other, the first real smile in ages.

Later that day, when the hallways were littered with rose petals and message tags from cookie-grams, I made my way over to my locker feeling exhausted but happy.

I gave a start as my locker door swung open and I caught sight of a stem poking out of the cubby. Ryan had already left me seven red roses, one before each period, the way he'd done the year before. He must have been trying to outdo himself this year because I'd caught him during one drop-off.

I'd placed the rest of my bouquet on the floor next to me until I could gather my books, and I pulled the rose out, intending to add it to the pile. I froze when the flower that emerged from the shadow of the cubby was not red but white.

The first thing to flash through my mind was the extra white rose David had asked for. But why would he . . . ?

I looked down the hall, hoping Ryan would be at his locker wearing a huge grin that would tell me this was all his doing. He was nowhere to be found. When I looked in the other direction, my heart stuttered. David stood at his locker, watching me through the corner of his eye. When he saw me looking at him, a dumbfounded expression on my face and a white rose clutched between my fingers, the corner of his mouth pulled up ever so slightly. He held my gaze for only a second before shutting his locker and walking away.

"Hey."

I jumped as a voice sounded next to me and turned to find Violet at my side.

"Hey." My eyes dropped to her hands. "Where are your flowers?"

Violet looked confused. "In Candy's car, why?"

"How many did David give you?"

"Six." She tittered. "He's so sweet."

"Six? Not eight?"

"I do know how to count, Kelsey. Three red plus three white equals six. Why?"

"Oh. No reason."

Violet held out two heart-shaped cookies wrapped in plastic. "Anyway, Candy told me to give you her cookie-grams. She says she's watching her figure. Gotta run, I'm late for practice."

I bent down and put the cookies in my bag, gingerly placing the lone white rose in my pile of red ones.

So David had bought eight roses but given only six of them to Violet. No—scratch that. He'd bought seven roses and given one to me.

Technically, I'd given the eighth rose to him.

Twenty

Connecticut
Winter, Sophomore Year

"Kelsey, please eat something."

David held a spoonful of chicken soup over the bowl my mother had brought to my room on a snack tray. The tray stretched across my legs, which were buried beneath the blue and green flowers of my comforter.

"I'm not hungry. I'm . . ."

"You're what?"

My chest constricted. "Humiliated."

That morning my mother had gotten out of bed and gone to the kitchen to start a pot of coffee. She'd heard my cell phone ringing in the study and, seeing it was David, picked it up. As she walked by the bathroom, she saw the door ajar and the medicine cabinet mirror wide open. That was when she found me, dead asleep on the bathroom floor with a bloody towel in my lap and a pair of scissors at my feet.

If she hadn't been holding the phone, and if she hadn't started screaming, everything would've been fine.

David put the spoon back in the bowl and put his hand on my arm. "Listen. Isabel isn't going to tell anyone. She could hear your mom through the phone, and I had to explain why I couldn't stay."

"You could've stayed," I said flatly. He'd slept at her house after the dance. Granted, so had a bunch of other people, but the knowledge still sat like a brick in my stomach.

"I felt bad enough that I missed your messages because my piece of crap phone didn't have service at the dance. So, no, I couldn't have stayed. I needed to make sure you were okay."

"You didn't have to tell her I tried to hurt myself, David!" Hot tears spilled over my cheeks and I turned away from him. "The whole school is going be talking about me now!"

He squeezed my arm. "All I said was that I *thought* you'd tried to hurt yourself. I'm sorry I even said that much. I swear I'll make sure she knows what really happened."

I shook my head. "Don't say a word to Isabel or anyone else. Except that I'm *fine*."

My mother crept into the room then. "You will be fine, no matter what. Understand?"

I grabbed the soupspoon and swirled it through the broth and noodles, not wanting to look at either one of them.

I didn't have to look to know they exchanged a glance.

"Are you going to eat that or play with it all afternoon?" my mother asked.

"Don't worry, Mrs. Crawford; I'm not leaving until she eats it," David promised. "I'll pour it down her throat if I have to."

Mom smiled. "You're a good friend, David. Let me know if you need me to hold her head." With that, she left the room.

David shifted on the bed. "Speaking of friends. I know you and Maddie aren't close anymore, but she doesn't hate you, Kelse. She just wishes you'd try new things and not be so quick to judge, that's all."

"Is that all?" I rolled my eyes and folded my arms across my chest. I had zero interest in continuing this conversation.

"You are pretty stubborn, in case you haven't noticed."

"Yep. So if you're not leaving until I eat, then I guess you're sleeping here." It took me a second to realize what I'd said. "Isabel won't like that."

"C'mon, Kelse. What do I have to do to make you eat a few spoonfuls?" His eyes fell on Wilma, whose tail and hind legs were sticking out from my comforter. He grabbed her. "Do I have to make out with your cat?" He squished her plastic nose against his mouth and closed his eyes. "Mmm, Wilma." Then he twisted her back and forth like they were having the world's most frenzied make-out session. "Mmm, Wilma, you sexy beast!"

A laugh bubbled up inside my chest. When he pretended to slip her the tongue, I had no hope of containing it.

"All right, all right," I said through a fit of giggles, snatching my poor, defiled cat away from him. "You're ridiculous. I'll eat!"

David let me slurp in peace for a minute, grinning like he'd accomplished something way more impressive than getting a few spoonfuls of soup into my stomach. Once I started eating, I realized I was starving. But I wasn't about to give him the satisfaction of admitting it.

"Happy now?" I said as I swallowed some noodles.

David's eyes grew darker and his mouth settled into a serious line. "No, I'm not happy. You scared the shit out of me, Kelse. And your family, too."

I dropped my spoon and twisted my hands in my lap. "I know," I said quietly. "I'm sorry."

"What were you doing on the bathroom floor? What were you thinking?"

A lump formed in my throat again, and I wished I'd had more sleep so I could switch off this annoying weepy Kelsey and locate my backbone. "That I was scared. That I didn't want my life controlled by some illness, and I didn't want to be the Sick Girl. That I wanted that damn hospital bracelet off my wrist. That—" I was dangerously close to crying now, so I tried to divert the onslaught by taking a breath and making a joke. "That I didn't want to die a virgin."

David laughed, a nervous laugh/cough combination

that told me I'd succeeded in lightening the moment, and also in making him slightly uncomfortable. "Wow. That's, uh, that's deep, Kelse."

I shoveled more soup into my mouth for the sheer purpose of having something to do. Something told me he wanted to stay far away from this topic. So, naturally, I had to pursue it.

"Wouldn't you think about it? If you thought you might be—" My breath caught in my throat, and I had to fight to push the rest of my sentence out. "Seriously ill? If you thought you might . . . never get to?"

He ran his hand back and forth over his hair and cleared his throat. "I guess."

That's when everything clicked into place. His fidgeting, his sudden change in demeanor, the guilty look on his face. David didn't have to wonder what it would be like to die a virgin.

He wasn't one.

Suddenly a huge chasm opened between us, like we'd been sucked into the postcard that hung beside my bed, staring at each other from opposite sides of a massive canyon filled to the brim with awkward.

I blinked. "Oh," I said softly. It must have been the only word in my vocabulary at that moment, because I said it again. David's ears turned bright red and he looked at the floor, the ceiling, anywhere but at me. I concentrated on breaking up a piece of chicken with my spoon, wondering if it had been Amy Heffernan who'd done the honors, or

Isabel Rose, or some other girl I didn't even know about. I wasn't going to ask him. It was none of my business, and knowing wouldn't have made me feel any less betrayed. I knew it was a stupid thing to feel, but it spread through my body like wildfire nonetheless.

My mind flashed back to the night before, when I'd thought about kissing him. I slouched over my soup bowl, afraid he'd somehow read my thoughts if I looked at him.

Don't think about it, I told myself. *You don't feel that way about him. It was the crazy talking, that's all. Now for God's sake, say something!*

Nothing came out.

The strained silence between us probably would have stretched on a lot longer if it hadn't been for the sound of my parents' voices approaching my door.

"Kevin, I think you should wait," my mother pleaded.

My father appeared at my door then, pushing it open slightly before he turned back to my mother. "Amanda, she can handle it. I want her to have something to think about, something to look forward to."

All three of them came into my room then: my father, my mother, and my sister. My father shook David's hand before pulling my desk chair over to my bedside. My mother stood behind him, her hands on Miranda's shoulders and a worried look on her face.

"How are you feeling today, baby girl?" my father asked, smoothing my hair.

"I'm fine, Daddy. I'm sorry." I'd said it a million times already, but I couldn't say it enough.

"Your mom and I aren't going to let anything happen to you. You know that, right?"

I nodded, but I knew my face betrayed my confusion. "What's going on, Dad?"

My father shot a quick glance back at my mother. She gave a slight shrug, as if to say, *Why are you looking at me when you're going to do what you want anyway?* My father turned back to me, smiling. "I have some good news. Or I hope you'll think it's good news. You girls know that I've been looking for work for some time. And while I have my book deal and that's fantastic, I really need something full-time because, well, I have two growing young ladies in my care and higher education isn't cheap."

I shuddered. Medical treatments had to be expensive too.

"I've been looking for work all over Connecticut, but nothing has panned out. Then, late last week, I got a call from another school system I'd applied to. Your mother and I have discussed it at length, and we think it could be a great opportunity."

"What other school system?" I asked suspiciously.

My father could barely contain his excitement. "Riverdale Junior High, in Rhode Island. Right outside of Newport."

Miranda gasped. I sat up straighter in bed and stared down at my father. "You were offered a job in Rhode Island?"

"Yes. But I haven't accepted yet. They don't need me

until next school year, and we wanted to discuss it as a family first." He looked over at David. "You're family too, David."

I'd forgotten David was still there. If he'd seemed uncomfortable a second ago, it was nothing compared to the way he looked now.

"But, Daddy, what if—"

I was going to say, *What if I'm sick*, but my father cut me off. "Kelsey, honey, I know you're going to be fine. But, if there's a chance you need some sort of treatment, we'd be better equipped to handle it if I have a real job lined up. And you and Miranda have always loved Rhode Island. I think this might be what's best for all of us."

"But this is home," Miranda said quietly. She looked shell-shocked.

"We're not making any decisions today," my mother cut in. She motioned for my father to get up. The clipped tone of her voice told me the silent treatment would be in his immediate future. "Your father wanted you girls to be aware, and now you are. We're not discussing it again until we hear about Kelsey's results. She has enough on her mind."

I had plenty on my mind. Plenty of reasons why this was the best thing that could have happened.

I didn't love Norwood. I'd lived there my whole life, but I didn't think of it as home the way Miranda obviously did. To me it was a place where I didn't quite fit in anymore, where everything about me would always be second best. Where I'd always be itching to be somewhere else.

On top of it, I now had the added bonus of not knowing if my health was about to go through the gauntlet the same way my reputation had. Everyone who'd been at Isabel's house that morning thought I'd tried to hurt myself. What if word of my little bathroom incident wound up all over school? I knew firsthand that teenagers weren't the most sympathetic species, and I'd had enough of people throwing things at my locker and looking down their noses at me.

Starting over somewhere new sounded like a gift.

Especially in the place where, for two weeks every summer, I felt like I was exactly where I belonged. Nothing made me happier than trading our tiny house and the claustrophobic overgrowth of our neighborhood for the manicured openness of Uncle Tommy's cabin. The ocean air brought me to life the minute it filled my lungs. I closed my eyes for a second, thinking about staring out at the sea, leaning against the sun-warmed railing of the Cliff Walk, or strolling through Thames Street with the breeze from the harbor whispering in my ear. Telling me it wanted me there as much as I wanted to be there.

Trying new things didn't sound like such a bad idea after all. I couldn't think of a single reason why I didn't want to move to Rhode Island permanently.

Until I saw the look on David's face.

Twenty-One

Rhode Island
Senior Year

"Ryan Andrew Murphy, this room is a disaster."

I stepped around a pair of jeans and a polo shirt that were crumpled on Ryan's bedroom floor, like a second skin he'd shed and then left there. Ryan took better care of his car than some people took of their pets, but you'd never know it by looking at his room.

There were two paths of uncluttered blue carpet, one leading to his desk and one leading to his bed. The rest of the floor was strewn with schoolbooks, college pamphlets, clothes, baseball memorabilia, and empty bowls with spoons in them. Ryan had a habit of eating cereal after dinner every night, and the routine didn't always include bringing the bowl back to the kitchen.

"I know," Ryan said with a guilty smile. His dimple made it a little harder to be disgusted. "My mom's been on me all week." He flicked on the TV, then pulled his sheets and white and blue plaid comforter into some semblance of neatness. He sat on the bed, patting the spot next to him. "Come over here. We've got a few minutes before Crowley and Candle get here. We can watch TV."

Watch TV, my ass.

Sure enough, the minute I'd settled in next to him, he rolled onto his side and kissed my earlobe. I kept my body stiff, trying not to wrinkle my white blouse. Matt and Candy and Ryan and I were going out to dinner, and I didn't want to get to the restaurant looking like I'd been playing Seven Minutes in Heaven. We'd invited David and Violet too, much to Ryan's chagrin, but David had gone back to Connecticut for the weekend to visit friends.

I tried not to think about which ones.

Ryan's lips grazed over my cheek, my jawbone, then my ear again, and soon I was giggling as he nibbled away. It wasn't long before his hand slid beneath my shirt, skimming over the bare skin of my stomach, and he leaned over me to kiss my lips.

Ryan had put his hands on my stomach plenty of times before, and he'd kissed me plenty more. So why my mind chose that particular kiss, that touch, to flash back to the last time someone who wasn't Ryan had held me that way, I'd never know.

It came back in a rush: warm, exploring fingertips on my skin, the taste of mint on his lips, the tenderness in the way he held me. . . .

I had to turn away from Ryan to catch my breath. He tried to move right back in and continue the kiss, but I pushed against his chest and turned my face. "Ry," I said. "Stop it. They'll be here soon."

Ryan moved to my neck, undeterred. "I can't think of a better way to kill a few minutes, can you?"

"Yes." I squirmed out from under him and straightened my shirt, sitting up on the edge of the bed. "We're going to clean up this room." To take the edge off my rejection, I added, "We can pick up where we left off later. Go wash your crusty cereal bowls and I'll put some of this crap away."

Ryan groaned, but he turned the TV off and did what I asked. I grabbed a pile of dirty clothes from the floor and took them to the hamper in the bathroom, then went back to his room and threw his closet doors open. He had at least three piles of clean, folded clothes in various locations that needed to be hung up, so that's where I started.

As I tried to get a third shirt onto a hanger, Ryan's cat brushed against my leg and scared the ever-living crap out of me. I dropped the shirt on the floor, but when I bent to pick it up, I got distracted by all the haphazard piles of shoes and tried to straighten them out. That's when I spotted a plastic shopping bag in the corner. I was half afraid I'd find ancient dirty underwear inside, or worse, dirty magazines or some other horror to make me regret my snooping. But curiosity won out, and I grabbed for it.

What I saw inside made no sense at all.

Normally I wouldn't have thought twice about finding a baseball jersey in Ryan's closet. Except that the number on the back was thirty-three, and the white letters across the shoulder blades didn't spell Murphy—they spelled Kerrigan. Why would Ryan have part of David's baseball uniform hidden in his closet?

I lifted the jersey out of the bag and saw four or five pouches of something green at the bottom. For a second I thought it was weed, and I felt rage bubble up inside me. *For all his talk about wanting a scholarship and needing to play baseball in college.* But my anger melted into confusion when I looked closer and realized the leaves inside were broad and spoon-shaped, and resting on top of Mrs. Murphy's gardening gloves. I opened a bag. This wasn't weed. It was . . . poison ivy?

"Hey, look who's—"

Ryan cut off when he saw me sitting there, jersey in one hand, bag of poison ivy in the other. I looked up to see Candy and Matt standing in the doorway with him.

"What is this?" I said.

Matt and Ryan exchanged a look. A look that told me I'd caught their asses in the act of something. And they'd better tell me what.

"It's nothing, Kelse," Matt said. "Ry's mom was ripping up some poison ivy in the yard the other day, so we stashed some. We were just going to play a prank on him, rub it inside his jersey. You know, haze the new kid a little. Harmless stuff."

I glared at both of them but mainly at Ryan. "You were going to put poison ivy in his jersey? What is this, fourth grade? Why would you do that?"

Ryan shifted uncomfortably and rubbed the back of his neck. "It's no big deal. We just wanted to throw his game a little, make sure he couldn't show off. The team was fine without him and he's so fucking cocky."

I shot a questioning look at Candy, and from the wide-eyed look she gave back, I knew she hadn't been in on this. I got to my feet, my jaw clenched and my hands still gripping the jersey and the poison ivy.

"'Cocky'? How can he be cocky when you haven't even had a real game yet? You sound like a jealous three-year-old, Ryan! You can't sabotage one of your teammates because you're holding out for some eleventh-hour scholarship! You need to face the fact that you're running out of options."

Candy mouthed the words *Oh, shit* and grabbed Matt by the arm, motioning for him to follow her and leave Ryan and me alone. "It's my fault, Kelse," Matt said as Candy tried to drag him away. "My idea. All me. Honest."

I held up the jersey. "Then why is this in *his* closet?" My death glare shifted to Ryan before Matt could answer.

"I can't believe you'd do something so juvenile. If you're that worried about college, didn't it ever occur to you to *study*?"

It was a low blow, but I felt only a mild twinge of guilt. Ryan wasn't stupid by any means, but he had a devil-may-care attitude toward school and that was no one's fault but his own. It had never bothered me before, but at that moment it bothered me a lot.

Ryan stormed over and grabbed the bag of poison ivy from my hand, snatching up the larger bag that contained the rest of them while he was at it. "Fine," he said, slamming everything into the trash can. "Happy now? I'll leave your precious *friend* alone."

Oh. So we were back to that again.

"Ryan, this is an idiotic thing to do to *anyone*. I don't remember Steve Koenig getting 'hazed' last year when he joined the team. Go ahead, try to tell me you're not doing this because you've had a problem with David since the second you laid eyes on him."

As the words left my lips, David's voice echoed in my head: *He's not the great guy you think he is.*

"Oh my God," I said, interrupting whatever response Ryan was about to make. "Has this been going on all year?" I stepped closer to him, every part of me daring him to lie to me. "Is that what the fight in the hall was all about? You started something with him, didn't you?"

Ryan's face turned bright red and his fists clenched

and unclenched at his sides. "Go ahead, take his side!" he exploded. "You would! You would think it was me!"

"I've asked you a hundred times to tell me what happened and you won't! How do you think that looks right now, Ry?"

Matt came over then, spreading his arms between the two of us. "Guys, enough." He put his hand on my shoulder. "Kelse, you're right. The poison ivy thing, it was a stupid idea. We'll wash the jersey and I'll give it back to David and pretend I took it by accident, and we can act like this whole thing never happened."

"And do *you* know what happened in the hall that day?" I asked pointedly.

Matt looked at Ryan through the corner of his eye, so quickly I thought I might have imagined it.

"All I know is that David came at Ry. That's all."

I inhaled and looked back at Ryan. "If there's something you need to tell me, please tell me now." My tone was softer, more pleading.

"Give us a minute," Ryan mumbled to Matt, who nodded and walked out, closing the door behind him.

"Babe." Ryan reached for me, and while I let him pull me closer, I kept my limbs stiff as boards. "I'm sorry," he murmured into my hair. "I didn't start the fight in the hall, I swear. But—but I know what really happened with you and Kerrigan."

My heart missed a beat. "'What really happened'?" I repeated.

"I know how you kissed him once."

I pulled away from him, eyes wide and heart racing. "*What?* Who—"

"I tricked your sister into telling me." My mouth opened, but Ryan held up his hand before I could say anything. "Don't be mad at her. Or me. I told her you'd already admitted it."

I wanted to be angry, but I had no right. I'd lied to him, and he knew it. No wonder he'd been acting like such an ass.

"Ryan . . ."

"Why didn't you tell me?" The anger from a few moments ago had disappeared. When I looked into his eyes, I saw only hurt. It killed me.

"I didn't want to upset you over nothing. You were so jealous when I hugged him; why would I tell you about a kiss that happened before I even knew you?"

"I don't care that you kissed him, Kelse—"

"*He* kissed *me.*"

"And you, what? Slapped him across the face? Kicked him in the nads?"

My hands twisted together. "No, but—"

"Then I don't care who started it if you didn't stop it. But I do care that you'd try to cover it up. I care about that a lot."

I sighed. "Ry, I'm sorry. I wasn't trying to be shady. You understand not wanting to talk about something, right? You didn't start the fight in the hall, and yet you don't want to talk about it, which doesn't make any sense to me."

I knew it was a cop-out. We were both being less than honest, and I'd basically implied that he didn't have to show all his cards if I didn't have to show mine.

And Ryan took the bait.

"Putting poison ivy in someone's jersey doesn't make much sense either, but I still thought it was a good idea," he said. I folded my arms and Ryan smiled. "Okay, not funny. I get it. I promise you, this is the first and last time I try to play dirty."

"First and last?"

He kissed the top of my head. "Unless it's with you."

I let him kiss me then, but it felt wrong. The nagging feeling that I'd missed something, that I'd been deliberately left in the dark, wrapped itself around me like thick fog.

Like David's shirt, still wrapped around my fingers.

Twenty-Two

Connecticut
Winter, Sophomore Year

The hair on the back of my neck stood up, and I knew it was happening again. I slammed my locker shut and turned around. Sure enough, two people a few lockers down immediately stopped their hushed chatter and averted their eyes.

Things like that had been happening a lot since the night I went to the hospital. If people weren't staring and whispering, they were asking how I felt, but in a very loaded way, like they thought I might crumple at their feet if I had to think too hard.

Honestly, I'd been feeling much better. I didn't have leukemia. Or aplastic anemia, or anything serious. My family and I had cried our eyes out with relief when the results finally came back.

After all the crap, all the drama, it turned out to be the sulfa antibiotics I'd taken for my sinus infection that started the whole thing. They'd caused my platelet count to drop, exacerbating a vitamin B12 and iron deficiency I hadn't even known I had. That's why I didn't get better after I stopped taking the antibiotics—I'd had more than one factor working against me. But my doctor seemed confident that supplements and some changes to my diet would prevent similar incidents in the future, and I was beyond glad that I didn't have to face what I'd feared the most.

Unfortunately, when it came to not having anyone find out about me spending the night in my bathroom with a pair of scissors, that was where my luck ran out. No one had said anything about it, but I was sure Isabel had told. Why else would everyone be acting so whacked? People didn't stare and whisper because a person had a blood transfusion.

Then again, I never thought people would react so cruelly to a nosebleed.

I couldn't prove Isabel had talked. Especially with her falling all over herself to make a phony show of concern for David's benefit. He never witnessed her fake smiles that turned into condescending smirks the moment he turned his back, or the looks she gave me—like I wasn't worthy of following her dog with a pooper-scooper. But he did see her accompany him to my locker, put her hand on my shoulder, and ask how I was feeling.

I wanted to take that hand and slam it in the metal door.

"Oh," I said. "I'm fine. Lucky that it was nothing more serious, but I wish I could've gone to the dance."

Isabel smiled, huge and fake. "Aw, Kelsey." She flipped the ends of my hair with her finger, immediately making me self-conscious about wearing it down. "There will be other dances. Getting better is what's most important."

"Riiight."

"Kelse, I'm going to walk Isabel to class," David said. "You want to walk with us?"

I slammed my locker shut, wishing I could have figured out a way to catch Isabel's head in it as I did. "No. I have to stop by the guidance office."

The only way I could convince my mother of my mental stability after the bathroom incident was to agree to a few sessions with the school psychologist, Mr. Petri. Even though she knew what she'd seen wasn't what it looked like, she was afraid of the toll everything had taken on me. I knew I didn't need his so-called services, but I would have done anything to make my mother stop hovering over me like I might fly over the cuckoo's nest on a moment's notice.

"Actually, David," Isabel said, "I have to go that way too. I'll walk with Kelsey."

I would've rather swallowed worms. "You don't have to."

Isabel ignored the disdain in my voice. "I want to."

"Cool. See you guys later, then." With that, David walked away.

Come back! Don't leave me here with her!

"So," Isabel said the moment he was out of earshot. "If you weren't trying to kill yourself, then what were you trying to do?"

"I wasn't *trying* to do anything. I had a rough night and—" I realized I'd let her unnerve me and wanted to kick myself for it. "Wait, how is any of this your business?"

She folded her arms and squared her shoulders. "David was white as a sheet when he left my house. Are you willing to sink that low to get his attention?"

A wave of dizziness passed over me. "Are you kidding me? I was sick, Isabel. How could you think I did any of that on purpose?"

"You were so sick that you forgot where your bed was?" She rolled her eyes. "Come on, Kelsey. You were playing at something. And whatever it was, it worked, because David went running."

I couldn't move. I couldn't speak.

"I know you hate me," she continued. Her eyes bored into mine. "But if you care about David, then let him make his own choices."

I should've told her to take her own advice. I should've said that David had never even wanted to go to the dance with her, that if he chose me over her, it would never be because I forced him.

Instead I watched as she turned on her heel and walked away, her hips swinging like the angry flick of a cat's tail.

I stood rooted to the spot with her words echoing in my head until I finally remembered how to move my feet. Then I turned and headed to my appointment.

I signed in at the reception desk in the guidance office, and the receptionist told me to have a seat in one of the chairs between Mr. Petri's closed door and my guidance counselor, Mrs. Malone's, office. I looked up to find one of the chairs already occupied. By Maddie, of all people, because apparently this morning hadn't sucked enough already. She sat there, twirling the ends of her hair around her fingers, avoiding my eyes and shifting around like she hoped the chair would grow jaws and swallow her.

"Hey," I said quietly as I sat down, dropping my book bag on the floor. Her mouth twitched into a fleeting semi-smile.

"Kelsey. How are you?"

There was that question again.

"I have to meet with Mr. Petri. So someone must think I'm not doing all that great." It was a lame attempt at humor, but I thought she'd at least crack a smile. She didn't.

"I heard about what happened. It isn't your fault."

Shit. So Isabel *had* opened her trap.

"Maddie, this whole thing got blown way out of proportion. I don't have an effing death wish."

"Of course not." She paused, studying the arm of the chair for a second. "But I'm glad you're getting help anyway." And there it was. She might as well have said, *Sure you don't.*

My fingers dug into the faded upholstery of the seat, but before I could force words through my clamped teeth, Maddie added, "And at least David got to you in time. Oh, and I heard your dad has a new job. That's good news, right?"

Her words knocked the wind right out of me. "David . . . *what?*"

Maddie's face went as blank as mine was horrified. "Got to you?" she repeated slowly, as if I hadn't spoken English my whole life. "Before anything got out of hand?"

I sank in my chair, the sound of keyboards clacking and coffee mugs clanging suddenly roaring in my ears. *Everything* was out of hand.

Mr. Petri's door opened then, and he ushered another student out. "So sorry to keep you waiting, Ms. Crawford—"

"Actually, I need one more second." I barely glanced at him.

I stood up and threw my bag over my shoulder, then turned so I could face Mr. Petri and Maddie at the same time. "I want you both to know that I didn't try to kill myself." I yanked the sleeve of my shirt up to my elbow, exposing the bandage covering the slice Miranda had made down my hand. "This happened before the dance, and it was an accident." I jerked up the other sleeve, where the cut from my dad's scissors was fading to nothing more than a scratch. "No one had to rescue me, because *nothing happened.*"

"Maddie?" The sound of Mrs. Malone's voice interrupted my speech. The door to her office had opened, and

Maddie made a beeline for it. She hesitated in the door frame and turned back to me, like she'd reached safe territory and suddenly felt brave.

"Maddie." My voice came out in a pleading whimper. "Why don't you believe me?"

She looked at the floor, still twisting a section of her hair into a taut funnel. "It just makes sense. Why you've been pushing everyone away."

"Why *I've* been—" I all but fell over. I wanted to do something, anything other than stand there like a dumbfounded idiot, but my brain refused to cooperate. So I stood there like a dumbfounded idiot.

"If you want to talk about it," Maddie said hesitantly, "I'll listen."

With that, she disappeared inside Mrs. Malone's office, and I stayed glued to the floor. She really didn't believe me. Worse, I'd seen her mock me, and now she was treating me like a charity case. And I had a feeling she wouldn't be the only one.

The next twenty minutes didn't help me feel any less like a leper. Mr. Petri was nice enough, asking questions about my childhood, my friends, my goals for the future. But to me, every question felt like a thinly veiled attempt to expose me as a wack job. When he asked how things were at home, I heard, *Do your parents make you want to kill yourself?* When he asked about my friends, I assumed he meant, *Do you not have any, and that's why you tried to kill yourself?*

It seemed funny, in a very unfunny way, that I'd been so worried about becoming the Sick Girl. I'd never thought about being the Girl Who Tried to Kill Herself, because, well, I'd never tried to kill myself.

Not that I would have had to think about it at all if it hadn't been for David's big mouth and his extremely crappy choice of girlfriend.

I stood the minute I sensed our meeting wrapping up. Every second that ticked by allowed for more gossip to spread like a disease, and I was anxious to get into the hall before it filled with more curious stares and thinly disguised whispers.

David had first period right around the corner, and I waited by the door of the classroom for the bell to ring. I ambushed him the moment I saw him, grabbing his arm and dragging him into an empty corner of the hall.

"What happened to not saying anything to anybody?" I hissed.

"What are you talking about?"

"How did Maddie know about my dad's job offer?"

David flushed. "I—sorry, Kelse, I didn't know it was a secret."

"You know what, David? When something's not your news to share, *don't share it.*" He mumbled an apology, but I barely heard it over my tirade. "What else did you tell them? Why does everyone think that I tried to kill myself and that you came to save my sorry ass?"

I waited for him to get angry, or indignant, or have any kind of reaction other than the one he had. He scratched the back of his neck and shifted from one foot to the other. "That's crazy, Kelse. No one thinks anything like that."

My eyes widened. "Yes, they do!" I told him about my run-in with Maddie, about what she'd said. "Am I supposed to let people think I'm a suicidal maniac? You have to make them stop this, because if she didn't hear it from you, then she heard it from Isabel."

David straightened, clearly offended. "I never said anything like that to either of them, and I've told you before, Maddie doesn't hate you. She wouldn't go around spreading rumors about you for the hell of it."

"Isabel would."

"Jesus!" David yanked a hand through his hair like he might rip it out of his head. "Do you realize anyone who was at her house the morning after the dance could be saying this shit? Shit, which, by the way, I hadn't heard a word of until right now."

"If they're thinking it, I'm sure they're saying it—"

"Kelse, listen. Who cares what people think? You know what really happened, and so do I. Don't worry about what anyone else says. It'll all blow over."

I couldn't believe those words had actually come out of his mouth. He made it sound like someone had insulted my shoes, or my choice of topic for a school project, and I should brush it off and get on with my life.

I narrowed my eyes at him, feeling my face flush with heat as I recalled Isabel's accusation. "Easy for you to say. You come off looking like a hero in all of this, like you rescued the pathetic little damsel in distress. I hope you know I'm not that desperate for your attention, David."

A flash of something shadowed his face, something that told me I'd hit a nerve despite the hardened expression that replaced it within a split second. He made a sound somewhere between a scoff and a snort.

"Trust me," he said. "I know."

Then, without another word, he turned and left me standing in the hall.

Twenty-Three

Rhode Island
Senior Year

"Are you coming down to watch us practice?"

I jumped at the sound of David's voice. I hadn't even heard him approach my locker. Then I racked my brain, wondering why he'd asked. He sounded completely casual, like watching the baseball team practice had been on my agenda for ages and he'd merely thrown out a reminder.

"Am I supposed to?" I asked. I couldn't remember promising Ryan I'd be at any of their practices.

"No, you don't have to. Candy and Violet said their coach is running late today, and they had time to kill. They're coming, so I thought you might too."

"Oh. They didn't tell me." Those biatches. "But I can't, anyway. I have a paper to write."

"Eh, you've got plenty of time. It's nice out too."

Even though we were on semi-hospitable terms again, it seemed strange that he'd want me there so badly. It made me wonder if he wanted me to see something specific, if maybe Ryan hadn't been honest about not playing dirty. I searched David's face for signs of something beneath the surface, but from what I could tell, he really just wanted me to watch him practice.

He smiled sheepishly, almost like he'd heard my thoughts. "I used to think you brought me luck, you know."

It was an innocent enough comment, certainly nothing that should've made my heart do a spastic little dance, but that's exactly what happened.

"All right," I said. "I owe you for the flower anyway."

His hand went immediately to his hair and he looked at the floor. "What flower?"

I landed a light punch to his ribs. "Nice try. How'd you get my locker combination?"

"I don't know what you're talking about," he mumbled.

"Fine, have it your way. Anyhow, I can only stay and watch until Candy and Vi leave for practice."

He flashed another grin at me and we fell into step beside each other. "Hey, why aren't you a cheerleader?" he asked. "I mean, I know you were never into that stuff before, but now I could totally see you doing it. Especially since they're your friends."

I shook my head. "They wanted me to try out, but in the back of my mind I guess I'm still kind of afraid. I think about how they practically had me on house arrest while my blood counts improved, and I still feel like one wrong move could send me back to the hospital."

He pressed his lips together and gave me a look of mock disapproval. "Now that's what I call a shame. You let your high school career pass you by without ever wearing a short skirt while shaking pom-poms and demanding football players b-e aggressive? A travesty, Kelse."

I laughed, bumping against him as I did. "I'd rather get my exercise on the Cliff Walk. You know that."

"Until you get to the 'scary' part."

"Ha! Wouldn't want me to break a nail, right?"

David ducked as I faked like I was going to whack him with my textbook.

"How did you meet Candy, anyway? I wouldn't have pegged her for your kind of people."

"Looks can be deceiving."

I smiled to myself as I recounted the first time Candy's and my paths crossed the summer before junior year. The summer I'd decided to reset my life.

It was at the salon where I had my hair highlighted, and Candy settled into her stylist's chair a couple of minutes before I vacated mine, hemming and hawing that she wanted to try something new but didn't know what.

"Maybe bangs?" her stylist suggested.

"Not unless I'm going to wake up eight years old again tomorrow, thank you," Candy countered. "I think I want to do something with the color." She gave me a once-over through the corner of her eye. "Now *her* hair looks awesome. Maybe we should get her opinion." I beamed, flattered as hell at already receiving my first compliment on my new look as she swiveled her chair to face me head-on.

"I'll bet red would look great on you," my mother piped up from the chair on my other side.

I nodded. "I was thinking the same thing."

At the beginning of my appointment, they'd handed me a color chart full of faux hair swatches in every rich and vibrant shade imaginable. I'd paused a few times to admire a burgundy red called Black Cherry, but ultimately decided I could never pull it off. That was the one I suggested to her. The girl who did my hair removed my smock, shaking off the remnants of what she'd trimmed. I smiled at Candy. "Hope you like it. I wish I could see how it turns out."

"You're leaving?" Her smock rustled and her hand emerged clutching her phone. "Wait, give me your number and I'll text you a pic when it's done." She grinned at me. "And then if I hate it, I can track you down."

A couple of hours later, I'd received a text: *Damn, I look good. We are so gonna party together.*

"The rest is history," I told David.

His face scrunched up. "Candy's hair isn't red."

"She's changed it a hundred times since then."

We both laughed and I had to marvel at how the simplest things could bring on the strongest sense of déjà vu. When I'd first started at Clayton, walking through the halls without him felt like I'd lost a limb. With Candy taking me under her wing, I'd made friends pretty quickly, but it wasn't the same. I missed having David's long strides fall into sync with my short, quick ones, the way our arms would brush together every so often, the way we didn't always need to talk.

At that moment, though, heading out the main doors with David, I knew we needed to talk. I needed to know for myself if Ryan had reason to be so paranoid, or if he was simply looking for excuses to torture the last boy who'd kissed his girlfriend.

Starting with: "So have you decided on a college yet?"

David shrugged. "Sort of. I've narrowed it down to two, but I haven't decided. Both offered me scholarships, but each has its pros and cons."

"Which colleges?"

"Um, I'd rather not say until I pick one."

I stopped in my tracks, squinting in the afternoon sun. "David! Since when are you superstitious?"

He looked at the ground and scratched his head. "Since my dad got sick, I guess. I need to sit down with him and talk about it."

I felt a bubble of panic expand in my chest. "He's not . . . ?"

"No, no. His scans have been good, his blood work is perfect. But he had stomach cancer, Kelse. You didn't see how bad it was. There were nights when he'd sleep on the bathroom floor because he'd get so sick and then he'd be too weak to make it back to bed. And you know how stubborn he is. I had to learn parts of his job because he didn't want them knowing he didn't even feel well enough to work from home. If anything ever happens to him, I need to be close by."

Not out of touch and out of reach like I'd been the first time.

"David," I said softly. "I'm so sorry I wasn't there for that. I wish I'd known. I would've . . ." I didn't finish, because I honestly didn't know what I would've done. I definitely *wouldn't* have continued to cut him off like a stubborn, slighted brat. I would've been there for my friend, regardless of whatever had happened between us.

Now was my chance to do better than sort of.

"I would've—"

"There wasn't much you could've done from here, anyway." A half smile curled David's lips.

He was letting me off the hook.

I must've looked as lost as I felt, because David put his hand on my shoulder and guided me in the direction of the path that led down the hill to the baseball field. "It's okay," he said. "So what about you? Have you picked a school?"

"I'm going to URI."

He stopped again. "What happened to the University of Arizona? The rest of the apple pie?"

"I wanted to stay close to home too. I've always loved it here, so there's no sense in leaving." I fiddled with my sleeve. "Apple pie is overrated."

I couldn't tell if David grimaced or if the sun was in his eyes. "Speaking of home," he said. "Why don't you come back with me one weekend—to Norwood?"

"I don't know, David."

"I saw Maddie the last time I was there. She asked about you. Lots of people ask about you. We could all go out to dinner or something."

"I'm not really interested in being in the same room with—" I clamped my mouth shut before I could say it.

David stepped in my path, making me stop short. "With who?"

Maddie, or any of her college freshman friends who might be home for the weekend.

I looked up at him. Neither of us spoke, but neither of us dropped our gaze.

"Kerrigan!" David and I both turned at the sound of Steve Koenig's voice. He stood in the distance, waving his baseball glove at us. "We were ready to send out a search party. Get your ass down here!"

David glanced back at me. "Go," I said. "Run."

Phew, I thought as he turned and sprinted off. I strolled down the hill in his wake, gripping the straps of my book bag as all the things he'd told me swirled around in my head.

I felt relieved that he had his act together concerning college, unlike my boyfriend. But at least now Ryan could stop acting like a sore loser and concentrate on taking the next step.

"Hey! Look who decided to grace us with her presence," Candy shouted as I approached the bleachers where she and Violet sat huddled together in their skimpy cheerleading practice shorts. Spring had definitely sprung early, but it was still only March and not warm enough to be bare-assed on a metal bleacher.

"Sorry, I forgot to use my mind-reading abilities to know I'd find you here. What did I miss?"

"We were just saying how cute Crowley's butt looks in those pants."

Violet looked Candy up and down. "*You* were just saying. Like, repeatedly."

I raised an eyebrow. "For someone who claims not to like him . . ."

Candy rolled her eyes. "I never said I don't like him. I'm playing hard to get. But let's be serious, ladies. What could possibly be cuter than *that* butt in *those* pants?"

Violet sighed. "My boyfriend, that's what. I swear, his biceps, like, haunt me."

I looked over at the diamond and spotted Ryan out in left field, and then David on the pitcher's mound. He rolled

his shoulders back, wound up, and sent a fastball hurtling at
Steve Koenig. Steve caught it, then took off his glove and
shook his hand, like catching it had hurt. It probably had;
David threw a mean fastball.

And he did look pretty frigging amazing while doing it.

I must've stayed quiet a beat too long, because I felt
Violet's and Candy's expectant eyes on me.

"What?" I said defensively.

"Um, insert moony comment about Smurf-Man here?"
Candy prompted.

Again, oops. "I didn't realize it was a contest."

"If I catch you checking out my boyfriend again, I'll cut
you," Violet said, only half joking.

"Sheesh, chill," I mumbled.

Though, from that point on, I made a concerted effort
to keep my eyes on my own boyfriend. It wasn't as easy as I
thought it would be. While Ryan looked delicious trotting
through the field and stretching his arm to catch fly balls
and adjusting his cap over his blond curls, David drove me
to distraction. I thought I saw him turn once and wink at
me—well, probably at Violet—the way he used to before his
best pitches. Like a silent code for *Watch this*. More often
than not, the crowd used to erupt into cheers after one of
those pitches.

I wanted to see if he'd do it again, and whether he'd
look at Violet or at me. But he didn't. Every now and then
he'd glance back and smile, to which Violet would wave

frantically, but that was it. After a while I convinced myself I'd imagined it.

When the girls took off for cheerleading practice, I stood up too, wanting to get home and make a dent in my history assignment. I tried to catch Ryan's eye to let him know I was leaving. He didn't see me, so I hopped down from the bleachers and waited a second to try again. That's when, through the corner of his eye, David spotted me on the sidelines. He rolled his shoulders, prepping for another pitch. As he turned his head to wind up, he looked over at where I stood.

And winked right at me.

Twenty-Four

Connecticut
Summer before Junior Year

No one came up to me for a final hug as I cleaned out my locker on the last day of school. Nor did anyone thrust their yearbook at me and ask me to sign it like their life wouldn't be complete unless I did. No one even told me to have a nice summer. Or a nice life. All around me, people were acting like they'd never see each other again, when as far as I knew, I was the only one aside from the seniors who was actually leaving for good.

A whooping ruckus startled me into looking down the hall toward one of the exits. Jared Rose literally came flying out of nowhere screaming, "SUMMER, BABY!" as he landed in front of the doors in the most acrobatic fist pump

I'd ever seen. Eric followed close behind, carrying Maddie on his shoulders. Then David emerged, with Isabel on his. Both girls were waving their arms and squealing as the guys grunted like celebratory apes.

I tried to ignore the way my heart instantly felt water-logged and heavy. But then David turned his head, and his eyes locked with mine. For an infinite second, neither of us looked away. Until his gaze dropped to the floor and he ducked out the door with Isabel's arms around his neck.

I slammed my locker shut, gulping the lump in my throat into submission. Let them act like I didn't exist. Once I walked out those doors, it would be like I never had.

"Mom?" I said as I brushed my hair in the bathroom mirror. It was one week before our final move—the one where, unlike all our other trips to Rhode Island in the past few weeks, we wouldn't be coming back to Norwood—and I had an idea.

"Yes?" I heard my mother's distracted response amidst the sound of bubble wrap being wound around something in her bedroom, followed by the squeal of tape ripping off the roll.

"Can I do something different with my hair when we get to Rhode Island?"

My mother appeared in the bathroom doorway. "Like what?"

"Maybe highlights or something? I don't know. I want a new look."

She smiled. "New life, new look?"

"Exactly."

Mom stood behind me and put her chin on my shoulder. We looked at each other in the mirror and she stroked my hair. "I think you're old enough," she said. "I'll make an appointment for both of us. We can have a mommy-daughter day before your first day of school."

"It sounds so sophisticated when you put it like that," I teased.

The sound of the phone ringing sent my mother back to her bedroom, but two seconds later she stood in the bathroom doorway again. "David is on the phone for you," she said.

My eyebrows pulled together. "He is?"

Things hadn't been the same between David and me since our tiff in the hall. He and I would exchange a few brief, strained words, and then I'd have to watch him with Isabel, walking and talking and laughing like she hadn't snatched up my self-confidence and my best friend from right under my nose.

I never did tell him what she'd said to me, how she'd accused me of milking my illness to get his attention. There never seemed to be an opportunity where I wouldn't look petty or childish, and after the way he'd eaten up her apology for the tissue incident and the way he'd defended her the last time we talked, I wasn't so sure he'd care anymore, anyway. It made the weight of everyone's stares and whispers that much heavier, and that much more unbearable.

By the time the warm weather had rolled around, I couldn't wait to get out of Norwood for good. Dad had accepted the teaching position in Rhode Island, and even Miranda had started to show semi-excitement about it. I'd been mostly excited all along, with only a tiny bit of trepidation about leaving the place where I grew up and, of course, David. Once he chose Isabel over me, though, the trepidation disappeared and all sorts of possibilities replaced it.

I planned to completely reinvent myself. My brush with death might've been a fluke, but that didn't mean it hadn't driven home the message that life as you knew it could be snatched away in the space of a heartbeat—and that maybe it was time to start living a little. Moving to Rhode Island was a second chance. To loosen up, do things differently, even if it meant not necessarily doing them right. No one at Clayton High would have to know that I wasn't the type who made friends easily, that I was actually pretty shy. I could pretend I wasn't, and they'd be none the wiser. I could pay more attention to my clothes and the way I looked— "try new things," like Maddie had supposedly wanted—and I wouldn't be seen as a poser or a sellout.

I'd be me—but better.

Most important, no one at Clayton High would ever judge me for what happened the night of the Winter Swirl dance, because no one there would ever know. My brand-new start was close enough to taste, and I couldn't wait to make a clean break.

"I think you should take the call," my mother said, holding the phone out to me.

At the same time I had the most unshakable feeling that making things right with David would be the one and only way to make me wish I weren't leaving.

I took the phone from her and walked into my bedroom, closing the door behind me. "Hello?"

"Hi," David said. He hardly ever called me anymore. My palms were sweating a little.

"Hi, yourself. Why didn't you call my cell?"

"I did. You didn't answer."

"Oh."

"I hate this, Kelse."

I wanted to respond, but only a small croak came out. Luckily, he kept talking, taking the pressure off me.

"I never see you anymore. We don't hang out, we hardly talk, and I don't want you to leave when things are crappy like this." He paused for a breath. "I miss you."

My heart cracked open like an egg and I felt my insides flood with warmth.

"You do?" I said quietly.

"A lot." I heard the smile in his voice. "I want to see you before you leave. Just me and you, one last time."

"David. You say that like we're never going to see each other again."

"For a while there, the way things have been . . . I was afraid we wouldn't."

So much for a clean break. But hearing him say he missed me, I couldn't have cared less.

* * *

David came to pick me up the night before we left for good. We'd planned to move at the beginning of summer, so my father would have time to set up his classroom and my mother could start her new paralegal job and my sister and I could get settled in before school started. The days had seemed to drag between the time we bought the house in Rhode Island and the time we could actually live there. But now I couldn't tell if the butterflies in my stomach were from the day finally arriving, or from nerves over having to say good-bye to David.

My bedroom door opened as I sat on the floor, zipping the last of my clothing into my overnight bag.

David poked his head into the room, smiling. "Ready to—whoa." His eyes swept over the barrenness of my bedroom, and he stepped inside, letting out an awed whistle. "This is weird."

"I know. It's really starting to hit me."

"No, I mean this is the cleanest I've ever seen your room."

I grabbed Wilma, the one thing I hadn't packed, and chucked her at his face. He caught her with a laugh and helped me up from the floor, pulling me into a hug.

"I'm teasing, Kelse. You know I'll miss you."

I nodded against his chest, afraid I'd cry if we started exchanging mushy-gushies. The sting of how much I'd missed him, how much I was going to miss him, hit me as I reveled in the familiarity of his hug.

Damn him.

"Ready to go?" he asked.

I nodded again. "You still haven't told me where we're going."

"Close by. I know you have a big day ahead of you tomorrow."

We piled into his car after disengaging Miranda from a leechlike hug around David's waist and giving a quick assurance to my parents that we weren't going far. And that I wouldn't be overexerting myself, even though I hadn't felt sick or tired in ages, thanks to the megavitamins I'd been taking.

"It is weird, isn't it?" I said, fingering the Saint Christopher medal clipped to the visor above my head.

"What's that?"

"That we met in Newport, but neither of us lived there. And then you ended up living down the street from me, and now I'm leaving. For Newport, of all places. For good."

"Well, it's not *exactly* Newport. You'll be on the outskirts."

"Close enough. But you know what I mean."

"Yeah," he conceded. "It is weird. Who knows? Maybe I'll end up there one day too."

"I'd like that."

"So would my grandfather," he grumbled. "He'd have a full-time cleanup crew."

I suddenly realized our surroundings were awfully familiar, and I sat up and looked out the windshield. "We're going to your house?"

David grinned. "Not exactly."

"Um, it looks like that's where we're going to me." But I trailed off as he drove past his house, right into the open field that sat alongside it, and then into the woods past that. "All right, I know you don't want me to go, but let's discuss options that don't involve killing me and stashing my body in the woods, m'kay?"

He rolled his eyes, but I barely saw it before something else caught my attention. "Oh my God, David, there's a fire! Look! Right over there, something's burning—"

I stopped, perplexed. David threw the car into park right in front of the fire, which I could now see was a carefully constructed campfire.

"I did that," David said. "I thought we could stay here and chill out for a little while."

"In your car?"

He smiled as he cut the ignition. "Give me some credit." He got out of the car and I followed suit, standing by the passenger door as he rummaged around in his trunk. David came forward with arms full of pillows and blankets, and arranged them on the hood of the car, propping the pillows against the windshield. I giggled as he helped me up onto the hood.

"Where are you going?" I asked as he disappeared into his backseat. He emerged holding a package of chocolate, a bag of marshmallows, and a box of graham crackers.

"What good is a fire without s'mores?"

"You thought of everything, didn't you?"

"Don't I always?"

With the s'mores fixings sitting on the roof of the car, we settled under the blanket. It felt strange to be under a blanket with a boy, even if it was only David. Or maybe *because* it was David. We were so close, and I was hyper-aware of his body next to mine. It was oddly intimate and completely natural all at once.

"So," I said quietly. "Does Isabel know you're here?"

David stared up at the sky, his hands cradling his head. "I don't see why she would. I haven't talked to her in a while."

"You're not with her anymore? Why didn't you tell me?"

"Because you barely looked at me the past couple of times I saw you. Besides, I don't know if we were ever really 'together.' We didn't have much in common. She didn't even like baseball."

"Or me," I snorted.

"She was jealous of you. There's a difference."

"No, David, the girl hated me. I never told you what happened." And then I proceeded to tell him about what she'd said at my locker after I got sick.

David sat up and looked down at me, a mix of anger and confusion on his face. "I can't believe you never said anything. I never would have bothered with her again if I'd known."

"I was afraid I'd sound like a jealous baby." I twisted the blanket around my hands. "Kind of like I did when I thought she started those rumors about me. Which, by the way, I still think she did. But I'm so sorry for taking it out on you."

He lay back down, his mouth twisted in a frown. "You know, if you weren't so stubborn, we could've had this conversation a long time ago."

"I know. But I was also afraid you'd take her side. You bought every crap line that came out of her mouth." I rolled a piece of fuzz from the blanket between my fingers and sneaked a glance at him out of the corner of my eye. "Why couldn't you see through her like I could?"

David looked at me. Then he reached over and took my hand. "I'm sorry, Kelse."

I pulled my hand away and looked down. I'd been angry about Isabel for a while, but I'd never admitted to myself how much it hurt. Confessing had the effect of putting it under a microscope; every pang felt magnified in clear, sharp focus.

We stared at the sky through the silhouettes of the treetops for a moment, listening to the snap of twigs and the chirp of crickets and the babble of the nearby brook. The longer the silence stretched, the sadder I became.

"Will you come visit me?" I said softly.

"Of course. You're not going *that* far." David thumped the hood of his car. "She may not be too pretty, but my old girl's a trooper. She'll survive a few trips up your way."

"And you could always stay with your grandfather."

"I guess," David mumbled.

You would have thought I'd suggested using a porcupine as a loofah.

"Or me!" I propped myself up on my elbow. "What am I talking about? You could stay with me!"

He laughed. "As long as you're not afraid I'll bring my Norwood cooties with me."

"Cooties," I snorted. "You're coming this summer anyway, aren't you? We can take a boat tour and eat taffy on the beach, like we always do. It'll be fun."

"That would be fun. As long as you're up for it, I'll do whatever you want."

My heart skipped with glee. Maybe I could have the best of both worlds after all. I leaned over and smacked a kiss on his cheek, except he moved and it landed on the corner of his mouth. My heart went from skipping to a dead halt.

Crap.

David's eyes widened. "What was that for?"

I scooted under the blanket and looked up at the sky again, embarrassed at the awkward turn things had taken. "Because I missed you," I said quietly.

David propped himself up on his arm and leaned over me. Even in the waning light, I saw the intensity in his eyes and I knew I should look away. This couldn't happen, not when everything was about to change so much.

But it did. In the next instant his lips were on mine. They were a warm, inviting contrast to the cool twilight air, tasting of mint and something else, something totally delicious that I couldn't put my finger on.

My eyes closed. I should have pushed him away. I should

have told him that it was too late for this, that he couldn't have picked a worse time to take things to the next level, and that, logically, this would never work.

But I didn't want to be logical. I wanted to keep kissing him.

My fingers caressed the soft skin at the base of his neck as he kissed me and I kissed him back. Part of me wondered why we hadn't done this before. Another part, another annoying, nagging, growing-louder-by-the-second part, knew it shouldn't have happened at all.

David pulled back and smiled at me, his thumb moving back and forth at the curve of my waist. My shirt had pulled up when I put my arms around him, and goose bumps erupted over my belly as he stroked my bare skin.

"I've wanted to kiss you again forever," he said.

"Again?" An impish look came over his face. "You son of a bitch!" I laughed. "You're talking about the time with the taffy! You told me that wasn't a kiss!"

"Only because you freaked out," David said with a chuckle. "You looked at me like I'd tased you."

"Well, what was I supposed to do?"

"I don't know. Push me down on the rocks and make out with me?"

I curled my fingers into the material of his shirt and yanked him down to me. "Like this?" I kissed him again, savoring the way he tasted and the feel of his hand stroking my rib cage and belly, so tender it was almost reverent. We were both breathless the next time we pulled apart.

"Yeah, like that," David said. He leaned in and brushed his nose against mine. "Can't help who you like, remember?"

"Are you saying you like me, David Kerrigan?" I'd meant to sound playful, since it was pretty obvious that he did like me, but it came out as a cross between desperately hopeful and totally panicked.

The smile disappeared from David's face, and I knew playful had worn out its welcome in this conversation.

"No." The word was gentle but firm. "I love you, Kelse. I always have."

Oxygen fled from my lungs like a fugitive prisoner. I no longer remembered how to form words, and the weight of his hung between us like humid summer air.

Part of me had always hoped, had secretly wished it might come to this, though I didn't fully realize it until he said the words. Another part of me knew he had no right to do this, not now. Not after he'd wasted so much time on the wrong person. How dare he kiss me, and hold me, and look longingly at me through those amazing lashes, and let his warm hand run over my bare belly and—oh, God, this had to stop.

Except he'd said it out loud, and there was no going back. So I did what any confused, terrified girl would do. I burst into tears.

I turned my face into David's arm, blubbering like an idiot against the sleeve of his T-shirt. His lips pressed against my temple. "What's wrong?" He trailed kisses down my face, the parts that weren't smashed up against his arm, anyway, until I felt him breathe a sigh against my earlobe. "I had to tell you," he whispered.

I jerked back. "You had to tell me *now*? I'm leaving tomorrow!"

I'm starting over tomorrow.

"I know." There was so much sadness in his face, in his voice, that I almost forgot to be angry. "But seeing you so sick this year, and then we were fighting, and now you're leaving . . . I thought . . . it's now or never." Half his mouth crooked up. "You know?"

"No! No, I don't know!" I sobbed. "You could have told me a million different times. Why didn't you?"

David's brow puckered into a frown. "Did I have to say it at all? Are you honestly telling me you didn't know?"

I turned my head, swiping furiously at my tears. "I guess I should've figured it out somewhere between Amy Heffernan and Isabel Rose."

"Kelse." David's hand covered my cheek, turning my face back toward him. "They don't matter to me. They never did."

"Really? Then which one did you sleep with? Or was it both?"

His face fell. "I—Kelse. C'mon."

"'Come on'?" I spat. "Now what? I move away, and you're left with all those stupid girls who throw themselves at you, and you're going to magically start telling them no? I don't want a long-distance relationship! I don't want to complicate things!" And then I said the worst thing I could've possibly said. "I don't want to love you!"

David looked at me like I'd asked him to quit breathing. His eyebrows pulled together, and he traced my bottom lip with his thumb. "But you do . . . don't you?"

I knew from the way he asked the question that I'd shaken his confidence in the answer. It didn't help that I let the black, silent space where my response should have gone grow, until it stretched into a gaping hole between us.

Finally, I sat up, fighting off the dizziness that came with the motion. I pushed the blanket off me and slid to the ground.

"I'm not doing this," I said. "You're ruining everything."

I heard twigs crunching beneath my feet before I even realized I'd turned and started to head through the woods toward my house.

"Kelse, wait!" David called.

I turned and saw him struggling to untangle the blanket from his legs. "Leave me alone, David," I called back. "I don't want to talk to you right now." With that, I broke into a run.

For more than a year, those would be the last words I said to him.

Twenty-Five

Rhode Island
Senior Year

Ryan's fingers crept around my waist seconds before his lips brushed against my jawbone.

"Excited about staying over tonight?" he asked.

I smiled and nodded, attempting to concentrate on the chunks of pumpernickel I was arranging around a bowl of spinach dip. Ryan had decided to throw a Saint Patrick's Day party, the same way he had last year when his parents took off for New York to see the parade. Remembering how trashed our friends had gotten, I'd insisted on having more than chips and Cheetos to serve with the alcohol. Preferably something that would absorb some of it, and limit the number of pukers and passer-outers.

From the slight slur in Ryan's words, I had a feeling my plan wasn't working very well.

I put the last of the bread on the platter and turned to face him, wrapping my arms around his neck.

"Remember what happened last Saint Patrick's Day?" he said, his dimple popping out with a mischievous smile.

Of course I remembered. Before the party got into full swing, he pulled me into his bedroom and closed the door. He immediately started pacing back and forth, adjusting and readjusting his baseball cap like it didn't fit his head anymore.

"Um, Kelse, I sort of have something to tell you," he said.

He looked so nervous that my first thought was, *Oh crap, he's going to dump me.*

My mouth went bone dry. "What's wrong, Ry?"

He let out a nervous breath, continuing to leave tracks in his carpet. "Okay, so there's gonna be drinking tonight, and what I have to say, I don't want it to come out while I'm drunk, because I want you to know I mean it."

"Mean what?" I squeaked.

Ryan finally stopped pacing. He stood in front of me and took my hands. "I mean, I don't know, because I've never really—but—you're fun and you're smart and you're smoking hot and I think—I think I might . . ." He paused and drew a sharp breath, blowing it out with a rush of words. "IthinkIloveyou."

A grin big enough to hurt my cheeks split my face. The old me never would've considered dating a guy like Ryan. I would've dismissed him as an immature, hard-partying jock, and moved on. And I would've missed out on so much. Like knowing he had a soft spot for animals, especially cats, and they loved him right back. Or that he still made cards by hand for Mother's Day every year. And that he could make me feel like the prettiest girl in the world by kissing my hand and smiling at me.

In that moment, watching him gather his nerve to put his heart on the line, giving myself permission to do stupid things felt like the smartest thing I'd ever done.

I wound up losing my virginity to him that night. Then I'd spent the rest of it sitting by his toilet, certain I was about to yak my guts up—not from what we'd done, but from the consumption of a little too much liquid courage. Not exactly the way I'd envisioned my first time, but hey.

I nodded, smiling at the memory as I kissed him. "Can you take it easy tonight? It's bad enough that I lied to my parents about sleeping at Candy's. I want you to be coherent when everyone leaves."

"It's Saint *Patrick's* Day, babe. You're asking me to curb my Irish pride?"

"You can have pride without a hangover. Paint a shamrock on your face, like I did. See?"

I turned my cheek to give him a better view of the small

green-and-gold shamrock Candy had painted just beneath my right eye.

"Cute." He kissed my forehead. "One more game of beer pong and then I'll stop, okay?"

"Fair enough." I kissed him again and grabbed the bread platter. "Can you handle bringing this downstairs?"

"Aren't you coming?"

"In a minute. I want to clean up the deck a little. Your buddies are slobs."

Ryan leaned in and kissed me again, the smell of beer mixing with his cinnamon gum. "You were more fun when you drank," he teased.

I lingered by the door to the basement, listening for thuds or crashes as Ryan made his way down. When I heard Crowley yell, "Food!" I knew he'd made it, and relaxed a little. I headed into the darkened dining room, where I had a view of the beer pong game in progress in the side yard.

When I first moved to Rhode Island, I'd tried to convince myself that I loved these kinds of parties, that I'd missed out by not jumping on the bandwagon sooner. At first, copious amounts of alcohol helped me believe it. But ever since I'd realized booze still held no real appeal for me, the glamour had quickly faded on the rest of it as well. I would've been perfectly content to curl up next to Ryan and watch a movie tonight, rather than watch my friends lose their inhibitions and fine motor skills inside big red plastic cups.

Ryan and Crowley ambled over to the beer pong table as David took his turn, sending the little white ball sailing into one of the cups on the other side of the table. Violet flailed and clapped, then threw her arms around his neck and smacked a big kiss on his lips. And another. And then one more for good measure.

As many times as I'd seen them kiss, it still made me gag.

I shuddered and headed back toward the basement door just in time to nearly get hit in the face with it.

"Are you hiding out up here?" Candy said. "I've been looking for you. We're about to take shots."

I made a face. "No thanks."

Candy ran her fingers through her hair. "Crowley says if I can down two shots of Hennessy, he'll let me chase it with his tongue. I told him to dream on."

"What is with you?" I'd never cared about Candy and Matt's cat-and-mouse game before, but all of a sudden I felt an overwhelming, inexplicable disgust toward the way she toyed with him. And an equally mysterious inability to keep my mouth shut about it. "Do you think he's going to wait forever? If you like him, why don't you just say you like him? Or better yet, act like it?" I snapped.

The second I saw the dumbstruck look on her face, I deflated. "I'm sorry, Can. I don't know why I said that. I think I need some fresh air. I'm gonna go clean up the deck."

I started to turn away, but she grabbed my arm. "No,

wait. Megabitch attitude aside, you're right." A devious smirk slithered across her lips. "I got this. Walk over to the dining room window. I want you to see something."

A few seconds later I watched her reappear in the side yard and come up behind Crowley, who stood pouring shots into glasses lined up on a bench. She tapped him on the shoulder. When he turned around, she grabbed his face and kissed him full on the lips. At first, he stared dumbly. Then he put his bottle down, grabbed her around the waist, and brought his lips crashing down on hers again.

I had to laugh as drunken shouts and cheers erupted around them. A few seconds later, as I stepped out onto Ryan's deck, my cell phone chimed with a text message: *That was long overdue. Now take your own advice.*

I sighed and shoved the phone into the pocket of my green hoodie. One of these days she'd forget this ridiculous idea of David and me as tortured lovers, if I ignored her long enough.

A roll of thunder sounded as I picked up empty and half-empty cups, napkins, gum wrappers, and various other debris. I tried to work faster than the approaching rain, and after a few minutes I had the deck looking fairly presentable. Just as I attempted to hoist a cooler full of half-melted ice over the railing, I heard, "Need some help with that?"

David emerged from the house and started toward me. Without waiting for an answer, he grabbed the other end of the cooler and helped me dump the contents onto the lawn.

"Thanks," I said.

"What are you doing out here all by yourself?"

"Cleaning up. What are you doing out here? Shouldn't you be canoodling with Violet?" I set the cooler down and tried to walk past him, but he blocked my path.

"'Canoodling,'" he repeated with a bleary-eyed grin. Then he brushed a stray piece of hair away from my face. "You and I 'canoodled' once. Remember?"

Oh boy. My chest caved in on itself and I had to remind myself to breathe. "Sounds like somebody's had a few too many." I patted him on the arm. "Yes, David, I remember. Now go back to the party. Go back to your girlfriend."

I tried to walk past him again, but he grabbed my wrist. "What if I told you I want you to go to prom with me?"

"What if— *What*?"

He stepped closer. "What if I want you to go to the prom with me?"

I stared at him, waited for him to laugh, to make fun of me for being so gullible. He didn't. He stared right back, his expression dead serious, and if he hadn't smelled like a brewery, I would've wondered if he wasn't so much drunk as insane.

"Then I'd say that's crazy, because you're going with Violet and I'm going with Ryan," I said evenly.

"Kelsey." He took another step closer to me, leaving barely any space between us. "You never even thought about going to the dance with me, did you?"

"Why would I think about going to the prom with you when we're both—"

"No, not that dance. The Swirl. It never even crossed your mind to go with me, did it?"

I swallowed, knowing I needed to get the hell out of there. But his fingers were twined loosely around mine and I stood frozen to the spot, his face just inches from mine. "You went with Isabel."

He leaned in, close enough that our noses nearly touched. "I wanted to go with *you*."

And that's when he tried to kiss me.

"Don't," I growled, my voice razor sharp. The corners of his mouth turned down and he pulled back a fraction of an inch. Then, before I could stop him, he leaned in and softly kissed the shamrock on my cheek instead.

My knees buckled. How dare he? How dare he breeze back into my life in his stupid green T-shirt that clung to his ridiculously sexy chest and try to act like the last year had never happened? How dare he come to this party, the party he'd only been invited to because he was dating my friend, and touch me so that I couldn't remember why I wasn't supposed to want him to?

"Am I interrupting something?"

Ryan.

That was why.

David turned around and I took a step back, glad his body blocked Ryan's view of me. I prayed he hadn't been able to see how close David and I had been two seconds ago.

"No," David said. "I was helping Kelsey empty out the coolers."

Ryan spit in the grass and folded his arms across his chest. "Vi's not feeling so hot. You might want to take her home."

I stepped out in front of David. "He's wasted, he's not taking her anywhere. I'll drive them home." I turned to David and in a tone of voice that left no room for argument said, "Come back tomorrow and get your car. You're not in any shape to drive."

When we got inside, though, it was obvious Violet wasn't in any shape to leave. She'd curled up on the couch in the basement and passed out, taking a wobbly swipe at Candy's head when we tried to shake her. Then she immediately zonked out again.

"She's done," Ryan said as he covered her with a blanket. "She can crash here tonight. I'll take Kerrigan home."

I put my hand on his chest as he came toward me. "No, you won't. You're almost as drunk as he is." I lowered my voice. "I'll take him, and I'll come right back. Promise."

Ryan nodded, though it didn't stop him from shooting a dirty look over my shoulder at David. I gave him one of my own as I nodded toward the sliding glass doors, indicating he should follow me outside.

The skies had opened up, driving needlelike raindrops into the ground. I threw my hood over my head and scurried to my car as fast as I could with my woven flats getting more waterlogged by the second. David sprinted beside me and we both slammed the car doors behind us, panting. The quiet that engulfed the interior felt deafening, even surrounded by the pounding of the rain.

I planned to avoid speaking, to avoid even looking at David for the entire ride. I threw my soaked hoodie across my headrest before starting the car and staring out the windshield while he stared out the passenger-side window. Then he ruined my plan, the way he'd been ruining everything lately.

"I'm sorry," he said. "I'm sorry for trying to—"

"Forget it," I cut off as the car backed down the driveway. I didn't want to hear him say he'd tried to kiss me, and I didn't want to think about it. "Just forget it."

"You hate me, don't you?"

"No. You're drunk and you weren't thinking straight. Now please, let's stop talking about it."

David nodded and turned back to the window. And even though I'd told him I didn't want to talk about it, I couldn't stop thinking about it. About the Winter Swirl, and how jealous I'd been when he'd gone with Isabel. How I'd figured out too late that he'd wanted to go with me, and how my whole life had taken a nosedive right after. How he'd told me Isabel didn't matter to him, even though he'd defended her when I suspected her of starting rumors about me. How, even after he knew what a spiteful person she truly was, he still sneaked back to Norwood on weekends to see her.

The next words I said detonated like a bomb before I could stop them: "Why are you still seeing Isabel?"

David's head whipped toward me. "What?"

"Isabel. Why are you still hanging out with her? If she never mattered to you, and if I was the one you wanted to go to the dance with, and if you never would have bothered with her if you'd known what a bitch she was, then why are you still bothering?"

He stared at me with a confused look on his face. "Who said I'm still seeing Isabel?"

"Why else would you go back to Connecticut? Your mother isn't there, your grandparents aren't there. What's the pull, David? Are you cheating on Violet?"

He let out a bewildered snort. "Let me see if I have this right. I tried to kiss you tonight, and you're all bent out of shape about *Isabel*?"

My voice lowered and I couldn't look at him. "I know you were with her the night before I left. At Maddie's."

"How do you know *that*?"

"It's not important," I mumbled.

His jaw dropped and he stared at me with a hardened look in his eyes. "Not that it's any of your business, Kelse, but I didn't even know she was going to be at Maddie's that night. I've seen Isabel *once* since I moved here. I applied to her school, and she offered to give me a tour. I haven't seen her since, and I've never cheated on Violet." He shook his head, his expression now one of disgust. "And for the record? If I do see Isabel again, it's because the biggest difference between you and her is that she wants me around and you don't."

He delivered his words with the precision of a surgeon, slicing me open with each one. Gone were the drowsy eyes and the sloppy enunciation, like he'd never been drunk at all.

Like he'd never . . . and yet he'd tried . . .

I turned to him as we pulled into the familiar gravel driveway of his grandfather's house. "Were you really even drunk tonight?"

David snorted again. "Right. I faked drunk because getting you alone is the focus of my entire life. Get over yourself, Kelsey."

"Excuse me, but I wasn't the one talking crazy about the prom and trying to kiss *you* tonight."

"And if I'd been sober, I would have realized it wasn't worth it. I don't even know you anymore."

"I'm so tired of hearing it!" I exploded. "I'm sick of it, David! So my hair color's a little different. So I'm not sickly, helpless, or pathetic anymore. Is that what's bothering you? That I'm not a broke nothing anymore? That I don't need you to play hero? Quit being such a jealous bastard!"

David's face fell and his eyes darkened. I knew I'd gone too far. I grabbed his arm as he reached for the door handle.

"Wait, David, I'm sorry," I said desperately. "I didn't mean it. I'm trying to tell you I'm still me."

But my voice trailed off as I said it, because I knew it wasn't true. The girl who'd left him behind a year ago would rather have died than to say something so hurtful.

He didn't look at me when he spoke. "I don't know *this* you. So if this is who you always were"—he turned ever so slightly, enough to let me see the total reproach in his eyes—"then I'm glad you never loved me. I never would have burdened you with my friendship if I'd known what you were really like."

He opened the door and took off into the rain. The sound of it roared through the car, almost as loud as my heart drumming in my chest.

With my lips set in an angry line, I cut the ignition and threw my door open. I stomped around my car as quickly as my shoes slurping through the mud would allow, and grabbed his arm again.

"How can you say that?" I shouted. "You were everything to me and you knew it! But you waited until the last second to say it, and then you wasted no time at all running back to that bitch! You only wanted me because you couldn't have me, and just because I didn't say I loved you on *your* terms, now I'm some horrible, unfeeling beast?"

Rivers of raindrops ran down our faces, spraying off our lips as we panted from equal parts chill and rage. David's voice was low and even when he spoke. "You don't love me.

You never did. I'm just glad I know it now, so I won't keep making a total ass of myself."

I clenched my fists at my sides and gritted my teeth. "It's *not true!*"

Now he raised his voice too. "When you left Norwood, you wanted to forget it. I never thought you meant *all* of it, me included. I poured my heart out to you like a total asshole that night, and you ignored every message, every call. You cut me out of your life!"

"I was scared!" My lips trembled and I struggled not to cry.

"Well you don't have to worry about it anymore. Because now I'm cutting you out of mine."

Some kind of strangled sound escaped me, and I dived at him, my chest colliding against his rib cage with enough force to knock my breath out of me. I captured his rain-soaked face between my hands.

I didn't even realize I was going to kiss him until he tried to turn away.

My palm dug into his cheek and I stood on my toes, smashing my lips against his.

He didn't respond, but he didn't try to pull back. I wound my arms around him and stood higher on my toes, refusing to let him breathe until he kissed me back.

When he finally did, sparks shot through my entire body. His lips parted, and I tasted the rain, the mint of his ChapStick, that other something so specifically David, all mingling with the faint trace of alcohol on his tongue.

One of his hands gripped my waist and the other pressed into the small of my back. I barely felt my feet leave the ground when he placed me on the hood of my car, pressing my body between his torso and the cold, wet metal, his lips never leaving mine.

My legs wrapped around him. My hands slipped beneath his soaked T-shirt, slid up his smooth back. I couldn't get close enough. It was the first time since that morning in the hall that I'd let myself feel this craving, this need to have him close to me. For a moment it was like no time had passed at all. The entire year melted away, and we were back in the woods. How I wished I could relive that night, when it was just me and my best friend, finally acknowledging something else between us.

Before we'd broken each other's hearts.

Twenty-Six

Connecticut
Summer before Junior Year

I ran through the woods until I broke into the clearing of my backyard, my underused muscles begging for mercy.

Even if I went inside and headed right up the stairs, my parents would ask why I'd come back so soon, and I didn't want anyone seeing the mess the last half hour or so had made of me. I curled up in a ball on the side of the house and hugged my knees, jumping a mile when my cell phone started to ring for the second time. David again. I hit ignore.

My head spun with everything that had happened. He'd kissed me. My best friend had kissed me, and he'd told me he loved me.

He'd waited until we'd hardly ever see each other to

go ahead and turn my feelings into a tumbleweed of sticky, tangled confusion. Maybe he only wanted me because he couldn't have me. Or because if I lived in a different state, I wouldn't be around to see how he handled—or didn't handle—girls who swarmed him at every opportunity. He could have his cake and eat it too.

How convenient. How selfish.

Yes, angry was the way to go. I wanted to be angry. Angry was so much better than sad. So I fumed until I felt it was safe to go inside, ignoring two more calls from David in the interim. I went straight into the bathroom and washed up for bed, then threw myself down on my mattress—literally, just my mattress. The bed frame had already been loaded into the U-Haul. I clamped my eyes shut and demanded sleep to take over. The sooner tomorrow came, the better.

Problem was, with my eyes closed, I couldn't control the images flashing behind my eyelids. As hard as I tried not to think about kissing David, it was the *only* thing I could think about. It didn't help that my shirt still smelled like him, and my blankets were a crappy substitute for the warmth of his body. So, naturally, it wasn't long until I started sobbing again.

Within minutes my bedroom door creaked open.

"Kelsey? Are you okay?" Miranda asked.

"I'm fine. Go away."

"But you're crying. Are you sad about moving?"

"No! I can't wait to go! I can't wait to leave this shit town and these stupid people. Leave me alone."

She ignored my order and came closer. "Are you crying because you're going to miss David?"

I meant to say, "David is an idiot," but a round of gasping sobs stole my breath, and "He kissed me" came out instead. The mattress dipped as Miranda climbed onto it next to me. "I swear to God, Miranda, if you ever tell anyone about this, I will never forgive you. Promise me you'll never tell."

Her huge blue eyes glistened in the dark. "I promise, but why is it bad that he kissed you? I thought you liked him."

"There's no point in liking him. We're leaving tomorrow and I'll never see him. I'm going to make all new friends and David will move on and I'll meet someone great and he'll be the guy of my dreams."

"Why do you have to go to Newport to find the guy of your dreams if he's right here?"

Her words were like icicles down my spine.

It was exactly what I hadn't wanted to think about: that I'd fooled myself into thinking the best things were yet to come, waiting for me to go to them. When in reality there was a very good chance I'd be leaving at least one of them behind.

I sat up, covering my eyes with my hands. "Oh, God," I moaned. "What did I do?" I threw the covers off me. I couldn't sleep tonight, not without seeing him again. And no way could I leave without telling him I loved him too. "I have to go. If Mom and Dad ask, I left something at David's." I threw on a pair of shorts before running out of the room, then doubled back. "Do not repeat a word of anything I told you." Miranda pretended to zipper her lip and then flicked her wrist to mimic throwing away a key.

I bolted through the woods, panting and sweating by the time I reached David's doorstep. Not seeing his car in the driveway did nothing to help the runaway-train pace of my heart.

Mr. Kerrigan opened the door, surprise and concern mingling on his face when he saw me. "Kelsey? Are you all right?"

I nodded, trying to keep the gasping out of my voice. "I'm fine. Is David here?"

"He's not, but come in. Sit down and let me get you a glass of water."

I started to protest, but he'd already made a beeline to the kitchen. I must've looked worse than I thought. I perched on the edge of the couch, ready to take flight again as soon as he told me where David was.

"I'm glad you're here," Mr. Kerrigan said as he handed me a tall glass filled with more ice cubes than liquid. He sat in the armchair across from me and gave me a smile that didn't match the sadness in his eyes. "I know I wished you luck with your move, but I don't think I've told you how much we're going to miss you."

"You'll still see me."

At the time I believed it.

"Of course. David's already been asking if we can head up to my father's early this year." The mention of David made me think of his lips against mine, and I was suddenly very aware of the water making its way through my stomach. Mr. Kerrigan looked at his hands. "You know, Kelsey, David is my proudest accomplishment. Knowing that he chooses to spend his time with people like you—good, salt of the earth people with smart heads on their shoulders—it makes me feel like I've done something right." The smile still played on his lips, but an unmistakable mist gathered in his eyes.

I put my glass on the end table next to me and stood up. Mr. Kerrigan did the same, and I wrapped my arms around him in a fierce hug.

"Thank you," I whispered.

He pulled away with a chuckle and held me at arm's length. "Look at me, getting old and sappy on you when you came here looking for my son."

I apologized and told him I didn't want to run off, but it was getting late and I'd need to head home soon.

"Do you know where he went?"

"He said he was going over to Hemlock Lane. A girl named Maggie's house? Or was it Maddie?"

"Maddie." The anticipatory butterflies in my chest grew strangely heavy. "I know this is going to sound weird, but can I borrow David's bike? I sort of need to find him."

I flew down the hill, pedaling as hard as I could, tempting fate to flip the whole bike over. Shadowed woods and angular houses with small, illuminated square windows blurred alongside me until the road began to widen and the treetops grew sparse and graceful, and I took a left turn onto the cul-de-sac of storybook colonials that composed Maddie's neighborhood.

I hopped off the bike, trying to get my breathing under control as I propped it against the car-lined curb edging the Clairmonts' property. My ears were met with the sound of voices coming from the backyard, and the crack of Wiffle balls against plastic bats. I tiptoed slowly through the grass, hesitating at the fence trellis that served as the entrance to Maddie's yard.

David stood in the middle of the lawn wielding a yellow bat. He picked up a ball from a bucket at his feet, tossed it into the air, and smacked it across the yard, where Eric ran to catch it, one hand in the air. Maddie and Jared Rose lay snuggling on a hammock a few feet away, the same hammock where Maddie and I used to swing lazily and read books and talk about our crushes. Maddie's older brother sat near a cooler on the patio, handing a beer to someone.

Isabel.

I angled my body behind the trellis posts as feelings warred within me, the desire to run to David and fling my arms around him battling a surging, overwhelming sensation that I didn't belong there. It was enough to keep me from taking one more step.

David had sought these people out after I pushed him

away. He felt comfortable turning to them, these same individuals who had slowly but surely edged me out of their lives.

Or maybe I'd edged them out of mine. I couldn't really tell anymore. Either way, I was literally very much on the outside looking in.

"Nice!" Eric yelled as David sent a Wiffle ball careening into the yard next door, and Maddie whooped from her spot on the hammock. He'd hit it like he had a serious vendetta against it. I was willing to bet no one else knew why. To any other person, it would've looked like a typical group of friends hanging out on a summer night.

As if the girl hiding behind the fence had never been part of their lives at all.

David threw the bat down as Eric ran off to retrieve the ball. Almost instantly, Isabel appeared in front of him, clutching her beer bottle against her abdomen and tentatively holding another out to him like a peace offering. I stood stone-still as David looked from the bottle to her, frowning. Isabel said something I couldn't hear. David said something back, something clipped and short. She set her beer down on the grass and put her hand on his arm, speaking more pressingly this time, more earnestly.

I knew what she was doing. Trying to wind her slimy tentacles around him and pull herself back into his good graces. Again.

David folded his arms across his chest. But he was listening to her. She rose up on her toes with the urgency of her speech. He looked off into the distance. His lips, those beautiful lips that had kissed me only a couple of hours ago, were set tight. When he looked back at her face, something passed over his. His eyes darkened with conflict, like he was on the precipice of forgiving her, once again, or telling her to go to hell.

And maybe it was a trick of the light, but in the next moment I swore I saw the slightest hint of a smile tug at his mouth, and I knew he'd decided. His fingers opened and he reached for the beer. Isabel let her hand linger over his as the bottle transferred from her grip to his. As he took a swig, they turned toward the house. And as they walked away together, Isabel's arm slid around David's waist.

I jerked back from the fence.

I couldn't keep doing this. I couldn't watch him find the good in people I despised and pretend it didn't kill me. After he'd kissed me and I ran, I'd told myself I needed to be angry. That it would help me believe I'd done the right thing. That it would make leaving everything behind easier.

Now I knew I'd been right.

That's why I turned around and headed back to the street, replaying what I'd seen and letting my imagination fill in the gaps of what I hadn't.

Whatever his decision, whatever that little scene had meant, I didn't want to know. David was going to be just fine without me.

And I was going to be just fine without him.

My last glimpses of Norwood blurred with tears as I rode back to the Kerrigans' house and propped David's bike against the garage door.

I turned off my cell phone, not wanting to know if David called again. And especially not wanting to know if he didn't.

I wouldn't turn it on again until I was under a different sky, in a different town, in a different state, just twenty-four hours later. It felt like a whole lifetime had passed in between. Everything felt different and new and scary and promising all at the same time. But one thing hadn't changed.

No matter how many times that familiar number showed up on my phone, my only answer was silence.

Twenty-Seven

Rhode Island
Senior Year

It was only when David's kisses moved from my lips to my neck that I realized the rain had stopped. He rested his head in the crook of my neck, right against my racing pulse, and smiled up at me.

I wondered if he could hear it breaking. My heart, that is.

I looked up at the sky, the rooftops, anywhere to avoid seeing the total contentedness in his eyes. The last time he'd looked at me that way, he'd told me he loved me.

I love you, Kelse. I always have.

I knew it was still true, but I couldn't let him say it. I didn't want to hear it, didn't deserve to hear it.

My body tensed when he leaned up and brushed his lips

against my ear, but he only whispered, "Come inside and dry off."

I nodded and let him help me down from the car. He didn't release my hand once my feet were safely on the ground, though, and when my Tiffany bracelet caught between our wrists, guilt bloomed like a lead flower in my chest.

"One second," I said, pulling my hand from his and running back to my car. I snatched my wet hoodie off the headrest, knowing it wouldn't do much good to keep me warm, but at least I wouldn't have to stare at the reminder of Ryan beneath my sleeve.

"Dad?" David called as we entered the house. "Dad? You asleep?"

"I'm in the living room, David. Everything all right?"

A lump rose in my throat. With everything he'd been through, everything he was still *going* through, his first concern was still his son. I could use a lesson in that kind of unselfishness.

"Everything's fine. Kelsey's here." I poked my head around David's back and waved.

Mr. Kerrigan's eyes widened. "What on God's green Earth happened to you two? You look like drowned rats."

David laughed. "We sort of got caught in the rain. I'm gonna get her a towel so she can dry off before she goes home." He turned to me and smoothed wet strands of hair away from my face. "Not that you have to leave right away. You can hang out, if you want."

The tenderness in his touch made my stomach sick.

I shook my head and looked at the floor. "I can't stay long."

Something flickered in his eyes, something I imagined to be a warning he ignored. "Come on," he said, leading me by the hand to the bathroom.

Once we were inside, he shut the door behind us and peeled his drenched shirt off his body, tossing it into the dryer.

It wasn't the first time I'd seen him shirtless. But it was the first time I'd seen him shirtless and felt my whole body react. The inside of my mouth grew as dry as the rest of me was soaked, and my heart still raced as if I'd run a marathon.

"Give me your sweatshirt," he said. I forced myself to look at the floor as I handed it to him, pretending the tiles were the most interesting thing I'd ever seen.

David slammed the door to the dryer and turned it on. Then he closed the distance between us until he had me sandwiched between his body and the bathroom door. The warmth of his skin radiated in the most cruelly inviting way as he kissed my hair and moved his hands beneath the hem of my shirt.

"Should we get you out of these wet clothes?"

"David!" I shoved him away and stepped around him, hugging my arms over my chest. "Your father is right outside!"

"Sorry," he said with a laugh. "Trying to make up for lost time, I guess."

He started toward me with his arm outstretched like

he meant to stroke my hair again, but I recoiled. His arm dropped to his side and his eyes narrowed in confusion.

I forced a weak smile. "Please just get me a towel, okay?"

He stepped past me toward a pile of folded clothes sitting on the washing machine. "Um, here." He held out a folded black T-shirt. "You can wear this. I'll get you some pajama bottoms. Leave your clothes here tonight and I'll wash them for you."

I blinked at the shirt in his outstretched hand and blurted, "I can't go back to Ryan's wearing your clothes."

I watched his face as my words registered, saw his smile falter and his arm drop ever so slightly.

"Right," he said cautiously. "Violet's there too. We should probably talk to both of them before they see anything like that."

I looked at him in bewilderment. "It's that easy for you? Don't you care about her?"

"Of course I care about her. But, Kelse." He took another step toward me. "I came here for you."

My knees wobbled. "Please don't say that."

David hedged another step closer, still holding his shirt. Still not wearing one. "Why wouldn't I say it? You went off on me once before because I waited too long to say something, and now you don't want to hear it?"

I pressed my lips together as if to keep my next thought from bursting free. It didn't work. "I went back for you that night."

David looked at me like the words didn't compute. "What are you talking about?"

"You want to know how I knew you were with Isabel? Because I *saw* you. I went to Maddie's to make things right, and you were already over it, David."

A kaleidoscope of emotions flashed across his face, everything from shock to disgust. "Over it? I was anything but *over* it, Kelse. I knew exactly what I wanted when I kissed you that night, and I thought you did too."

"I don't know what I want," I said helplessly.

Anger flashed in David's eyes. "Funny, but I thought what happened out there was your way of telling me you *do* know what you want. I guess it was more like your way of shutting me up?"

"David, Violet is my friend and I—" My voice cracked. "I love Ryan. I can't do this to both of them."

"You love him," David repeated robotically.

I nodded.

"So you figure you'll hurt me instead since, hey, you did it once already. Must be like riding a bike by now." The bitterness in his tone made every hair on my body stand on end.

I started toward him but stopped short, knowing I'd only make things worse. "I wasn't trying to hurt you. Then or now. But you and I are both with other people, and it doesn't make sense to throw them away because we got caught up in the past. This was a mistake."

David's jaw clenched. He turned away and gripped the

edge of the washing machine, the muscles in his arms and back defined with tension. Considering his nail beds were white against the surface of the washer, his voice came out surprisingly even when he spoke. "So you want to pretend nothing happened."

When I didn't respond, he glanced at me out of the corner of his eye. I tried to swallow even though my tongue felt like an overstuffed pillow, and nodded. "I'm sorry."

He turned to face me and for a split second held my gaze. Challenging me. Waiting for me to break down and throw my arms around him and kiss him again. A split second more and I might have done exactly that.

"Fine," he said. "Then everything I said before you *didn't* kiss me still stands."

He stormed past me and out of the bathroom, slamming the door behind him. A whimper escaped my throat and I buried my face in my hands. The last thing he'd said before I'd kissed him was that he was cutting me out of his life. He'd gone from never wanting to see me again to wanting to leave his girlfriend for me, and then back again.

I didn't want him to leave Violet for me, and I didn't want to leave Ryan for him.

Did I?

I paced the floor, telling myself I'd made the right call even as tears burned my eyes and fled down my face. I told myself that what I'd done had everything to do with loose ends and guilt and the heat of the moment creating a massive black hole in my judgment, and nothing to do with lingering feelings for David.

All those things explained everything. Everything except why my body ignited all over again every time that kiss replayed in my head. Then I'd think about Ryan and a heavy, cold guilt would come crashing down on me.

I stood in front of the mirror and demanded my reflection to get ahold of itself, smudged mascara, tangled hair, and all. The remnants of Candy's shamrock bled down my cheek. I grabbed a tissue and wiped my face with one hand while scraping my fingers through my matted hair with the other. Half of me hoped Ryan would still be drunk enough to accept whatever explanation I'd give him. The other half didn't know how I'd be able to face him at all.

My jeans were stuck to my skin and filthy. My sweatshirt couldn't have dried after such a short time in the dryer, but I couldn't stay there to wait for it. David didn't want me in his life, much less in his house, and Ryan would be worried if I didn't get back soon. And suspicious, like he'd been since day one. Book smarts might not have been his thing, but my boyfriend was obviously no fool.

I snatched my sweatshirt from the dryer and sucked in a deep breath as I reached for the doorknob. Light from the TV still flashed against the walls down the hall, but Mr. Kerrigan wasn't on the couch when I got to the kitchen. Another wave of guilt washed over me as I assumed he'd heard the door slam and gone upstairs to see if David was okay.

As quietly as I could, I slipped out the door to the back porch and into my car. I immediately grabbed my purse from the backseat and called Ryan on my cell phone.

"Kelsey?" Ryan slurred. "The hell's taking so long?"

I couldn't tell if I'd woken him, or if he'd broken his promise and kept drinking after I left. Part of me hoped for the latter. Because after what I'd just done, I deserved to be lied to.

"Sorry. David was really drunk. I had to . . . help him inside. How's Violet?"

"Out cold. Crowley and Candle are gonna crash in the basement with her. Hurry up and get back here so you can crash with *me*."

"I'll be back soon." I paused. "Ryan?"

"Yeah?"

For a moment it was all there on the tip of my tongue. I wanted it off my chest, and I wanted him to forgive me. But the words retreated to the back of my throat, and I had to say something else or suffocate on them.

"I love you."

"Love you too, babe. See you soon."

Tears threatened again as I hung up the phone, until a glint from the bottom of my purse distracted me as I put it away. I reached in and came away with something silver and round in the palm of my hand.

"Oh, God," I said aloud.

It was the Saint Christopher medal Ryan had given to me on the first day of school. The one that had reminded me of David because he'd had one exactly like it clipped to the visor of his beat-up Chevy. The one that made me freak out about my past even before I'd known the damn thing would be a premonition of the future.

Staring at it in my hand, I felt like it mocked me, reminded me of how badly I'd screwed up both then and now. Finding it at that exact second had to be the universe's way of flipping me off.

My fist closed around the medal and my teeth gritted. I opened the car door and prepared to throw the medal as far as I could, but my arm wouldn't cooperate. It froze in midair and my fist refused to release.

So with a frustrated noise ripping through my chest, I flung it back to the depths of my purse, started my car, and tried to get used to the rock of self-loathing that would sit in my stomach from that moment on.

Twenty-Eight

Rhode Island
Senior Year

The picnic tables were finally open again in the senior lunch area, but I found it hard to pay attention to the sunny sky or the warm spring breeze, or even the excited prom chatter happening at our lunch table.

"My dress is red, so your vest has to match," Candy informed Matt.

"I'll be rocking a cummerbund and a bow tie. None of this vest shit for me," he replied.

"As long as they're red, you can wear your underwear on your head and she won't care," Violet cut in.

Matt grinned and turned to Candy. "Now there's an idea. By the way, my underwear will be black and lacy so make sure yours match."

Violet turned to David and batted her eyes. "My dress is pink, baby. Do you think you can get a pink tie so everyone knows we're together?"

I stifled a laugh. While Ryan had a whole collection of pink polos, I'd never seen David wear pink in my life. He was the male equivalent of a girly girl—a boy-y boy?—and he'd never go for it.

"Whatever you want," he said, and planted a kiss on her neck.

My sandwich nearly fell out of my mouth. I had to force myself not to gape, not only at what he'd said, but at what he'd done. Violet had always been PDA Offender Numero Uno in their relationship; she was the clingy one. While David had never rejected her advances, it was only recently that I could remember him being the initiator. Ever since I'd turned him down, in fact.

"Kelse? Hellooo?"

I blinked at the realization that Ryan had been talking to me. "Sorry, Ry. What?"

"I asked what color your dress is."

"Oh. It's white with silver beads. So as long as there's no gold in your tux, anything will match."

Ryan's brow puckered. "You seriously didn't hear a word I said, did you? I asked so you could tell me what kind of flower you want."

"Anything is fine," I mumbled guiltily.

"Oh!" Violet cried. "Do you know what would be so pretty with my dress? An orchid!" She batted her eyes at

David again. He pulled her closer and whispered something in her ear, to which she promptly erupted into giggles. They carried on like that for a full minute—his face buried in her hair, nibbling at her neck, telling her things the rest of us couldn't hear while she yelped and giggled and wiggled.

My sandwich threatened to come back for an encore performance.

The end-of-lunch bell sounded then, and Ryan shot to his feet and gave me a hurried kiss good-bye. "Gotta run," he said. "I'm one tardy away from a week's worth of detention."

Everyone scattered, me included. But instead of heading to class, I lingered by my locker, knowing David would pass by on his way to his next period. We hadn't spoken at all since Saint Patrick's Day. When he said he planned to cut me out of his life, he'd meant it—he didn't even look at me anymore. He treated me with the same indifference he'd have for a dead bug or mud on the bottom of his cleats.

If he didn't have anything to say to me, fine. But I had a few words for him.

I hissed his name as he breezed by, acting like he hadn't seen me at all. My hand shot out and grabbed the sleeve of his T-shirt, and I pulled him into an alcove of lockers tucked into the corner of the hall. "I need to talk to you," I spat.

He looked me up and down, like the idea of talking to me bored him senseless. "So talk."

"Whatever you're trying to pull with Violet, you need

to stop. Don't you dare use her to get back at me."

David's face contorted like he'd eaten something vile. "Violet is my girlfriend. What the hell are you talking about, 'using' her?"

"You were ready to drop her like a bad habit when— you know when. Now she's your frigging snuggle bunny? You've never acted this way with her. Never. And if you're doing it to make me jealous, I'd say that's a pretty douchey way to get back at someone."

His jaw tensed. "You are something else, you know that? You really think it's all about you." He stepped closer and lowered his voice. "I held back with Violet because of all the unfinished bullshit between you and me, and now I don't have to. So if she and I are closer, it's not because I'm trying to get some twisted revenge on you. I don't care what you think anymore."

A tiny gasp escaped me. He'd more or less said, *I'm over you.* Which was exactly what I'd wanted for all these months, wasn't it? I should've felt relieved, but the words digested about as easily as a wad of slime.

"Good," I said, trying to pretend he hadn't snuffed me out like a candle. "You shouldn't care."

"Then we're finally on the same page."

He turned to walk away, but I called after him. "David? Has she asked you why we're not talking? Has she noticed?"

David grimaced. "I haven't told her, if that's what you're asking. But I'm sure she's noticed. She isn't stupid."

"Don't you think it looks worse if we don't talk at all? We either need to come up with a reason why we're not, or we should at least be civil."

David looked like he didn't quite buy my logic, and honestly, I didn't even know where that had come from. If Ryan had noticed the wall between David and me, he hadn't said anything either. Probably because he wanted nothing more than for David and me to loathe the other's existence, and he'd have no problem with our relationship staying on a never-ending bad spell. Eventually he'd want to know why, though, and Violet would too.

"Civil, huh?" David said. "I guess. Especially since we'll be in the same limo for prom and everything."

"Right. Venomous hatred becomes kind of obvious in small, enclosed spaces. So let's work on keeping that in check." I forced a smile, but David's mouth stayed settled in a solemn line.

"I don't hate you, Kelse."

My insides seized. Definitely hadn't expected that.

A nervous laugh bubbled in my throat. "I'll bet I'm off the hook for that dance, though."

"What dance?"

Heat crept up my neck and I waved him off, embarrassed that he didn't remember asking me to save him a dance for another time the night he'd gone to the Swirl without me. "Nothing. I don't hate you either, David. And . . . I'm happy for you and Violet."

The corner of his mouth twitched and he nodded almost imperceptibly. As we went our separate ways, I couldn't feel the satisfaction I should've. The conversation had more or less been a success: He wasn't using Violet as a pawn, and we'd established that we didn't hate each other. Yet I felt gutted. I almost wished we hadn't talked at all.

Because knowing he hated me would have been a thousand times easier than knowing he didn't love me anymore.

Twenty-Nine

Rhode Island
Senior Year

"You look *gorgeous*!" my mother squealed as she stepped back from a cloud of hair spray. It was prom night, and she'd arranged my hair half up, swirling and curling around sparkling silver clips, with the rest cascading down my back in loose curls. And she'd applied enough product to ensure it would stay put for at least a week.

"You did a great job, Mom."

My mother's brow furrowed. "Then why do you look so sad? Is everything all right with you and Ryan?"

"Ryan is fine. But Dad's not here."

"I know, baby. He felt so bad that this was the only night they could reschedule his book signing. But he told me to take lots of pictures and video so he can see them when he gets back."

"Don't you ever miss the way things used to be?" I asked as I fiddled with a hairpin on my vanity. "When Dad was around more often? Everything seemed so much simpler back then."

My mother knelt down next to me. "What's this about, Kelsey? Are you starting to get nervous about going away to college? Because you'll be close enough to come home whenever you want. Daddy and I hope you will, actually."

"I guess." I couldn't quite put my finger on the source of my melancholy, but separation anxiety probably had at least something to do with it.

"And just because Ryan will be in North Carolina doesn't mean you'll never see him," my mother continued. Ryan had finally given up on holding out for the schools he'd wanted in South Carolina or Florida. He'd enrolled at North Carolina by the skin of his teeth, four days before the cutoff. And two days after his parents had threatened not to pay for any school but that one.

"I know. And Candy and I will be roommates, so at least I'll have her."

"Exactly. Sometimes change is for the best."

Ha. I'd thought that once too.

I stared at the floor and she patted my leg again, smiling. "No more sad faces tonight, baby. It's your prom. I want you to go and have a great time." Her grin widened. "After I take pictures of you and your sister, of course."

Once Mom had snapped some pictures of me with Miranda, they walked me out to my car. The plan was to meet at Ryan's, where the limo would pick us up, and then my friends and I would all sleep there afterward. Unlike Saint Patrick's Day, I had my mother's permission, because his parents would be home.

"See you in a few!" she called as she and Miranda piled into her car. When we pulled up in front of the Murphys' house ten minutes later, the lawn buzzed with color and people. Violet in her pink dress, Candy in her red one, Steve Koenig and his date having their picture snapped by various sets of parents. Finally, my heart fluttered with excitement.

Ryan came out of the house looking like a dream, all blond curls and blue eyes and dimples. "You look so pretty, babe," he said as he took my hands in his. "Ready to party?"

I smiled and gave him a quick peck, not wanting to smudge my lipstick. That's when I saw David and his father emerge from their car. My breath caught in my throat as I watched him walk toward the house in his tux, his hair freshly cut, his face clean shaven, and a plastic box in one hand. Just like the first day of school, and just like that night in the rain, it felt like time had melted away and nothing had changed. He looked every bit as handsome as he had in my hospital room, and I had to fight the knee-jerk instinct to go running to him.

Violet did instead.

With everyone finally accounted for, we took pictures

and pictures and more pictures. When we'd finally snapped photos in every possible configuration, the limo pulled up and our parents retreated to their cars. Just as I was about to disappear into the cave of LED lights and black leather, a hand touched my wrist.

"Kelsey, honey," Mr. Kerrigan said. "I want you to take a picture with my boy, if you don't mind. For old times."

I looked over his shoulder at David to make sure it was all right with him. When David held his arm out to me, I stepped into the spot at his side where I'd always fit so well, and we smiled like we hadn't spent the past two years finding every possible way to hurt each other.

Prom was perfect, right up until it wasn't.

It was held in a renovated Civil War–era hotel, in a banquet room that overlooked the Cliff Walk and the Atlantic. I would've been perfectly happy to dance with Ryan on the veranda all night, listen to the waves lap the shore, and fall in love with Newport all over again. But Steve had smuggled in a flask of some ungodly smelling booze, and the moment Ryan knew about it, he had a hard time focusing on anything else. I started to get irritated at the way they kept sneaking out to the Cliff Walk, coming back a little more off balance each time.

When I found my table mysteriously empty yet again, I headed toward the bathroom to touch up my makeup. I made it only halfway there when I felt a tap on my shoulder.

"Where do you think you're going?" David said. "I'm here to collect my dance."

"David." I sighed. "If you're drunk again—"

"I'm not drunk. Your date keeps leaving you alone and you owe me a dance. So?" He gave me an expectant look and I raised an eyebrow, wondering if he really remembered or if this was a shot in the dark. As if he'd read my mind, he smirked and said, "I figured out what you were talking about."

"You don't have to do this. That was a long time ago and I know I'm not exactly your favorite —"

"Enough of the martyr crap. Come on, let's go."

"But-but where's Violet?" I stuttered as he led me toward the dance floor.

"Outside with everyone else." He stopped so fast that I almost smacked into him as he turned to me. "I won't make you dance with me if you don't want to." His hand dropped from my arm. "We're supposed to be civil, but if it's too much. . . ."

It wasn't until he said it that I realized how much I didn't want to go back to my table. I hoped I didn't look as terrified as I felt. "It's one dance. No big deal."

That's what I told myself anyway. But I was hyperaware of the slow music vibrating through my body as he put his hand on my waist, and of the familiar mix of mint and citrus in the way he smelled, and of the fact that even if my tongue hadn't felt like a dry wad of cotton, I still would've had no idea what to say to him.

"So this is what it's like to dance with you," I said when I couldn't think of anything else.

He smiled down at me. "Not so bad, right?"

"No." We swayed together for a few more beats and then, as if I had no control over my own mouth, I blurted, "I would've gone to the Swirl with you if you'd asked me."

David pulled back and looked at me. "Where did that come from?"

"Because you said I never considered going with you. But you never asked."

"True. I guess not knowing when to open my mouth is kind of my MO, huh?"

"Just sayin'," I replied with a laugh.

We'd started dancing in the middle of a song, and when it ended a few seconds later, I felt a twinge of disappointment as a faster beat replaced it. I stepped away from David, ready to head back to my seat. Or out to the veranda for some air.

He caught my hands as they dropped from his neck. "Hey, where are you going?"

"The song is over."

A wicked grin spread across his face. "That was only half a dance. We're not done here." Before I could protest, he lifted my hand above my head and spun me around. The squeal of laughter that peeled from my throat took me completely by surprise, but I went with it. I loved the song playing, and maybe it possessed me, but I smiled more in that three and a half minutes of spinning and shaking and laughing with David than I had the whole night.

By the end of the song, I had the lapels of his jacket twisted in my hands and his hands had found their way back to my waist. We were breathing hard and laughing, and everything felt a thousand pounds lighter. Which had to be why Steve Koenig chose that moment to come up and put his drunken arm around David.

"Kerrigan," he bellowed. "Better watch it. Murphy's looking at you like you're about to get another scar to match the one he already gave you."

My smile dissolved slowly, but David's fell right off his face. "What? What's he talking about?" I asked.

David stood up as straight as he could with Steve's two-ton arm clamped around his shoulder. "His scar," Steve said, chucking David's chin with his free hand. "Ain't it cute?"

My whole body felt limp. I looked David dead in the eye. "Tell me what he's talking about." As the words left my lips, someone came up behind me. I didn't have to look to know it was Ryan.

David glared over my shoulder at him. "Let *him* tell you," he said. With that, he shoved Steve's arm off him and walked off the dance floor. Violet must have been standing next to Ryan, because she was scampering after David by the time I turned to face my boyfriend.

I folded my arms across my chest. "Do you want to tell me what, exactly, Steve means about David's scar?"

A drowsy smile floated on Ryan's lips. "It's nothing, babe." He put his hands on my arms and tried to pull me closer. "Koenig's too wasted to know what he's saying."

I yanked my arm away from him. "He may be drunk, but he knows exactly what he's saying. And you have about two seconds to fill me in, Ryan, or you won't be smiling anymore."

My tone alone wiped the smirk off his face, and a mixture of panic and defeat flashed in his eyes. "Not here," he mumbled. "Come outside with me."

Ryan turned in the direction of the veranda, and I stormed off behind him. Neither of us spoke when we got outside, even when the glass door clicked shut and muted the music to a dull, vibrating bass.

"Well?" I said.

Ryan sat in one of the whitewashed chairs and raked his hand through his hair. "I'm sorry, babe."

"What are you sorry *for*?"

He leaned back and let out a frustrated breath. "Here it is. So over the summer, Coach B. told Steve and me about this kid who might be transferring over for senior year, and he asked if we wanted to go to Connecticut with him to watch him play one day, so we did. You remember?"

"No. Where was I?"

Ryan shrugged. "Touring a school, I think. Anyway, we went, and halfway through the game, we knew we were fucking screwed if he joined the team. It's one thing to be good, but to be good *and* have an in with the coach? Why not just sign our scholarship money over to charity?"

A cold feeling started in the pit of my stomach and spread throughout my body. "So what did you do?"

Ryan fidgeted and rubbed his temples. "The more we thought about it, the more wired we got. By the time we got back to Steve's house, we were off-the-wall pissed. Neither of us wanted him on the team, and Coach was acting like he fell face-first into the Fountain of Youth or something, already treating this kid like a fucking god." He paused, pressing his lips together as if trying to keep his anger from boiling over. "Steve's brother overheard us and he told us we should do ourselves a favor and make it harder for this kid to play."

I stood frozen to the spot, not believing what I'd heard and not sure I wanted to hear more.

"We knew he was moving over the summer because of everything he told Coach," Ryan continued. "So when he got here, we watched him for a while. We'd sit in the car, parked outside his house, and have a few beers. We joked about breaking his hand or his arm and then taking his glove for a trophy or something, but I didn't think we'd ever actually do anything."

He stopped and looked at me, his eyes pleading. "Go on," I prompted, my voice cold and hard.

"One night he left the house while we were there, and we followed him. We wound up sitting in the parking lot at a drugstore, and the more we waited, the more this . . . *thing* built up inside me. I can't even explain it, Kelse. By the time he walked out to his car, I snapped. I didn't even tell Koenig before I got out of the car; I just did it. In my head, the plan was to slam his hand in his car door and walk away. But he fought back, and I lost it. The next thing I knew I'd smashed his face into the door and Steve was pulling me off him. I went nuts. I got loose long enough to grab the medal out of his car, and then we took off."

My whole body shook. "So the medal you gave me on the first day of school, the Saint Christopher medal—that was David's?"

Ryan looked at me with sad eyes and nodded.

"Let me get this straight." My words were slow and jagged with the struggle to contain the disgust roiling in my chest. "You took David's medal as some sort of trophy after you beat him up for being better than you at baseball?"

Ryan jumped out of his chair so quickly that I almost stumbled back. "He's not better than me! He's nothing, and everyone acts like the sun rises out of his ass, including you. Because wouldn't you know it, the next time I saw him after that night was the morning you wrapped yourself around him like a fucking anaconda."

For a second I could only stare in bewilderment. Then, finally, I found my voice. "How could you do it, Ryan? What's wrong with you?"

"I told you, I don't know. It was wrong. *I* was wrong, and I'm sorry."

"So sorry that you tried to put poison ivy in his baseball jersey?"

"Come off it, Kelsey!" Ryan exploded. "You think I don't know the only reason you care about any of this is because it's him? I could've done it to anyone else and you would've been over it in five seconds. But because it's your precious *David*, it's the end of the world."

"Not the end of the world, Ryan." My windpipe felt pinched shut and I struggled to get my next words out. "The end of us."

Ryan's face went pale.

"You're joking. Kelse, you don't mean that." He started toward me, but I stepped behind a chair, blocking his path.

"I mean it, Ry," I said as I headed down the steps toward the Cliff Walk. "It's over. I need to go find David."

"Kelse, *wait*." Ryan threw the chair out of his way and came after me. Given that he was faster than me on days when I didn't have three-inch heels on, I had no hope of outrunning him. He caught my arm and spun me around to face him. "How can you say that? I love you, you know I do."

"Ryan, I can't even look at you right now. Let go of me and leave me alone."

"But I want to talk—"

"LET GO!" I'd yelled loudly enough to get the attention

of the other people milling around the expansive lawn, some of whom were chaperones, and Ryan knew it. He dropped my arm, looking exactly the way I felt on the inside: ready to crumble.

"Promise you'll come find me when you're ready to talk?"

I nodded, fighting back tears. As much as his confession horrified me, I knew he meant it when he said he loved me. The defeated look on his face all but shattered my heart.

I couldn't watch him retreat, head bent, sadness in every line of his body. I turned toward the Cliff Walk and slipped off my shoes, knowing what my next step needed to be. For the second time in my life, I was about to turn my back on a boy who loved me. Except this time, I'd do it for all the right reasons.

Thirty

Rhode Island
Senior Year

I jogged toward the Cliff Walk, shoes in one hand, hem in the other, as the salt of the ocean air mingled with the salt of my tears rolling over my lips.

In the distance I spotted David and Violet strolling toward the hotel. He'd given her his tuxedo jacket to wear, and I suddenly realized how cool the night had grown. I ignored the goose bumps that sprang up on my own arms as I got closer to the water and wiped my tears impatiently. Violet and David stopped short when they saw me barreling toward them. By the looks on their faces, I must have been the definition of a hot mess.

"Kelse?" David said. "What happened?"

I walked right up to him, ignoring Violet. "Why didn't you tell me?"

"He didn't even tell *me* until two minutes ago. Why would he tell you?" Violet huffed.

David put his hand on her shoulder. "Meet me inside, Vi. I need to talk to Kelsey."

Violet's face twisted with indignation. "I'm not going inside! Anything you need to say to her you can say in front of me." She put her hands on her hips and shot him a look that could fry eggs.

David asked me to give them a minute before pulling Violet to the side. I stared at my toes on the sidewalk, trying to allow them some privacy, but it was obvious that asking to be alone with me had landed him on her shit list. She kept pulling her arm away from him and shrieking incredulous *no*'s left and right. Finally, she stalked away from him, clearly against her better judgment. As she passed me, she stopped in her tracks. "Thanks for ruining prom, Kelsey," she spat. Her lip quivered, and I saw it in her eyes before she stormed off: She'd actually fallen this time.

I looked at David, unable to focus on her tantrum. I had more important things to apologize for.

He put his hands in his pockets and bobbed his head toward the trail as if to say, *Let's walk.*

"Why didn't you tell me?" I repeated as I fell in step beside him. I shivered uncontrollably, though I couldn't tell how much of it was from the breeze.

"Would it have changed anything?" he asked quietly.

"Yes! Yes, it would've." My lip trembled. "Maybe. I don't know."

"Maybe what? Maybe you would've felt sorry for me? You ripped my heart out and stomped all over it. Why would knowing this have made any difference? I didn't want pity friendship."

"You weren't afraid he might hurt me after what he did to you?"

David raised an eyebrow, and a choked sound escaped his throat. "Kelse, no. If I thought that for a second—"

I waved him off, shaking my head in frustration before he could say more. It was a stupid question, and we both knew it. The Ryan Murphy who'd been my boyfriend would never dream of raising a hand to me. But Ryan Murphy the baseball player was obviously an ass hat.

"I feel like I don't even know him," I whimpered.

"Pretty crappy feeling, isn't it?"

My words came out in a choked whisper. "I'm sorry."

"Don't apologize for what he did. It's not your fault." He scuffed the pavement. "Besides, I told him I wouldn't tell you. You needed to hear it from him, not me."

Typical David. Always trying to do what he thought was best for everyone else.

"I'm not apologizing for him. I'm apologizing for me. You keep forgiving me, for every stupid, hurtful thing I do to you, and I don't know why."

We paused as we reached the end of the sidewalk, where the boulders loomed, irregular lumps in the moonlight. David looked at me, taking in the shivering, sniffling wreck before him. "I'm kind of an idiot when it comes to you. And *I* don't know why."

Then he held out his arms to me. I stepped into them, letting him hold me and rub my back and wrap me in warmth until I finally stopped shaking.

I sighed against his chest. My arms dropped slowly and I reached for his hand, not ready to let go of him yet. "Do you want to keep going?" I asked, nodding toward the rock trail.

His eyes widened with surprise. "Keep going? This was always the end of the road for us."

I nodded, threading my fingers through his. "Maybe I'm not scared anymore."

David's grip tightened around mine, but he didn't move. When I looked up to search his face, he kept his eyes cast down. The corners of his mouth curved into an unsettled line.

"We'd better get going, Kelse," he said as his hand slipped from mine. "It's gonna be a *long* ride home."

"Long" wasn't quite the word.

Awkward? Yes.

Quiet? Unbearably.

Nauseating? Abso-frigging-lutely.

Between Ryan and me, and Violet and me, and Violet

and David, there was enough friction in the limo to start a fire. I sat between Candy, who held my hand the whole way, and Molly, Steve's date. I didn't want to be next to Ryan, but I didn't want to cause more trouble with Violet by sitting anywhere near David.

I spotted my car as we pulled up to Ryan's house and felt a huge surge of gratitude that I hadn't carpooled with Candy like she'd wanted to. Now I could go home and cry over the ruins of the night without having to bother anyone else, or worse, having to stay there because no one had enough brain cells left to operate a vehicle. Except for David, and Violet would have none of that.

"Call me tomorrow," Candy whispered as she hugged me good-bye. "Are you sure you're okay?"

I nodded into her shoulder. "I'll tell you everything tomorrow." I'd only given her the ten-second version of the story in the bathroom after David and I came back from the Cliff Walk. There were too many nosy people and not enough time for more.

She squeezed my hand before heading toward Ryan's front steps, where he held the door open for everyone filing into his house. Everyone except Violet and David, who took off in Violet's car together. When Candy disappeared inside, Ryan looked over at me.

"Come on," I said, opening my car door and indicating he should get inside. "You wanted to talk. Let's talk."

I threw my shoes and purse in the backseat as Ryan

trotted over to my car and slipped into the passenger seat. The door shut behind him and instantly the tension became palpable again, like he'd sealed us inside a vacuum.

With the exception of a few furtive glances out of the corners of our eyes, we didn't look at each other. "I'm so stupid," Ryan said to his hands after a moment of terse silence. "I can't believe I did what I did. I just wanted to get into a good school, that's all."

"And the fight in the hallway that day?"

"I started it," he mumbled. "I said stupid shit about him, about his father—"

My anger flared. "Don't tell me any more. You realize it was for nothing, don't you? David had his choices narrowed down ages ago, while you were still resorting to pranks and acting like a jealous kindergartner." Ryan twisted his hands and turned toward the window. "All for nothing," I repeated.

"So it's really over then?" Ryan asked quietly.

I looked over at him and felt myself break into a million pieces. In the year and a half we'd been together, I'd never seen Ryan cry. But at that moment there were unmistakable tears rolling down his cheeks. Seeing him that way killed me, and my own eyes filled with tears instantly.

"I'm sorry, Ry."

"I shouldn't be surprised." He wiped his cheeks with the back of his sleeve and stared out the window again. "You haven't wanted me since the day he got here." His shoulders jolted with a silent sob.

"Ryan," I bleated. "I'm sorry." I wanted to tell him everything, tell him that he wasn't the only one who'd done something despicable. Part of me wanted him to know how I'd kissed David and then come back and slept in his bed like nothing had happened. How I was just as disgusted with myself, if not more, than I was by what he had done. But watching him break down, I knew there was no point. I'd only hurt him more.

Ryan lunged across the center console and pulled me into a crushing hug. I didn't know how long we sat there, holding each other and crying. I just knew that when he left my car, I felt so alone and so hollow.

He'd been right, of course. When I'd left Norwood, I'd wanted to believe all things perfect were around the corner, waiting for me to find them. I hadn't stopped to think about what I'd be leaving behind, which turned out to be a huge piece of my heart. Specifically, I'd left it with David. Once I got far enough away, I'd been able to pretend I hadn't, and falling for Ryan had helped me keep my delusions going. But the truth was, I'd never been completely his—and the girl he'd fallen for only half existed. Seeing David again had sent my illusions crumbling around me. I'd just been too stubborn to see it.

Sitting in my car, bereft and broken, I saw everything crystal clearly. I'd hurt them both. And now I'd lost them both.

Thirty-One

Rhode Island
Senior Year

Emotional hangovers suck every bit as hard as alcohol hangovers, if not worse. I found that out firsthand when I woke up the next morning feeling like a steamroller had had its way with me. My eyes burned, and without even looking in the mirror, I knew there must have been bags the size of eggs beneath them. My whole body felt heavy and useless, and I had no intention of leaving my cocoon of sheets, let alone my room.

A light knock sounded at my door. "Kelsey?" Miranda called softly.

Great. Unfortunately, sheets weren't a very effective barrier against nosy little sisters.

My door swung open and Miranda stepped inside in all her bed-headed glory. Only my sister could manage to wake up looking like she'd gone to battle with her pajamas and lost. Though I probably could've given her a run for her money on that particular morning.

"I thought you were sleeping at Ryan's house," she said suspiciously.

I rolled over to face the wall. "I didn't."

"Did something happen?"

"A lot happened. I don't want to talk about it."

There was a long stretch of silence, so quiet that I wondered if she'd left the room. But when I turned over again, there she stood, blinking her big eyes at me. "Did you and Ryan break up?"

"Yes."

She shifted and picked at her cuticle. "Did he figure out that you still love David?"

I shot up in bed. *"What?"*

Miranda rolled her eyes. "Don't be dumb. If you and Ryan broke up, it's either because he figured out you still love David, or *you* finally did."

I gaped at her, speechless. A fresh batch of tears seared my eyes. Had I been the only one too stupid to figure it out?

My head slammed against my pillow and a new round of sobs took control. I couldn't have cried any harder, or any uglier. And my sister couldn't have been any sweeter.

Just as she had the last time I'd made a mess of everything, she climbed onto my bed and stroked my hair until I didn't have any tears left to cry.

I spent Saturday in sad shape. I wouldn't leave my room, and I wouldn't talk to anyone but Candy. She told me Ryan had slept in his room instead of down in the basement with the rest of them, but he'd at least joined them for breakfast. I knew she'd left out any details that would break my heart all over again, and I loved her for it. When I asked about Violet, a long pause followed.

"She'll get over it," Candy finally said.

"It's not like I can help that Steve dropped a bomb on me in the middle of prom. She's acting like I purposely spoiled her fun."

"You know Vi. She can't stand any drama that's not her own. And it burns her buns that David has such a soft spot for you."

"Well, she has him. I don't."

"That would change in a millisecond if you wanted it to."

I frowned into the phone. "Not anymore, Can. I blew it. Majorly."

"You're majorly a moron if you believe that."

It was the first time I cracked a smile all day.

When I woke up the next morning to the sound of rain thrumming against the house, I thought it would make me even more of a zombie. Rain always sapped my energy and made me cranky. At least it had, until it became the thing I associated with the best kiss of my life.

The more I thought about it, the more restless my limbs became. I itched to do something productive. I knew there was nothing that could counteract the damage I'd already done, but maybe I could find something that would at least be a step in the right direction.

I threw the covers off me and went into the study. A few minutes later I emerged with a freshly printed chocolate chip cookie recipe. I stuffed it in my purse, and after brushing my teeth and hair, hopped in my car and returned a little while later with all the ingredients. My mother looked completely baffled when I came into the kitchen and plopped my bags on the counter.

"Kelsey? What are you doing?"

"Making cookies," I replied, grabbing a baking sheet from the cabinet.

"Are you okay? You haven't made cookies in ages."

"I'm fine. I promised Mr. Kerrigan I'd make him some and I never did. Better late than never, right?" My mother nodded and visibly relaxed. I raised an eyebrow at her. "Did you think I was going to binge on them or something?"

"No! But you've had a rough weekend. I had to ask. Do you want any help?"

I told her I didn't, and she left me alone in the kitchen after a quick kiss on my forehead. For hours I turned out batch after batch of delectable-smelling cookies. I'd forgotten how much I loved the whole therapeutic process of mixing and measuring and sampling. It made me wonder how many other things I'd forgotten about myself since I moved to Newport. Enough to hurt David, and that was plenty.

With the last batch cooling and the mess cleaned, I hopped in the shower. I wanted nothing more than to throw the cookies into containers and drive over to the Kerrigans' house, but my mother insisted on feeding me first.

Finally, clean and fed and feeling human for the first time in forty-eight hours, I started down the familiar road to the heart of Newport.

Thirty-Two

Rhode Island
Senior Year

The closer I got, the more it seemed like a bad idea.

What if no one was home?

What if Violet was over?

What in the hell was I expecting to happen, anyway?

The questions needled into my gut like pins into a pincushion, but I kept driving anyway.

I couldn't tell if I was disappointed or relieved when only Mr. Kerrigan's car sat in the driveway. Maybe a little of both. At any rate, I wasn't going to turn back. Taking a deep breath, I grabbed two containers of cookies and scampered through the rain to the back porch.

Mr. Kerrigan's face lit up when he saw me on the other

side of the door. "Kelsey!" he cried. "Come in, come in! Are you looking for David?"

"Actually, I'm here to see you." I held the containers out toward him. "I believe I owe you some cookies."

"Oh, what a sweet girl you are. You cheered my evening right up."

My face fell. "Why do you need cheering? Is something wrong?"

"No, no! I'm fine, nothing like that." He guided me into the kitchen and pulled out a chair, but I stopped short and gasped when I realized how different it looked. "You remodeled the kitchen!" I cried. The cabinets were new and white and the stone countertops gleamed. "It looks amazing!"

"So glad you like it! David and I did most of the work ourselves. Have a seat and I'll get us some milk. You can help me make a dent in these wonderful cookies, not that I'll need help once David sees them."

"Um, where is David?"

"He took Violet to a movie. Should be back soon." He took a carton of milk from the fridge. "Nice girl, that Violet. A little flighty, but she's good to my boy." He paused to pour the milk. "Anyhow, what I meant before is that it's been a bit crazy around here. Getting David ready for college, getting the house ready for the market, getting ready to move again. David is a huge help of course, and it's a godsend that I work from home. But still—whew—this year went by in a blink."

He placed a glass of milk in front of me with a flourish and a smile, but I didn't smile back. He'd lost me a few seconds ago. Somewhere around "getting ready to move again."

"Move?" I repeated. "Move where?"

"Back to Connecticut, of course." That must've been when he noticed my dumbfounded expression, because he tilted his head and looked at me in confusion. "We'd only planned to stay here for a year. David didn't tell you?"

Cold spread through my insides even though I hadn't touched my milk yet. "He didn't say a word." As usual.

Mr. Kerrigan nodded as if it made perfect sense. "He cared a lot about you, honey. He still does. In fact, I think you were a big part of the reason he agreed to come here so easily."

I already knew that. Because David had told me.

"But why go back to Connecticut? I thought you inherited this house? Now you have to find another one?"

He shook his head. "We never sold the house in Connecticut. When my father died, this house was in my name, but I never intended to keep it. There's no mortgage, but the taxes are high, and it's too much house for David and me. I gave him a choice; we could rent out the house in Connecticut and live here while we got this house ready for the market, sort of a last hurrah before we said goodbye. Or, we could stay in Connecticut. Drive up here on the weekends and do what we needed to do in our free time. With my health being what it was, it didn't make sense to do all that traveling. But I didn't want to pull David out of school, so I told him the decision was his." He smiled again. "You'd be surprised how little convincing it took."

Suddenly I wanted to be back in my sheet cocoon in the worst possible way. In September I'd hoped David's arrival in Rhode Island was a figment of my imagination—a huge misunderstanding. Now I hoped the same thing about this conversation.

"So you're leaving again?"

"Not until after graduation. But definitely before the end of the summer, whether we have a buyer by then or not."

"But I thought—"

The sound of the kitchen door opening interrupted my question. David came into the room, swatting at raindrops that shone like glitter against his black hair. "Hey, Kelse," he said. "What are you doing here?"

"You're leaving." I'd meant to phrase it as a question, but it came out sounding like an accusation. Neither of us broke eye contact, but neither of us knew what to say.

Mr. Kerrigan pushed himself away from the table and stood up. "Look at these cookies Kelsey made for us!" He grabbed one of the containers and pushed it into David's abdomen. "Why don't you take these upstairs and show her your fish tank?"

David looked at his father as if he'd spoken complete gibberish.

Mr. Kerrigan patted his shoulder. "I think she'd like to see your fish."

"Yeah," David said, finally getting the hint. "Come on up, Kelse."

It had been ages since I'd been in David's room at this house. It felt foreign and familiar all at once, with the same wooden bunk beds against the right wall and the window at the far end with blue sailboat curtains. The biggest difference was that it no longer looked like a temporary, unlived-in bedroom. His baseball memorabilia dotted the dressers and walls. His hooded sweatshirt hung on his desk chair, the same desk that had always been mostly bare. Now it held his computer and his schoolbooks and, of course, the fish tank. And a framed picture of him and Violet.

It looked like the bedroom of a normal teenage boy, not a room where he stayed for a week or so each summer. It looked lived in, though apparently he wouldn't be living in it much longer.

"Is there something else you forgot to open your mouth about?" I asked as the door shut behind me.

"Why would I tell you?" He tossed the container of cookies on the desk and dropped into the chair. "We weren't even friends for most of the year. It's like I said; I didn't want pity. I just wanted to know what would happen if you and I were in the same place at the same time again."

"Does Violet know you're moving?"

"She does now. It's part of the reason she was so pleasant at prom."

"This doesn't make any sense. That day when we talked about choosing colleges, you told me you planned to stay close to home."

"I do plan to stay close to home. I'm going to UConn."

"UConn? Then why did Violet tell me you were going to Massachusetts like she is?"

David grimaced. "Wishful thinking on her part. UConn and UMass both offered me scholarships. She thought if she kept on me, I'd pick the one closer to her. UMass is less than two hours from here, but it's more than three from Connecticut." He shrugged. "She's not too happy with me, but I had to go where I'd be close to my dad."

"So now you're leaving," I said again.

David sighed and stood up. "Why does it matter, Kelse? You love it here. With or without me."

"I do love it here. But I want you here with me."

"Why?"

I crossed the room and stood in front of him. Tentatively I traced the shadowed pattern of raindrops on his T-shirt with my finger. "It's raining. What do you think about when it rains?"

"What do you mean?"

My heart galloped like a racehorse, but I forced myself to look him in the eye. "I think about kissing you every time it rains." I sucked in a shaky breath. "And every time it doesn't." Then I leaned up on my toes, and pressed my lips against his.

It ended too fast—fast enough that I wasn't sure what happened. Then I realized he'd pushed me away. Not roughly, and not in a way that made me think he was angry. Just enough to let me know that it wasn't going to happen. I looked at him with questioning eyes.

"Sorry, Kelse," he said softly. "Not this time."

"Why not?"

"Because I have a girlfriend, and because you broke up with Ryan two days ago. I'm not gonna be your rebound."

His words hit me like a slap in the face. "You know you're not a rebound. How can you say that? I'm finally trying to do what's right here."

"So am I. What am I supposed to tell Violet? 'Thanks for being Kelsey's stand-in, but your services are no longer needed'? That's not fair."

I took a step back and folded my arms over my chest. "If she's only my stand-in, how is *that* fair?"

"That's not what I meant. She's already upset because she thinks you had something to do with me choosing UConn. I can't stand here and kiss you again when I've told her a thousand times that there's nothing going on."

"You almost broke up with her last time. What were you going to tell her then?"

"I honestly don't know. But it doesn't matter, because you didn't want to be with me. Again."

I let out a frustrated breath. "What was I supposed to do? I made a whole new life for myself before you got here. I had my friends, I had my boyfriend. I thought everything was perfect. Then you show up out of nowhere and tell me how much I've changed and start kissing my friends and confusing the hell out of me and no matter how much I want to hate you, I can't!"

David's lips settled into a frown. "That's the part I still don't get. I never did anything to deserve you hating me. I told you I loved you, for Christ's sake. Why would you hate me for that?"

I sat down hard on the lower bunk and buried my face in my hands.

"I didn't hate you for saying you loved me. I hated you for making me want to stay. And then breaking my heart all over again when I tried to tell you."

"Kelse, it wasn't—"

I held up my hand. "I know. I was so stupid back then. I thought it had to be all or nothing; if you could be happy without me, with people I didn't know how to relate to anymore, then you didn't need me at all. I had this idealized image in my head of what life would be like when I got here—what I'd be like—and taking the next step with you didn't fit in the picture." I paused for a second, the photo of the Grand Canyon that used to hang by my bed flashing through my mind. I thought I'd crossed the valley to the perpetually coveted other side when I left my old life behind. And yet, here I was, staring longingly at where I'd already been. "And then what if it didn't work? I would've lost my boyfriend *and* my best friend."

"So you decided to throw me away instead?"

"I can't stand what I did to you, but part of me hated you for being the person I could never be again, and making it look so easy." My breath shook. My confession had surprised even me. "But, David, you wouldn't be here, in this house, in this *state*, if you didn't want to give it another chance." I looked at him with pleading eyes. "Can't we make it work?"

Some kind of exasperated sound tore from his throat and he pushed his hand through his hair. "We wouldn't be together this time, either. Not physically. You'll be in Rhode Island and I'll be in Connecticut, just like before. We had all year to make this work." He held my gaze, both sadness and resolve in his eyes. "It's too late."

A sound like the ocean rang in my ears, one that must have signaled all my blood rushing to my feet. The room spun and my legs wobbled when I stood up. David started toward me. "I still want us to be friends, Kelse."

Friends. We'd started as friends, but it wasn't what I wanted anymore. I'd wanted more for a long time, longer than I'd even realized. But I'd missed my window, and begging wouldn't change anything.

I nodded woodenly. "And I want you to know that if I could go back and do things differently, I would."

The briefest flicker of a smile crossed his lips and he stepped forward like he might hug me, but I turned toward the door. The thought of touching him was too much. I only wanted to get out of there and be alone with my humiliation, pronto.

"Guess I'll see you at school tomorrow," I said hurriedly. The knowledge made me want to vomit.

I didn't know how I'd make it through the next couple of weeks until graduation. As I tore out of the house and back into the rain, I only knew that all my perfect illusions had burst like bubbles. Of course, if they'd ever really been perfect, then what happened in David's bedroom wouldn't have mattered. But it did matter, because I'd made the biggest mistake of my life when I let him slip through my fingers last year.

And now I'd made the same mistake all over again.

Thirty-Three

Rhode Island
Senior Year

Being locked in a torture chamber would've felt like a trip to the Bahamas compared to the last days of school.

Ryan barely looked at me, and David went overboard trying to be the friend I didn't want. Even though Violet knew her theory about David's choice of college was ridiculous and claimed to be over it, things were strained between us, too. It felt like sophomore year all over again. Everything had fallen apart overnight. Eyes and whispers followed me wherever I went. Once again, I couldn't wait for a new start.

Graduation finally came and went on a warm, sunny afternoon, and then it was all over. I felt sad and relieved all at once. It was time to focus on things to come instead of the past, and planning for college seemed like the best distraction. So a few days into summer, Candy and I sat in my bedroom making a list of the things we would need for our dorm room.

"How about a TV?" I asked. "Do you want to bring yours or should I bring mine?"

"Doesn't matter," Candy replied. "What about a futon? Do you think we can fit a futon? Matt's going to need somewhere to sleep when he comes to visit."

"Ew!" I wrinkled my nose. "When that happens, let me know so I can go home. I'm not sleeping in the same room with you and Crowley getting it on."

"We haven't gotten anything on." She flashed a wicked grin. "Yet."

"It's on the agenda, then?"

Her grin grew even wider. "Tonight's agenda, actually. He has no idea I'll be making a man out of him later."

"No offense, but gross."

She picked up a pillow and chucked it at my head. "Consider it payback for all the times you burned my retinas making out with Smurfy. Oh!" She sat straighter, like she'd remembered something important. "Can I borrow your strawberry lip gloss? Matt likes the way it tastes."

"If I can find it, you can keep it."

I fished through my drawers and my purse, but the lip gloss was nowhere to be found. "Are you sure you don't still have it?" I asked.

"No. You let me borrow it at Ryan's party and I gave it right back."

"Oh, right. Then I think I know where to find it."

I dug around in my closet, searching for the purse I'd had with me on Saint Patrick's Day. I hadn't used it in a while, and sure enough, the lip gloss turned up at the bottom of it. Right next to the Saint Christopher medal I'd almost thrown into the woods that night.

"Stupid thing," I muttered, plucking it from my bag. "It keeps turning up like a bad penny."

"What is that? A medal?"

"David's medal, actually. The one Ryan took from his car the night he busted his chin." I cringed, thinking about it.

Candy stuck her lower lip out. "I still can't believe he told you no." She was the only person who knew about the night David sent me packing.

"I can. I deserved it."

"No, you didn't. He's been in love with you forever, and you finally tell him you love him back and he says *no*? Sorry, but I'm calling bullshit on that."

Something inside me fluttered. "Oh my God," I murmured.

"What? What's wrong?"

"I didn't actually tell him. I told him I wanted him with me and I wanted to make things work, but I never came out and said I loved him." I'd had two chances to say it, and I'd blown them both. I stared forlornly at the medal. "Now I won't get to."

"Yes, you will. Tell him right now." Candy grabbed my cell phone off my vanity and held it in my face. I swatted her arm away.

"He wants Violet. He told me so."

"No, he doesn't. Listen, you know I love Vi, but boys are toys to her. So David kept her occupied a little longer than most. It still won't last. He means more to you than he ever will to her." She held out the phone again. "And I know that because I saw the look on your face the first time she kissed him. Remember?"

"It's too late. He said so himself. Besides, it's not the kind of conversation you have over the phone, and I'm out of excuses to run over there."

"Um, dumb ass?" Candy took my hand, the one that held the medal, and brought it up to my face. "You're holding your excuse in your hand." She batted her eyes and raised the pitch of her voice. "'David, honey, I have something that belongs to you and I want to give it back. And by the way I love you and I want to have your babies.'"

I couldn't help but giggle. "Hey, Can, you know who else I love?"

"*Moi?*"

"Damn right."

I circled the block three times before I had the courage to finally stop my car in front of David's-grandfather's-house-turned-David's-house.

Not that it would be his much longer. Mr. Kerrigan had told my parents at graduation that they already had an offer, and would probably be out by the end of July. Gone from my life for good.

I couldn't bring myself to get out of the car right away. I draped my arms over the steering wheel, resting my head against them and trying not to hyperventilate until it occurred to me that David might look out the window. For whatever reason, the embarrassment of being seen staked out in front of his house like a stalker felt worse than any embarrassment that might come from what I was about to do.

After all, he'd already turned me down once.

I fingered the Saint Christopher medal in the pocket of my jean shorts as I made my way down the driveway. My toenails were painted fuchsia, and I stared at them as they passed over the gravel, letting the splash of color against the muted stones act as a temporary distraction. If I thought of anything else, the odds that I'd vomit would be exponentially worse. Or better, depending on how you looked at it.

My stomach contracted when I glanced up and saw David on the back porch, already watching me from the swing. Looking at him felt like taking one of his fastballs to the gut. I had no idea how I'd ever managed to convince myself I wasn't in love with him. I loved him so much it hurt.

"Hey," he said, standing up. "What brings you here?"

"Um, hey." I climbed the steps, realizing the minimal

exertion it required couldn't be the reason for my heart pounding. I'd never been afraid to talk to David in my life, and yet there I was, at serious risk of passing out at his feet. "I didn't come to bother you. And I won't stay long because I know you're—" I meant to say "leaving," but the word refused to come to out. "Packing. I just wanted to give you something."

"You don't have to give me anything." He leaned against the railing and shuffled his feet against the floorboards.

"It's yours, anyway."

I produced the medal from my pocket and placed it in his outstretched palm, but at the moment when I should have pulled back, something happened. I couldn't do it. Instead I folded his fingers over the medal and held his hand in both of mine.

"Remember the first time I saw this?" The breathless words tumbled out on top of each other, and that was it. After all the time they'd been bottled up, there was no stopping them now. "It was next to the card that Amy Heffernan made you, and I think—I think even then, though maybe I didn't know it, or I guess didn't want to know it—I was jealous. I hated that you were interested in girls like her. I couldn't stand having to share you. Not that I blame them. Not that I blame you." I shook my head, wishing I could at least filter the things spilling out of me, even as the relief of saying them propelled still more from my mouth. "I hated that you could have anyone you wanted, and most of all, I hate myself for not figuring out sooner that all *I* wanted was *you*."

I pulled his arm around me, flinging my own arms around his neck and burying my face in his shoulder.

"David," I whimpered as he put his hand on my back in an infuriatingly benign way. "I'm sorry." I buried my face in his shirt. "I know you don't want me, and I know I ruined everything. But I love you. And I can't take this anymore."

David's hand stilled against my back. He stayed quiet and motionless long enough to make me wish I could hurdle the railing and pretend I'd never been there.

"Say something." I sighed.

A pause. "Your timing sucks."

"It's no worse than yours."

"Guess I'll give you that."

We both laughed awkwardly and I pulled myself away from him. "Listen. I know we've been through this already, but I had to say it. You know how that goes." I managed a half smile, but David dropped his eyes to the medal rotating between his fingers.

Defeat. Again.

My stomach twisted and I knew I had to take the high road while I still could. "I get that you want to treat Violet better than I treated you. So as long as you're happy—"

"I'm not with Violet."

I must've misheard him. "You—what?"

"I'm not with Violet," he repeated. "We broke up. No

drama or anything; we just didn't see it working long distance."

I tugged at the frayed edge of my shorts, swallowing hard. "Oh. I, um, didn't know." So he wasn't with Violet anymore, but he still didn't want me. Talk about hitting rock bottom.

David placed the medal on top of the porch railing and pushed it away with one finger before flattening his palms against the wood on either side of him. He didn't look at me.

"I should go," I said. "Moving sucks and you probably have a ton to do."

I started toward the steps, a lump already burgeoning in my throat. I looked up when David blocked my path.

"You know that saying, 'If you can't be with the one you love, love the one you're with'?"

"That's a stupid saying. The one you love and the one you're with should be the same person."

"So you still think you can't be with someone if you're not together physically? Because I think you're wrong."

He wasn't making sense. He'd just told me he and Violet ended things to avoid long distance, and now he was contradicting himself.

I drew back, the lump in my throat ready to burst. "I don't know what you're saying, but—" I tried again to get around him, but he stepped in front of me again and cut me off before I could finish my sentence.

"I'm saying the only person I'd have a long-distance relationship with is you."

I must've looked like an owl, staring at him with big, blinking eyes. One second I stood glued to the spot, wondering what in the hell I was supposed to say to that. In the next I barely registered that I'd been gathered up in his arms. My back collided with the outer wall of the house, but I hardly noticed that either. All I felt were David's lips pressed against mine, his arms wrapped around me, my body molded against his.

I didn't care why he'd done it. I just knew I wanted it.

I kissed him with everything I had in me, trying to memorize every second of his lips and his scent, in case it never happened again. I had no idea how much time had passed once our kisses became softer, slower, and we finally had to stop to catch our breath.

The moment my lips were unoccupied, the babbling started again.

"We can do this, can't we? Long distance isn't so bad, right? And we can see each other on the weekends and maybe one of us can transfer later on—"

David shut me up with another kiss. "I told you your timing sucked."

"I know. But we've already tried forgetting each other, and it didn't work. Don't you at least want to try?"

The tip of his nose brushed mine and he leaned in to within a hair's breadth of my lips. "Why didn't it work?" he said softly.

"Because I can't forget you." I moved in to kiss him, but he didn't let me.

"And why not?"

"You know why."

A smirk spread across his completely edible lips. "Tell me again."

"Because I love you." I moved in, but he dodged me, and this time his expression turned serious.

"You mean it, Kelse?"

Now it was my turn to smile. I took his face in my hands and said the words I should have said a long time ago, the words he hadn't hesitated to say to me.

"I always have."

ACKNOWLEDGMENTS

There are so many people I need to thank for making this book a reality. First, my agent, John M. Cusick, for pulling me from the slush pile and being the last person I ever would've expected to believe in and love this story. And for being exactly the right person to represent it. I still can't believe it's been three years since the phone bomb that made my dream come true.

To my editor, Sara Sargent: I cannot thank you enough for loving this novel the way you do. Never in a million years did I expect to get an e-mail saying that you'd been reading *Last Year's Mistake* on your morning commute—two years after it was first submitted to you. On Valentine's Day, no less. Thank you, thank you, for not being able to forget this story. Thank you for coming back for it, and for helping me make it the book I always meant for it to be. You are this novel's very own David. Working with you has been a gift.

Special thanks to the rest of the Simon Pulse team, especially Jessica Handelman for the gorgeous, sexy cover, and the copy editors who caught all my embarrassing mistakes. I am eternally grateful to everyone who had a hand in making this book not just presentable, but badass.

To the people who took the time to read and offer critique in *LYM*'s awkward early stages: Leigh Ann Kopans, Chessie Zappia, Maggie Hall, Megan Whitmer, Jenny Kaczorowski, Tristina Wright, Jamie Grey, Alexa Hirsch, and Katie Mills.

Your time, insight, observations, and kind words were key in making this story something I could be proud of.

A big hug of thanks to Brenda Drake for hosting the contest that ultimately scored *LYM* its two offers of agent representation, and another huge hug to Marieke Nijkamp for not only critiquing my early drafts, but writing the pitch that changed everything. You, Maggie, and Dahlia Adler are CP gold and I'm so lucky to have stumbled into your paths. I'm not sure I would've hung in as long as I did without the three of you and many epic, novel-length e-mails. Never leave me.

To my family: thank you for putting up with years of my antisocial behavior as I buried my nose in books at every party and gathering. Diana, I know how much you hated waiting for me to finish "one more chapter"—but look where it got me! Mom and Dad, you always encouraged my creativity, always told me my stories were good. You believed I could do anything I wanted, and now I have. I love you.

I owe a big debt of gratitude to my in-laws, Linda and Domenick, for having us over for dinner every Saturday night while I was writing this book, and for the random pots of soup you'd bring over just because I loved it. You didn't know it then, but you were giving me the free time I needed to get my first draft done. Thank you for that!

And to Aunt Gloria: this might not be the book I wrote while you were taking care of Andrew and me, but you've saved my life in a thousand other ways, and I am so very grateful to you.

Last but not least, to Dom: Thank you for not laughing at me when you caught me in our study writing my first novel five years ago. If you had, things might've happened very differently. You're my husband and now Daddy to our sweet little boy, but I'll never forget that you were my very own YA romance.